SOUTHSIDE

SOUTHSIDE

A Novel

Michael Krikorian

Oceanview Publishing

Longboat Key, Florida

ISBN: 978-1-60809-055-6

Published in the United States of America by Oceanview Publishing, Longboat Key, Florida
www.oceanviewpub.com

10 9 8 7 6 5 4 3 2 1

PRINTED IN THE UNITED STATES OF AMERICA

To Jeanine, the lovely daughter of Tony and Rose, and to Nancy, the curly-haired chef of my dreams.

ACKNOWLEDGMENTS

First, I want to thank my cousin Greg Krikorian who got me into journalism and paved the way for my writing.

Two of my other cousins, Dave and Jeff Arzouman, helped build my writing foundation by providing adventures that bordered on the legal.

If it hadn't been for Miles Corwin, this book wouldn't have been professionally published. Miles told me about Pat and Bob Gussin and the crew at Oceanview Publishing.

So many writers to thank, but a couple stand out. In the mid-1990s, Michael Connelly got me back into reading after a decade-long lapse. More recently, Michael Koryta became a grand champion of *Southside*.

Thanks also to Jim Murray, the great *L.A. Times* sports columnist.

In different ways, so many people helped along the way. To name a few: Suzanne Tracht, Ralph Waxman, Chris Feldmeier, Phil Rosenthal, Bonnie and Alan Engle, Jason Asch, Alex Glass, Conrad Hurtt, Ellen Nadel, and the living legend Caryl "Carly" Kim.

Thanks to my uncle Harry for pushing me to not give up the fight and to Larry Silverton for his stories and daughters, Gail and Nancy.

Here's to Sal LaBarbera, the best homicide detective in America, and to his storied opponent on the opposing corner, Cleamon "Big Evil" Johnson, the most charming gang leader I've ever known.

August 2004

Payton and Marcus walked toward the car wash on Central Avenue
and 89th Street in the lethal neighborhood of Green Meadows. To
meet some girls? No. Both were in old-fashioned romances with
their one and only loves. To buy drugs? No. Neither used nor sold
drugs. Just out for a stroll to gaze at one of those meadows this 'hood
was named after? Hell, there hasn't been a green meadow 'round
here for three-quarters of a century.

Even years later, no one, not even the detectives, had been able
to figure out why they—or anybody, for that matter—would walk to
a car wash.

The two were not gang members. Still, they must have known
the inherent danger of two guys from the Eastside of Central crossing
over to the Westside.

The simple act of crossing that avenue on foot was risky, if not
straight-out reckless, here on the Southside of Los Angeles.

The shot caller was sitting on a porch fifty yards away when he saw
the prey and haphazardly sentenced them to death.

"Poison Rat, you wanna earn some respect 'round here and live
up to your name? See if you really got some poison in you or you
just a rat?"

"I'm ready. Ready for a promotion, blood."

"There, them," said the shot caller, nodding, not even pointing,
to the two guys crossing Central. "The two fools from the Kitchen.
Crabs heading for the car wash." "Crabs" was a derogatory term for
Crips.

"Man, I know them guys. They ain't Kitchens," said the young thug, referring to the Crip set that ran the "Kitchen" neighborhood of Central Avenue.

"Rat, where they live?"

"Other side of Central."

"What 'hood is that?"

"Kitchen."

"Then where they from?"

"Ah'ight. Ah'ight."

The shot caller motioned toward a teenage homeboy in the alley adjacent to the house where the shot caller sat on his throne. The kid ducked down the alley and, twenty seconds later, reappeared and approached the porch, casually carrying a Food4Less paper shopping bag by its flimsy handles like it was half full of groceries.

He handed it to the shot caller who pulled out its contents: an Uzi and a clip. He checked the clip and shoved it into the gun. He held it up for observation as nonchalantly as someone holding the sports section on a lazy Sunday morning. He then handed the weapon to Poison Rat.

"This here ain't full auto," the leader said. "So just squeeze and squeeze away. Thirty times. You feel me? Take about three seconds, maybe five with your fat-ass fingers. And I don't want or hear 'bout one bullet left in this motherfucker. You feel me?"

"I feel you."

"Get up close, don't say a word, pull, then jam to the alley. Li'l Gun'll be there in the truck, and you guys hit it. Get outta here for a couple days. Go to Vegas or sumpthin'. I don't wanna see you for a while.

"Understand?"

"I got it, man. Be bool."

" 'Be bool'? Nigga, you the one better be bool. Now go do it." Bloods, whenever they could, or remembered, avoided the dreaded letter "c."

The shot caller knew he should've left the area, given himself an alibi. He knew he'd be questioned. No doubt about that. But he just couldn't leave. It wasn't in him to leave. Not when a thrill far too enticing was just seconds away.

The two young men had crossed Central Avenue. Poison Rat met them at the car wash. After the first nine shots, he stood over them and pumped in the last twenty-one till he clicked on empty.

Three blocks away, his head underneath the hood of an '89 Ford Ranger pickup, adjusting the jets on the carb, a mechanic heard the long burst of rapid gunfire. Even here on 92nd and Central, the northwestern border of Watts, that was a lot of shots during the day.

Like he did whenever he heard gunfire, even a single shot, the mechanic thought of the love of his life, his son. He still remembered an article in the L.A. *Times* a year or so ago that calculated if every neighborhood in the entire city had as many homicides as this area, there would be more than 11,000 killings a year in Los Angeles.

The mechanic worried, too, about his wife, but not nearly as much. Their relationship was shaky at best, and she was most likely away at work at the hospital. Or in a Compton crack house.

The mechanic told his boss he had to walk up the avenue, just to check. The boss who owned the ramshackle auto repair was accustomed to this. He told a customer, "Hell, a car could backfire and my man here would think it was a bullet fired into his son's heart."

The mechanic walked quickly toward the car wash. From a block and a half away, he could see there were a few people gathering. Most folks around here knew better than to go to the scene of a shooting. A second shooter, an ambusher, could be lying in wait.

The man's walk turned to a trot. Then he saw, through the small standing group, two bodies sprawled out. He started to run.

Forty feet away, a lady, one of those standing near the bodies, noticed the running man rapidly approaching. She raised her hands over her head, crossing them frantically. "No! No! Mr. Sims, no. Don't come over here!"

He panicked. His body released a cold sweat. He ran past the woman to the fallen men. He couldn't recognize the faces of his son and his son's friend. But, he recognized the jersey. Number 34. His heart died right there at that car wash.

December 2013

The oak door opened and light slashed darkness at the Redwood Saloon. Danny, the bartender, eyed me and gave up his customary greeting.

"Hit 'n' Run!"

I had earned that sobriquet from my frequent forays in and out of this haunt on 2nd Street between Broadway and Hill in downtown Los Angeles.

I worked a block and a half east at the *Times* as the paper's street gang reporter and if the day was slow—no triples, no doubles, no kids under ten shot, no grandmas over seventy, no desperate assistant city editor pestering me for briefs—round three or so I'd head to the Redwood. Danny would see me enter, and by the time I got to the bar, a shot of Early Times was waiting to be swallowed. I drank the harsh whiskey as a tribute to my grandpa, my mom's dad, a tough Armenian from the fierce city of Van who started every American morning with a shot of E.T.

I'd lift the shooter, down the shot, leave a fin, grab a couple of peppermints for later, pop a stick of Big Red for now, walk back into the brightness, and return to the job I loved. I'd be back at the paper quicker than most of my fellow metro reporters took to get a cup of coffee and read another Plaschke column on why the hell there was no NFL team in America's second largest city.

This had gone on for years. When it started, having a drink during the day wasn't a sin for a journalist, though it was already thought to be old-school. But, back then, old-school was cool, even fashionable. Not that I ever tried to be cool or fashionable. I was just old-school for real.

Now, by 2013, drinking during the day was considered cause for concern, in a league with insubordination, relying on one anonymous source, or tonguing out a fifteen-year-old girl while on the education beat. Fuck 'em. Part of the romance of being a journalist was going to a bar and having a drink. Damn, I loved that. Whenever I heard Coltrane's "My Favorite Things," it made the list. But, I did make some concessions. Rarely did I have more than one drink and never three. Plus by now, I'd switched to vodka—usually Stoli, sometimes good old Smirnoff. This was after a surly old-time photojournalist named Boris Yaro told me vodka didn't smell. Maybe it didn't reek like whiskey, but it still fouled my mouth.

So today I got a Stoli on the rocks. A double. It wasn't a hit-and-run situation. This day I was done at the newsroom and heading down to 74th and Hoover to hook with King Funeral, the ancient forty-seven-year-old shot caller of the Hoover Criminals, one of California's biggest and deadliest black street gangs. I had already talked with him once, sort of a get-to-know-each-other preinterview. Didn't tape it, didn't even take notes. This night was to be the real interview.

That was my specialty, street gangs. No other reporter wanted to deal with them, even though gangs were the single biggest social problem in Los Angeles, often accounting for more than seven hundred homicides a year in the city and a thousand in the county, the County of Angels. The killings had dropped dramatically over the last few years, city officials were quick to boast. Now, there was "only" one a day.

Covering gangs was a natural fit for me. After graduating from high school, while my classmates sought out respected universities, pragmatic trade schools, or meager employment, I ventured, like a wide-eyed tourist, to America's most dangerous neighborhoods. I carried a past armed with its share of demerits, some of them attained in the slums of the South Bronx, East St. Louis, the Westside of Baltimore, and the South Side of Chicago, the rest on the streets of Compton, South Central, and Watts. The Southside of Los Angeles. The worst side, the best side, depending on what you were looking to get out of life.

Typical of the isolation racial groups felt in Los Angeles, many black residents here partitioned the Southside into either the West-side or the Eastside, the dividing line being the Harbor Freeway.

Of course, the editors at the *Times* didn't know the details of that boisterous time of my life. Didn't know about my arrests and my felony convictions, either. When I was hired, I simply threw out the form requesting a background check. A secretary later called to say she didn't get it. I told her I had filled it out. She said she'd double-check. That was the last I heard about it.

Later, when the LAPD and L.A. County Sheriff's Department came around the newsroom annually to update press credentials, I'd be sure to be out of the office, not a rarity. Later, when the metro editor's assistant came by to remind me about the police press passes, I'd always say something like "Okay, I'll get on it." But, I never did. I didn't want a background check run on me. After a while, it was forgotten. At crime scenes, just my regular *Times* photo ID did the job. On the very rare occasion a rookie or persnickety cop asked for my credentials, I'd just say I left it at the office or home. Fortunately, a lot of street cops were familiar with my byline and even my face. I was on the streets a lot.

Danny asked, "What's doin', Jack?" only half expecting an answer. Danny's about sixty, full head of black Mexican hair, thickly rimmed black eyeglasses, muscular, hairy forearms. He never drinks behind the bar and he's been calling me Jack for close to eleven years, though that's not my name.

"How many dead today?" asked Sharky Klian, the badass Armen-ian bail bondsman sitting at the end of the bar.

"It's dead, Shark," I told him. "Only one."

"When's the next big story coming out, Jack?" said Danny. "Let me know, Jack. I want to read it. But, you gotta be careful, Jack."

"Careful? He's got a fuckin' death wish," said Sharky, who or-dered a French Connection, which is Courvoisier, Hennessy, and Grand Marnier. Cognac with sweetener. A waste of good brandy.

Sharky has three black belts, goes about six two, two forty-five and is never far from a fifteen-round 9mm SIG SAUER P226 Elite.

"Why don't you ask Danny for a French kiss while you're at it, ya fuckin' *bahduk*," I said, using the Armenian word for fruit.

"He's not my type, Jack," Danny quipped.

"Fuck both of you assholes."

I never correct Danny on the Jack thing because it's good to have an alias at a bar so close to work and, besides, Jack's a cool name. Not that mine ain't.

One day he was reading this article by me that someone told him to read and he realizes Jack's not my real name. The next time Danny saw me he called me by my real name, Michael. "Danny," I schooled him, "at the 'Wood, my name is Jack."

I ordered another Stoli, took a few sips. It started to get my blood feeling pleasantly cool and loose.

"I'm heading tonight to interview the leader of the Hoovers."

"At night, Jack?"

"Night's the best time to talk to a criminal. They think they can get away with anything in the dark, even stories. In the day, they ain't so colorful."

"What'd I tell you, Danny," Sharky said. "This guy is lookin' to die young."

"Too late for that, Shark," I told him. "When you gonna hook me up with the Armenian Mafia guys?"

"I told you, there's no such thing."

"Yeah, sure, you're right." I finished off the Stoli, feeling pretty damn good. As usual, I gave Danny a good tip, five on ten, grabbed the mints, stepped past the red phone that is the hotline to the *Times*, and walked out.

I was walking down 2nd Street about thirty feet from the Redwood, and off to my left a car slowed. That's not unusual. They all do. Broadway's coming up. But this car, a Regal or a Cutlass, stopped, the passenger door opened and the driver got out that way, leaving the door wide open.

Black man. Medium height, medium age. A purple rag on his head. Grape Street Crips. Old for a Grape shooter. Run or charge? Charge. It was too late. He started squeezing. I don't remember a whole lot. I remember noise. I remember fire flashes. I remember searing, gut-wrenching punches, like from a horizontal high-speed pile driver ripping into me. I remember the buildings going sideways.

CHAPTER 1

The Monday the reporter got shot was one of those glorious winter days in L.A. that made it easy to understand why countless, clueless masses in the rest of the planet believed the City of Angels deserved its nickname.

Looking north from the third-floor editorial offices of the *Los Angeles Times*, the view was urbane and civilized. All it took was three floors up to blot out the grime, the homeless, the graffiti, the dealers, and the horns of irate motorists. Directly across First Street was a magenta-and-gold bougainvillea-filled open space that two years earlier was a thriving heroin mart where dope fiends laid on slabs of weedy, broken concrete and numbly stared across the street at the shimmering twenty-eight-story City Hall. A Column One piece by Nora Zamichow had forced the mayor and city council members to look out their windows and clean up the embarrassment in their front yard.

Beyond downtown, just twenty-five minutes away by McLaren P-1, were snowcapped mountains beckoning skiers to call in sick and play Franz Klammer at Mt. Waterman.

In the *Times*'s newsroom, a football field of pods with a core of glassy offices where editors conspired, even veterans were impressed.

"Well, the mountains came out today," bellowed Eric Malnic, a sixty-three-year-old alcoholic who had been a reporter for forty-three years and hadn't had one sneaky gulp of his beloved 100-proof Smirnoff Blue since the Iranian hostage crisis. He didn't notice—or give a damn—that, as usual, no one paid a smidgen of attention to him.

The newsroom, as a whole, paid little attention to anything. Like the Sunday paper delivered to nearly one million people, everyone was wrapped in their own world.

It was a rare occurrence when that world opened and the entire staff was on the same page: September 11, 2001; March 21, 2003 when missiles descended upon Baghdad; April of 2004 when the paper won five Pulitzer prizes; President Obama's 2008 election and 2012 reelection; the 2013 Patriot's Day bombings at the Boston Marathon; and the day reporter Michael Lyons was shot.

At 5:55, fifty-five minutes after the first, seldom-met deadline had passed that Monday, Lyons had been walking on 2nd Street, heading back from the Redwood Saloon. He had taken two hits—upper right chest and right side—but, as the paper's LAPD reporters quickly learned from sources, Lyons was not dead and would not die from the wounds.

Still, in the newsroom there were tears, dismay, and heartache. There was real emotional unity. But even the shock and the poignant outpouring didn't last long. It was replaced by wagering faster than you could say Seabiscuit. The wager? Who finally shot Mike. The reporters put together a betting pool.

The list of potential assassins was deep. He had amassed some serious enemies over his twelve years on the staff.

There were street gangs he had outraged by writing about them, bringing extra scrutiny and harassment from police. Gangs such as the Grape Street Crips from the Jordan Downs Housing Project and the Bounty Hunter Bloods from the Nickerson Gardens Housing Project, both in Watts. The Rollin Sixties Crips in Hyde Park, the Eight Trey Gangster Crips headquartered in St. Andrews Park, Geraghty Loma and Arizona Maravilla in East Los Angeles, and Armenian Power in Hollywood and Glendale.

There were the husbands Lyons had infuriated over the years by entertaining their wives.

The gambling began.

"Okay, okay, okay," said Morty Goldstein, the paper's old-school day cops reporter, a bespectacled, portly ex-Berkeley radical who had developed a taste for USDA prime beef and old Bordeaux. He never hit the streets, never left his desk, but had more cop contacts, more cop cell and home phone numbers than the new chief of police himself.

"Let's see," Goldstein said. "We got all the gangs, the husbands, including that chef. Also that guy that confessed to Michael."

"Krebs," said another reporter within the gathering crowd.

Rex Krebs, who killed two college students, had confessed to Lyons in a jailhouse interview and landed on San Quentin's death row solely because of the interview. At sentencing, in open court, he screamed his biker pals would kill Lyons.

"The Armenian Mafia," said ace general-assignment reporter Carly Engstrom, a foxy, temperamental thirty-five-year-old half-Korean, half-Swede who had been Lyons's pod mate for years. For over a year, Lyons had been trying to expose the Armenian Mafia in all their prey-on-their-own wickedness.

"Right, the Armenian mob," said Goldstein, grabbing a pad off his desk, easily the most cluttered in the newsroom. He started a list as he leaned back in his chair.

Nona Yates, the newsroom's premier researcher, maneuvered to the core of the group of gathered reporters. She grimaced and shook her thick, long auburn mane. "Holy Sonny Barger. Mike's near death and you people are betting on who shot him? I can't believe this shit. Michael was the—Michael *is* the coolest motherfucker in this whole newsroom."

"Sorry to destroy the image, Nona, but Mike was overrated," said assistant metro editor Ted Doot, who had moseyed to the rim. "You know how many times I had reports from nightside copy editors that they smelled booze on him. He should have been suspended long ago."

Nona Yates took a moment to size up Doot. He was a reasonably proportioned man of thirty-eight except for his incredibly tiny, shiny, bald head and his equally freakish large buttocks, which she guessed weren't bald. She tried to shake off that image.

"If not for his cousin," the pompous, Oxford-educated Doot continued, "he would never have been hired here. Glorifying gang members is what he did best. Killers. If there is any betting to do, I'll wager he was smashed when they finally shot him."

Doot's stinging appraisal of a wounded reporter was further proof to the reporters that he was not human, but rather a heartless cyborg for the paper's equally heartless editor of California coverage, Harriet Tinder, a hard-working troll with no neck and the personality of dandruff, which she had in vast reserves, like the Kirkurk oil fields. Many people dismissed Doot simply as "Harriet's bitch." But, his timing was off today. The staff, which normally put up with his put-downs, was not in the mood this time.

Carly Engstrom was first to speak. "Ted, the guy just got shot. Can you at least wait till he wakes up to write him up? And I believe the editor of this paper hired Mike, not Greg," referring to Lyons's cousin, Greg Mahtesian, also a *Times* reporter.

Doot stared at Engstrom, but said nothing, silently calculating his revenge for that young hotshot calling him out in front of everyone. He'd just report her slutty little mouth to Harriet Tinder.

Nona Yates ignored Doot. She'd been sober for twelve years and it was times like this she got nostalgic for her old self: a twenty-eight-year-old Jack Daniel's-slugging, meth-snorting biker chick with keys to Angel clubhouses in Oakland and Ventura. Now, at forty, she had learned to ignore the ignorance. So she just muttered "mother-cunter" and let it alone.

To the relief of several, Doot waddled away.

Nona started to walk away. "Betting on Mike. Shame on you."

"Nona," Goldstein called out, "Greg's at the hospital. Michael's going to be okay. No vital organs were hit. He got lucky. We got lucky. In a weird way, this might be a good thing for Mike. He'll come back stronger than ever and be even more a legend on his streets. In a sick way, I'm almost envious."

"That isn't sick, Morty. That's just stupid." Nona shook her head.

"Nona," Goldstein said. "When Mike hears about this, everyone betting on who shot him, us making a pool. Come on. It'll be newspaper folklore. Lyons is going to love this story."

CHAPTER 2

Officers from LAPD's Central Division had responded to the shooting. Central handled calls for service in the downtown area—north past Chinatown and the Dogtown projects to the warehouses near the Pasadena Freeway; south past the Staples Center, home of the Lakers, Clippers, and Kings to the Santa Monica Freeway; east past skid row and the artist's lofts to the railroad tracks and the Los Angeles River; and west from the Figueroa Street high-rises to the Harbor Freeway.

Central Division's main responsibility was keeping a lid on the bubbling cauldron that was skid row, a twenty-block toilet of humans flushing down the drain, most of them going with the flow, only a handful struggling against the mighty, dirty tide. There was no master plan to clean up the area, just contain it, the way you let roaches roam a corner of an East St. Louis tenement hallway after giving up trying to kill them all. Let the bums run amok east of Spring Street, but keep them away from the Biltmore, the grande dame where old money still threw eighty-thousand-dollar weddings, away from the Water Grill and its sesame-crusted ahi tuna tartare and market price Santa Barbara spot prawns, away from Frank Gehry's wavy Disney Concert Hall that drew in the Hancock Park crowd.

But in the last several years, there has been a gradual subduing of the grim and colorful sidewalk culture that defined skid row. Though East Fifth Street and its tentacles still teemed with homeless, most of the cardboard condos were swept away. Long vacant office buildings were turned into lofts occupied by young, employed Caucasians who preferred mixologists to bartenders and Central

Coast craft brews to Heinekens. The Varnish, a bar modeled after a speakeasy, set the new standard for cocktails that took a few minutes to concoct, and many others followed. An Ace Hotel was going up on Broadway. Restaurants with high critical ratings, like Baco Mercat, Spice Table, and Church and State, were booked solid nightly.

Still, glamour crime was exceptional in Central. Those who died there rarely had funerals. They were just dropped in the East L.A. dirt by four illegals with a backhoe. And though the *Times* was in Central's jurisdiction, the paper hardly ever wrote about their own backyard. In 2006, there was an excellent series by columnist Steve Lopez about a skid row cellist that was made into a movie, but usually coverage amounted to the annual "Downtown is Booming" story, the goings on at city hall and the occasional celebrity trial at the Criminal Courts Building. That was about it.

Michael Lyons was not source rich in Central. So when officers arrived at the scene of the shooting on 2nd and Broadway, in front of the very building where the LAPD compiles and analyzes its crime statistics, they didn't know the victim. Though he had his license in his wallet along with $227 in cash, including a C-note stashed in a semihidden compartment, and a *Times* picture ID, they didn't put it together.

It wasn't until homicide detectives were called in that the significance of the shooting became clear. Most of the city's homicide dicks, many of whom rolled on all shootings even if they weren't life-threatening, knew of Lyons.

He had done gang stories like no one before and most of the homicides in the city were gang related. Those stories had won him admiration to the point where the police would tell others in their division, "Lyons got a gang thing today," and they would actually read it. And often they would respond by cracking down on the gang. Bigger the story, harder the crack. It was always curious how Lyons could get gang members to go on the record, knowing it would be brutal for them in the days following publication. To the police, it just reinforced the stupidity of gang members.

Those stories never glamorized gang life, but they probed deeper into the "why" of it all, the ultimate futility, the almost certain sad conclusions. But, more than anything else, they brought a human element to even the most notorious killer. Lyons's stories brought to life people whose entire biography in most other reporter's articles were simply summed up in two words, "gang member."

So, when detectives showed up, they knew this was big local news. And they knew the case would be taken away from them. Detective Megan Tropea of Central Division called the head of LAPD's Robbery-Homicide Division, which handles high-profile cases.

"Tatreau."

"Jimmy T, Tropea here. Got a good one for you."

On the phone, at his Mission Viejo home, forty miles away, Captain James Tatreau waited, heard nothing. "All right, Megan. I'm waiting. Or do I have to guess. Is this *Jeopardy!*? Who got it?"

"Well, Jim, actually on *Jeopardy!* you are given the answer first and then you answer by asking the appropriate question."

"Megan, who the fuck got shot?"

"Michael Lyons."

"No shit? Dead?"

"Not yet. Hit pretty bad from what I hear. He's at County USC. Got it near the Redwood."

"Damn. He gonna make it?"

"Two in the torso."

"Fuck. TV's gonna be all over this. They like that crazy nut. Actually, so do I. We're taking it."

"That's why I called."

"Stay there till I get some guys over."

"Of course."

Jimmy Tatreau hung up. Went to his closet. He had his own, separate from his wife's and just as packed. As head of the elite Robbery-Homicide unit, Tatreau often took high-paying security consultant jobs on the side. With that money, he put most of it into his passion—clothes. He would need to dress well for this one. This was gonna be a natural for the press. One of their own. Maybe even national press. Jimmy T chose his favorite and most expensive Italian suit, a charcoal Kiton he had had made for him in Naples a year ago. With it, a $270 Paul Stuart sky-blue dress shirt he picked up on Madison Avenue during a recent homicide conference in New York. Slipped on some black New & Lingwood Stamford loafers. As Jimmy T began calling detectives, he pondered which Hermes tie to wear. He might be on the *Today* show by morning.

On 2nd, a narrow, busy street that led to the freeways, Detective Tropea had officers tape off the block. By the time the crime-scene tape was up, the television media were already there.

CHAPTER 3

Dr. Charles Wang was only thirty-one, but he had already seen more than a thousand gunshot wounds, from distant grazes to intimate sawed-off blasts. He was the head of trauma surgery at Los Angeles-USC Medical Center in Lincoln Heights, the busiest hospital for violent crimes in California.

So when Wang saw Lyons's wounds and the striking amount of crimson staining the front of his muscular body, the doctor wasn't particularly concerned. In fact, he took a ten-second look, wiggled some body parts, and surmised that Lyons would not only survive, he would not sustain permanent damage. Wang knew from the patient's color and the extent of blood flow that no artery had been hit.

One of Lyons's wounds was a through-and-through to his extreme right side just beneath his rib cage. If you had to get shot near the greater stomach area, this would be the ideal place. You couldn't plan it any better. The more serious wound hit just inside his right armpit, three inches below his collarbone. Lyons would be in severe pain. He'd have some impressive scars. But, thought Wang, Lyons was one lucky reporter.

The doctor knew the reporter. Lyons had interviewed him for a long, mesmerizing profile of a fifteen-year-old gang member, a Fruit Town Brim who had been shot two different times in the head, once with a .45, and survived. Wang had saved the kid's life both times. By the end of the story, the kid had gone back to gangbanging.

Michael Lyons was semiconscious as he was wheeled into surgery. "Mr. Lyons, Michael. It's Dr. Wang, Dr. Charles Wang. Can you hear me? You've been shot, Michael, but you are going to make it. Can you understand me? You are going to be all right. Do you understand? Try to relax and we'll get you through this in good shape."

Michael looked up at the doctor as two orderlies pushed the blood-and-sweat slimed gurney. Dr. Wang walked alongside and kept talking gently. As he walked, he had his hand on Mike's forehead, comforting him.

In all the confusion, in all the pain, in all the surrealism of this incident, Michael was still aware enough to know that the last thing he wanted to do was panic. He didn't want to for two reasons. One was a lesson he had learned a long time ago in the South Bronx when that part of the borough had been the national poster slum for urban decay. It was something his best friend there, Jose "Baby" Rolon, the leader of the Reapers street gang on Daly Avenue, told him after Jose had been shot eight times. "Mikey, if you ever get shot, don't panic. That's the way to survive. You panic, you die. You panic, your heartbeat goes up and more blood pumps out. You got it? Low heart rate means less blood coming out of you. It's that simple."

The other reason for not panicking was that it simply wasn't cool. Sky Masterson would not panic. Nor would Shane. Or Luke. Or Rick Blaine. Or Frank Bullitt. No way. The last thing he wanted was an article or the TV news to talk about how he was panicking. How pathetic would that be? Maybe he'd soiled himself. Pissed himself, too. But, that stuff was natural after getting shot. Nothing could be done about that. He must be doing all right if he thought that was his biggest concern.

The doctor spoke reassuringly. "You've been remarkably calm. Have you been shot before? This old hat to you? You look bored." Michael looked at Dr. Wang. "That's okay. Don't talk. I'm going to take care of you. By the way, the television cameras are here. Lots of them. You're a big star."

Michael nodded ever so briefly and then he passed into a slumber, deep and peaceful.

CHAPTER 4

Throughout that chaotic Monday evening, local television stations broke in with teasers.

"Crime reporter gunned down in the heart of the city. Film at eleven."

"Writer shot downtown. Film at eleven."

The local news programs all led with the shooting. It was a natural. A huge L.A. story with an excellent cast—a reporter, a bar, guns, gangs, downtown, a well-known girlfriend. Had Lyons been killed, it would've been a national story.

Like all reporters, Lyons yearned for page A-1, but with his neglected Southside beat rarely got them.

Most of his night crime stories didn't get much space in the paper—even homicides, especially if they were in the ghetto. Still, Lyons covered them with gusto. But, so often those killings would be briefed—a two-inch capsule—and the next day there would be another homicide and yesterday's killing was all but forgotten, except by the dead guy's family and friends, the guy who shot him, and the overworked detectives.

Michael and some reporters called certain shootings "SIWA": Shooting In White Area. Reporters and column inches were assigned to shootings in accordance with property values and victims age. A shooting in Watts, South Los Angeles, East Los Angeles, or McArthur Park would not make the paper unless the victim was a child under ten, a grandma over seventy, or an incredible hard-luck story. A lightly grazed thirty-five-year-old white female in Santa Monica was good for a eight-inch story inside. A wounded fourteen-year-old boy in the Beverly Center got at least the front of the second section called LATEXTRA. The extraordinary Holmby Hills, Bel Air, Beverly Hills, or Pacific Palisades homicide guaranteed A-1 for days.

Of course, a SIWA meant more coverage, more reporters, usually three, sometimes more. At least one of them would hit the streets and that would almost always be Lyons, who had the best feel for pavement.

Michael understood this was simply the way it was at all the papers. He had been initially disappointed to learn that even the vaunted *L.A. Times* followed that standard policy. Homicides in his Southside beat were often reduced to briefs, the one-inch digest. That was just the way it was.

But, how could he really complain? He was a staff writer at the *Los Angeles Times*, even with all the layoffs and buyouts, still one of the nation's best newspapers, a paper where thousands of journalists, rookies and veterans alike, would auction their ideals to be on staff.

Breaking news clusterfucks were not Michael's forte, though they could be exciting. He preferred to go where television cameramen never tread. To alleys and projects when there wasn't breaking news, but stories of everyday life. To waiting rooms at prisons and jails. The struggling life. The doomed life.

I saw the curved metal railing above me, the cheap thin curtains that partially privatized the bed. I felt the meagerness of the blanket. I've had better blankets at Men's Central or Wayside. I saw wires leading away from me.

A male Filipino nurse came in. He said nothing and took my vitals: blood pressure, temp, pulse. I numbly stared at the ceiling and wondered what is it with Filipinos and nursing? Just once, once before I die, I'd like to see a Filipino doctor.

Almost in automatic mode, as the male nurse was wrapping up that blood pressure device, I went into the same routine I always did with Filipinos.

"From Manila?"

"Yes."

"Ever been to the Tondo?"

All Filipinos responded identically, with a smile and look of amazement. "You know Tondo?" was the response. Always. Like Tondo was a person.

I usually told them that I had heard about it from my father, Tony, an Oakland-raised Vietnam vet who'd been to the Philippines and spent time in Manila's infamous Tondo slum, a teeming hellhole with rats the size of wolverines, shirtless, barrel-chested men in alleys with machetes, and whores who should've been in grammar school.

But today, all I said was, "Heard about it." The nurse left after adjusting some drip. I tried to look down my body. Much of my torso was bandaged. I felt my head, no bandages. If I didn't move much, I felt no pain. The drip must be morphine.

Then I panicked. Full-bore anxiety attack. With it came a spasmodic jolt of cold sweats. Was I damaged? Was I paralyzed? Could I fuck again? I thought about my girlfriend, Francesca.

I tried to breathe in real deep. It hurt. Even morphine has its limitation. I tried to remember facts I loved, to test my brain. The birth and death years of Alexander the Great?–356 to 323 B.C. Number of Mantle World Series home runs? Eighteen. Relief. A few more to double test myself. Francesca's address and phone number. Got it.

I quoted from *The Iliad* opening, the Robert Fagles translation. *"Rage, Goddess, sing the rage of Peleus' son Achilles."* It was one of only two lines from *The Iliad* I knew by heart.

Okay, I'm not brain dead.

I moved my feet. They moved, as did my toes. My hands and

fingers worked. With trepidation and long, slow breaths, damn the pain, I touched my penis. It stirred enough to calm my greatest fear.

I lifted and twisted my neck. Moved my arms, I didn't feel that bad. I smiled and drifted off. Morphine did that to people.

A few hours later, I woke, disoriented. I wondered if word had spread. Was anyone here? My girlfriend? My sister? Of course, they must know. I looked up at the TV. That Filipino nurse was there, watching the news.

I remember the car pulling up. I remember it was an older American car, probably GM. It stopped and a man, a black guy, getting out because I noticed the purple rag he had. Grape Street Crips. I thought this guy was old for a Grape, maybe even fifty. And then I got shot. That's it. Maybe, I thought, when this dope wears off I will remember more.

For many years I had lived with an ominous feeling something dreadful would befall me that would send my life spiraling downhill to its ultimate sad ending. Sometimes I felt this dread hover about me like a swarm of hornets and knew soon their stings would lay me out.

I'd dismiss it as foolishness, as drama, as booze-spattered anxiety. As long as I was vigilant, nothing really bad would happen to me. I'd be on the lookout for the ax and when it swooped, I'd dodge it as gracefully as Manolete sidestepped horns. But the feeling would return. I could be simply talking to a friend or alone in my ride and I'd sense doom racing toward me with intent to imprison, paralyze, or kill.

Often the dread would feature me killing a baby while driving drunk. The worst of the worst. As real as I could, I would imagine, no, not imagine. Imagination is for good things. I would conjure up this terrible scene, strain to feel its horror. I would envision the mangled body of this dead infant, the grieving, angry family, my own heartbroken family. The revulsion that my life would be. And I would languish in that thought and then, when all was doomed in this conjured life, I'd rejoice in reality.

And that's how I felt in this hospital room. Rejoiced. That long-awaited dread had come calling, had fallen on me hard, but it hadn't killed me. Fuck that dread. For the first time in years, I felt no need to worry. There was no more doom lurking. Damn, I felt good.

I put my feet on the floor and stood up. I was wobbly, but I was standing. Life was a grand adventure. The phone rang. It was Francesca.

People often did not believe me at when I told them Francesca Golden was my girlfriend. Just the day before getting shot, I was at little café on Virgil Avenue called Sqirl, and when I spoke proudly of this romance to a friendly foodie seated next me, she called me a liar. I wasn't at all surprised.

Even in Los Angeles, where bizarre bedfellows get few glances, our relationship was treated with curiosity, perhaps even suspicion.

Francesca is the reigning goddess of the Los Angeles restaurant world, a beguiling curly haired brunette drizzled with allure. She has a nose with a slight, sexy bump in its middle that reminds me — and me alone — of the old Masta Kink at the Formula One circuit in Spa, Belgium. See what I mean? And her eyes, her eyes are hazel, the green like wet emeralds, the brown so gentle, almost caramel, making them very sensitive to light. She almost always wears sunglasses, sunshine or rainfall. She almost always wears Marni, her favorite designer.

Francesca Golden had grown up in an especially affluent section of Encino in the San Fernando Valley. Despite the fancy address, she had a wild streak. While in the fourth grade, she stole cosmetics from Sav-On Drugs, got caught, and retired from the thieving life. In the sixth grade she hopped a freight train off San Fernando Road in Glassell Park and rode it alone to the distant land of North Compton where she took a taxi home, financed by her older sister, Gail.

Francesca found her true passion in food and trained at the

mythical restaurant of Fredy Girardet in Crissier, Switzerland. She opened a bakery on Wilshire Boulevard that, on a good day, rivaled Poilane, and a restaurant, The Tower, with her husband, Bernard Fezetta, a master sommelier from Alsace. Soon Francesca became revered in Los Angeles. She expanded the bakery. She made her first million at twenty-seven.

The couple had a daughter Zoe, but by the time the child was three, Francesca and Bernard had split. She opened a new restaurant on her own called Zola, after her child born in L.A.

Five years ago, Francesca went to Napa Valley for a West Coast James Beard benefit dinner. It so happened a friend and frequent customer of Zola was also in Napa Valley that week. He was a convicted violent felon and, though he was white, hung out in the housing projects of Watts, in the barricaded alleys of Green Meadows, in pool halls of North Compton with guys named Mad Dog, Honcho, Snipe, and Big Evil. He was usually dressed in Target black and thought Marni was an old Sean Connery movie. His bank account never soared and he was not handsome. Somehow though, long before she had ever even kissed his mouth, he knew Francesca was made for him. That guy would be me.

I had come to get away from the city, to drink wine and eat well, and to start work on a book I'd probably never finish. I wrote three pages that day, ran three miles, then called Francesca whom I knew was doing a food event in the Napa Valley. She told me to join her and her friends Hiro and Lissa for dinner in St. Helena at Terra Restaurant.

We got toasted—not wasted—at the dinner. Dumol's Eddie's Patch Syrah 2001 did the trick. I maneuvered her away from her trusted friend and pastry chef, Dahlia, and walked her to my car where that old wild streak of hers surfaced. We made out on Railroad Street and I took her back to my room, room 17 at the nearby El Bonita Motel. It was the night of my nights.

Even though I worried come morning, the foodie legend in bed with the longtime customer would turn awkward. So I wasn't surprised, yet I was sad when Francesca awoke, kissed me once on the lips, and walked out. I was pleasantly surprised, no, nah I was euphorically stunned when, fifteen minutes later, she returned with coffee and a lone croissant from the Dean & DeLuca just down Highway 29.

That night we went to Bouchon, little bistro sister to the French Laundry in the wine burg of Yountville. We kissed at the dinner table like young lovers. I knew this would not be just one weekend and, in all my life, I've never been happier. During dessert, we struck up a conversation with an elderly couple at the next table. After about fifteen minutes of banter, the lady at the table asked a question that I'd fondly repeat dozens of times over the years. "How do a famous chef and a crime reporter get together?"

Five years after that, we're still together. I like to sing her praises to people and I love to end by saying, "There's only one thing that makes me suspicious about her. Have you ever met her boyfriend?"

I thought of that question as I listened to Francesca's opening phone salvo. "Small wonder people don't believe you when you tell them I'm your girlfriend."

"Aren't you going to ask how I am?"

There was silence for several seconds. I took that as a beautiful sign. Francesca wasn't much for a breaking voice. Then she said, "You know, I hope they do say I'm your girlfriend when they show you on the news tonight."

That made me silent for several of my own seconds. "I hope they do too."

CHAPTER 5

In a change of the natural order, detectives—Sal LaBarbera and Johnny Hart—had taken to interviewing reporters.

LaBarbera and Hart were not in the Robbery-Homicide Division, which handles high-profile cases. They were from Southeast Division, aka 108th Street. Captain Tatreau wanted them because they were homicide detectives who knew Lyons well and covered the same unruly beat he did.

LaBarbera was New York street-smart and Hollywood leading-man handsome, six foot even, well built, full head of black hair, with a Bronx accent that came on hard when he needed to be tough or when he was joking. A smart dresser, decked out in a black Ralph Lauren blazer and gray slacks, oxblood Cole Haans.

Hart was six three, a motocross-racing, snowboarding, black-belted blond bachelor who was heading for a life of California dreaming until his nephew was killed by a stray bullet in Gardena. So he entered law enforcement, sheriff's first, then LAPD. Simple as that. He found that walking an alley in Watts looking for a sniper was a bigger thrill than pulling a hole shot at Glen Helen motocross track or skiing the west face of KT-22 in Squaw Valley.

They set up shop on editor's row in California editor Harriet Tinder's mid-size office. Before they began to interview other reporters, the detectives scanned Lyons's nearby desk. They noted the books on the top shelf. There were the usual suspects: the tattered *Webster's Dictionary*, a new-looking *Roget's Thesaurus*, a never-opened *Times* stylebook, several *Best Newspaper Writing* annuals and Miles Corwin's seminal *The Killing Season* about a summer with homicide detectives from LAPD's South Bureau.

The first reporter they interviewed was Greg Mahtesian, whose father was Mike's mom's brother. Greg was a rock-solid reporter who often broke major news with his strong FBI contacts. Since September 11, he had been the paper's go-to guy for the Feds.

"Greg, Johnny, and I both know Mike and we think he's a classic guy," said LaBarbera. "He's a guy that I trust, and that's about as high as a compliment a detective can give a reporter." Sal reached out to pat Greg on the shoulder.

"Appreciate that," Greg said.

"Your cousin is either one tough SOB or crazy," Hart chimed in. "Maybe both. He'd go places at night alone and unarmed that I'd only go with a partner and backup. Guy like that, though, he's bound to get some enemies. We're thinking this wasn't random. Not at five p.m. on 2nd and Broadway."

An hour later and several reporters later, Hart turned to LaBarbera, the two of them alone in the editor's office. "You remember that story Lyons wrote on Big Evil?"

"Of course."

"That's when I met him, when he was working on that story."

"Best gang story the *Times* ever had," LaBarbera said. "Lyons hung with Evil tight. And I know it wasn't just a bullshit story."

"I know it," said Hart. "You remember Leslie Harrington, the deputy D.A. on Evil's case, right?"

"Of course. What the fuck. How could I forget? What about her?"

"Even Leslie told me Lyons knew things about Evil that she didn't know, and if she knew then what he knew, she would've gone for the death penalty."

"Once," LaBarbera said, "I met Mike down on Hoover. 'Round 57th Street. 'Bout ten, twelve years ago. At first we thought gang, drug-related. You know, three Mexican guys in one house. But, turns out, this guy living at his cousin's house? He got pissed about something and wasted his cousin and his friends. So Mike is there walking the 'hood for hours, gets the whole story. Finds out all these details about the vics. I remember the cousin, the dead one. He was working sixty hours and going to school to be a nurse. I always remember that."

"Umph, a male nurse," said Hart. "Usually they're Filipinos."

"Anyway," Sal continued. "'Bout seven or so, he calls me. All pissed. He said the city editor told him, 'It's just Hoover Street. We're gonna make that story a brief.' Man, he was so pissed. I thought he was gonna go off. I had to kind of cool him down myself."

"Sounds like Lyons," said Hart.

Hart and LaBarbera considered their suspects. The chef ex-husband of Lyons's girlfriend had been in Colorado when the shooting occurred. Most killings or shootings are committed by the favorites—rival gang members, fellow gang members, husbands, wives, neighbors. But, long shots do come in. Even Man o' War got beat once. By a horse named Upset.

CHAPTER 6

As Lyons floated in and out of his morphine-induced stupor, editors and reporters gathered in Editor Duke Collinsworth's large office to discuss how to advance the story.

"What's new? What do we have?" asked Collinsworth, a distinguished, silver-haired man who looked like a prototype editor. A sixty-three-year-old Southern gentlemen who enjoyed twenty-year-old Pappy Van Winkle's Family Reserve bourbon with one drop of water, had a wife he met at Duke forty-four years ago, a long, slow smile, and a quest to reverse the recent cutbacks that had badly gutted the paper. "How we going to play it today?"

"Well, my sources tell me detectives don't have any eyewitnesses yet, but they think it was gang related," said Goldstein.

"No eyewitnesses. It was at 2nd and Broadway at rush hour. There must've been at least twenty cars within a hundred feet. Have a news aide count cars at that corner for ten minutes," Collinsworth said. "Someone saw that shooting. Any thought the gunman had a silencer?"

"No," said Goldstein. "The bartender at the Redwood said he heard the shots from inside the bar."

Collinsworth shook his head. "A real whodunit. This is a great story. Too bad he's one of us. Anyway, what's going on with the police?"

Goldstein prattled on without saying anything of substance until Tinder cut him off. "How about we do this for a follow? Something like detectives are pursuing leads, including a list of potential suspects that they gathered from colleagues of Lyons. We update his condition. Have Greg get a quote from Mike. Even if it's just 'I'm doing better' or whatever. Go over what Mike covered again. Pound some pavement. Do about twenty, twenty-two inches."

Collinsworth settled back in his worn, brown leather chair that had been with him since he became the editor of the *Charlotte Observer* a quarter century ago. His hands and fingers formed a teepee, his starched, white dress shirt covered elbows resting on the chair's soft leather arms. "That sounds right. And try to keep a lid on this betting pool. The blogs might have it already, especially *L.A. Observer*. But this pool, as of right now, it's history. You hear me, Morty?"

"Yes, sir."

"We'll go with what Harriet suggested. But, if there is nothing new tomorrow, I'm having editorial get on this. We'll do a, 'How can one of our own get shot downtown, broad daylight, two blocks from the LAPD's Police Administration Building with no witnesses and no suspects? Is anyone safe here?' That type of story. The lead editorial. Heck, I'll write it myself. And I'll admit, that pool idea was classic. Now destroy it."

Wednesday evening, I continued to improve. Francesca brought me a bowl of ultrasweet tangerines called Paige mandarins. I wanted to wrap them in newspaper and put them on a radiator to savor their intoxicating aroma, the routine M. F. K. Fisher wrote enticingly about. We did that last year in small, charming Left Bank hotel, a long way from my sterile hospital room in Lincoln Heights, a block from the county morgue.

The morphine had already been replaced by Demerol, but I did not request it until night fell. There were even times when, in a strange way, I actually relished the pain for I felt it strengthened me, made me a better person, more appreciative of those who suffered far, far worse than I. I was earning my right to write the blues.

I was feeling better that night. Euphoric, even. Shortly after my night shot, Francesca kissed me good night and sang softly into my ear a few lines from her favorite song by her beloved Van Morrison, "Brown Eyed Girl."

And Francesca never sang. My eyes got wet.

The next day LaBarbera and Hart stopped by Los Angeles County-USC Medical Center. LaBarbera rapped once, hard, on the open door to my room. I knew that knock. I dispensed with the small talk.

"So who shot me?"

"Not much to report yet, but we'll get him," said Hart.

"What about the first forty-eight hours? How long has it been anyway? Kinda losing track of time."

"You been watching too much TV. Mike, we're lookin' at all angles. Tell us everything you remember about what happened. Every little thing."

"Like I said on the phone, I didn't get much of a look at the guy. It happened so fast. I had just left the Redwood."

"Were you drunk?" asked Hart.

"I don't get drunk, but I'd had two drinks. Two doubles. Stoli."

"That would fry me, but go on."

"So I'm walking along Second Street, right near Sharky's Bail Bonds, and I notice this Buick or Olds pull up."

"Two door, four door?"

"Two. I'm pretty sure two."

"Go on."

"At least I'm remembering more than I did the other day, whenever that was, when I was deep on the morphine."

"Congratulations. Go on."

"The car pulls up to the curb, and this black guy gets out. He's like maybe forty-five, fifty, and he's got a purple bandana covering his head and forehead and a semi, a nine apparently, and he starts shooting. That fast. I think there's nowhere to run, so I think about a charge, but he's too far away and then I go down. Whole thing is maybe two, three seconds at the very most."

"Color of the car?"

"I couldn't say, other than it wasn't light, like white or beige or yellow."

"Color of the black guy? Dark, light skinned?"

"Dark, but not like African dark."

"Height? Weight?"

"Like I told you on the phone, nothing special, wasn't tall, wasn't short. Wasn't fat, wasn't skinny. I know you're getting tired of hearing this, but it happened so quick. I'd say he was somewhere between five eight and five eleven, say somewhere between one sixty and two hundred. The thing is there was nothing really distinctive about him."

"Say, Lyons," said Hart, "you ever think about taking a 'Describe People' class? The FBI has them. You could sure use it."

"Fuck you, Hart."

Hart laughed.

"Actually, what you gave us does help," said LaBarbera. "Narrows it down at least a little bit. We can do a lot of eliminating. On the phone you didn't give me any numbers, but you were out of it. Did he say anything? Anything at all?"

"If he did, I didn't hear it."

"Was anyone on the sidewalk near you?"

"No. Not that I remember."

"You said he had a purple rag on. You recently pissed someone off from Grape Street? Fuck some married women down here?" Hart asked.

"You're a funny guy."

"Whaddya mean funny?"

Sal cut them off. "Don't start with that routine, you two clowns. Jordan Downs, go on."

"I haven't even been to Jordan Downs in months. You know I'm loved down there. Maybe the purple bandana was to throw off the scent."

"That's what Sal and I were thinking. Shooters don't advertise anymore."

"So none of our fine citizens have stepped up. I know there had to be thirty people who saw it. Second and Broadway? Please."

"We got one plate called in, but it turned out to not even be an actual license plate number," said LaBarbera, "And what we have got from anonymous tips goes with you that it was an American car, like a Buick or an Olds or Pontiac."

And, as for suspects," said Hart, "even your colleagues had a list of like fifteen, twenty suspects."

"Yeah, Greg told me. But, hell, half of those suspects were husbands of women I kissed in the last ten years. They don't count. They didn't have balls to fuck their wives, let alone shoot me."

"Coulda hired out," said Hart.

"I don't see it."

"So, it's most likely work related," LaBarbera said. "We thought maybe the Rollin Sixties. You did that big piece on them a couple years ago. We came down hard on them after it ran. They had to be pissed."

"But, like you said, that was two years ago. They don't remember back that far. Plus, Wild Cat was one of the first people to call me in the hospital. I've known Cat for a long time, and we've always respected each other. Used to write him when he was in Soledad and Corcoran. Sometimes send him twenty-dollar mail orders. Guys inside, they don't forget that shit. They love you for that."

"Yeah, we talked to him today. He spoke highly of you. I don't know if I'd be proud of that, but you probably are."

"Damn right," I said. "The Sixties didn't do this."

"You're right about that," said LaBarbera. "If they did, you'd be dead."

"Let me ask you guys something," I said, scooting up a bit on the pillow that had the consistency of hour-old cement. "Do you think I have to worry about whoever did this coming here to finish me off?"

"*Finish you off?*" said Hart with exaggerated tone. "Who are you,

Don Corleone? Sal, how many times you think this guy has seen *The Godfather*?"

"Fuck you, Hart," I said, trying to hide a smile.

"Hey, Johnny," LaBarbera said. "Maybe we should get Luca Brasi to stand in front of the door."

"Fuck that, Sal," I said, moving toward relaxed. "That overrated motherfucker is sleeping with the fishes."

They laughed, said their goodbyes, but not before LaBarbera told me he would tell hospital security to keep a guy on the floor just to play it safe.

"Tell you the truth, Mike, I think whoever did this to you wasn't a pro," said Hart. "There were nine shell casings we picked up on the sidewalk and curb. Two hits outta nine. Not exactly the Sundance Kid."

Later that night, in his office, true to his word, Duke Collinsworth wrote a scathing editorial of the LAPD. The story ran in Thursday's paper.

ARE WE SAFE NEAR PAB
by Duke Collinsworth

The Mayor and the Police Chief like to quote statistics that crime is down. And it is, according to their stats. But, are we safe in Los Angeles? Not really. Can we count on the police to track down our assailants and, as the cliché often used by politicians, goes "Bring them to justice?"

Apparently not. The employees, the family here at the *Times* tasted this bitter reality this week when one of our own, Michael Lyons, was gunned down under a sunny sky just one block away from our editorial offices, two blocks from City Hall and three blocks from the Police Administration Building, PAB, the LAPD's new headquarters.

Lyons was shot and seriously wounded as he walked along 2nd Street near Broadway shortly after five pm. We have tracked that intersection and within a 30 second period up to 100 cars pass that corner. Someone saw something. Yet all the LAPD can say is, "We are vigorously pursuing all leads."

What leads? This happened three short blocks from police headquarters. They like to say the downtown area is safe. Come to Los Angeles. But is it? If a gunman can get away, even for two days, with shooting someone in daylight in downtown Los Angeles two blocks from City Hall, what hope is there for the victims in housing projects in Watts, in alleys of Boyle Heights and in the parks and crowded apartment hallways of Rampart Division?

Mike Lyons has a dangerous beat for a city reporter. He covers street gangs and, I imagine, knowing him, when he is healthy, he will return to this beat he loves. Between 50% and 60% of the homicides in Los Angeles are gang related and Lyons, who personally convinced me we should create a beat solely devoted to gangs, felt we, as the newspaper of record in the West, needed to cover them more thoroughly. I agreed and he was given that beat.

The LAPD needs to cover gangs better, also. They need to protect us. As their car says "To Protect and Serve." Maybe they should add "And to Find the Shooters."

How can we be safe in Los Angeles if we are not safe on Broadway and 2nd Street? The LAPD needs to find the shooter and send a message to other shooters. Our citizens need to know if you shoot someone, be it a reporter from the *Los Angeles Times* on 2nd Street or a grandma on 114th Street in Nickerson Gardens, you will be, in the blowhard words of our politicians, "hunted down." Get on your jobs, detectives, and find the person who shot my reporter. Let the city, let the country, let the world know, shooters can't get away in Los Angeles.

CHAPTER 7

The editorial was met with scorn throughout much of the city. It resulted in a rare union: residents from the city's roughest neighborhoods and the police that patrol their streets. They agreed the *Times* only cared because it was one of their own who got popped.

That afternoon, LAPD called a press conference in front of the Police Administration Building. Uniformed LAPD Chief of Police Charlie Miller, flanked by finely attired Captain Tatreau, police brass, and city officials, stepped to the microphones set up near the entrance to the PAB. A SWAT team was out of sight inside the lobby and, in the nearby parking lot, another thirty or so officers were ready for trouble.

"Everyone ready?" Miller asked the TV news crews. And, of course, as is always the case at any police news conference, one station's cameraman wasn't quite ready. He squeezed in between his friends at competing stations, adjusted his camera, gave a thumbs-up. Miller began: "We're here to give you an update into the investigation of the shooting of *Los Angeles Times* reporter Michael Lyons, who was seriously wounded downtown early Monday evening as he walked out of the Redwood Saloon on 2nd Street.

"Because of the nature of the case, I have assigned two detectives from South Bureau Homicide to work with Robbery-Homicide to lead the investigation, Detective Sal LaBarbera and Detective Johnny Hart, both of whom have worked the gang units and who both know Mike Lyons. As a personal aside, I have met Lyons on several occasions and have always admired his work. This case has garnered special attention from us not because Lyons is a *Times* reporter, but because of the when and where of this audacious shooting. We cannot let criminals turn our downtown into a free-fire zone.

"As for the investigation itself, we are pursuing a number of leads, some of which I cannot get into, much to the apparent chagrin of the *Times* editorial board. Obviously, they have never run an investigation of this type.

"Nevertheless, I can tell you we are in the process of interviewing people and are going over some of Lyons's stories in search of clues. We do ask the public for their help. There were many cars and people near the intersection of Second and Broadway at five p.m. Monday, and we need to hear from you. Even if you think you have nothing to tell us, we would still like to talk to you. This can be done over the phone and anonymously if need be. I'll take a few questions now."

At the news conference, news radio reporter Howitzer Hal Hansen, with his cavernous voice, overpowered the others and got in the first question. "Chief, can you tell the people of Los Angeles, particularly the people who work downtown in the heart of this great city, that they are safe?"

"Yes, I can, Hal. There are, unfortunately, many shootings in this city, but the numbers are down dramatically. I repeat, dramatically, from five, ten, even twenty years ago. Daytime downtown shootings are extremely rare. It just does not happen often. If it did, this would not be major news. So I want to encourage the people — residents, tourists, and workers alike — not to fear downtown Los Angeles. This was a very unusual incident. You do not have to be fearful of walking downtown.

"I need to emphasize that reporter Michael Lyons dealt with street gangs. That was his beat. He was known for doing some dangerous street reporting. We are definitely looking into the distinct possibility that one of his stories upset some bad guys. We've been going over his stories and looking for clues. The average citizen of this city does not go out of their way to deal with gangs as he did, and we believe that may have contributed to this shooting."

A reporter called out, "Are you calling this a gang-related shooting?"

"No, we are not. Not yet. Well, not unless you consider the *Los Angeles Times* to be a gang." Some polite scattered laughter rippled through the crowd. Not much. "But seriously, we are looking into the strong possibility that it was gang related."

Channel 7 was next. "Chief, I know you say things are safe here. Still, this shooting was only two blocks from city hall, just three blocks from police headquarters."

"Sounds like you read today's editorial," said Miller.

"We all did, Chief. We all did. But, doesn't this send a message to the gangbangers that they can blast away in daylight three blocks from LAPD headquarters and get away with it? Won't this spark even more bloodshed? Isn't this a problem?"

"It is a problem for criminals to shoot two blocks from here and it is a problem for them to shoot a hundred and three blocks from here on Grape Street in Watts. The media are focusing on the Lyons shooting and, believe me, I understand the news angle here. But, last night there was a homicide on Fifty-Fourth Street and Ascot. The *Times* made it a one-inch brief and, as far as I know, none of the TV stations, including yours, even carried it. But, within two hours, two suspects were in custody. I want to let the public know that we are out there doing our job, in Watts, in Boyle Heights, in Pico-Union, in Hollywood, in Venice, in San Pedro, in the Valley, and right here in downtown."

Howitzer Hal started in again, "Chief, can you say—"

"Hold on, Hal. The message is not that the gangbangers, if this was indeed gang related, can get away with it. They will not get away with it. Whoever did it will be brought to justice. It might take another day, it might take a month, but we will get the shooter. That's the real message."

Though several reporters yelled out questions, Miller cut them off. "We ask the public's help as we do in all cases. This is not the police versus the criminals. This is the police and the public versus the bad guys. The public is a key ally. We need the public in this case and in all cases. The police with the public's help, the public with the police's help. That's the way we all win. Thank you very much."

CHAPTER 8

To be merely wounded during a crime and get mentioned in the *Los Angeles Times* is rare. On many an occasion, Lyons had told an editor about a wounding he had heard on the police scanner or learned from making a cop call. The editor's reaction was usually, "Let me know if he dies."

There were basically four ways to get in the paper with just a wound.

If the victim was some type of celebrity, such as a rapper or athlete of middle to major note, he or she would get in. Hollywood movie or television stars do not get shot. They are never around real violence.

If a student is wounded on a high school campus, even just grazed in the finger, most likely that will make the paper unless it happens at Manual Arts, Jordan, Fremont, Jefferson, Locke, Washington, Crenshaw, Dorsey, Gardena, Compton, Carson, Roosevelt, Garfield, Centennial, Morningside, Inglewood, or Banning high schools. At those schools, the wound would have to be more than a nick.

If the wounding occurs at a major venue—say the Grove, Los Angeles County Museum of Art, Rodeo Drive, Disneyland, Santa Monica Pier, Beverly Center, places like that—it gets major play for sure.

About the only way for a commoner to make it in the paper with just a wound is when that victim is a real hard-luck, against-all-odds success story.

•　•　•

Debra Sady Griffen was a classic example of the "I'm gonna make it, come hell or high water" story. Two years ago, in three weeks' time, her parents were killed on Crenshaw near Imperial Highway by a drunk driver; her older sister, Denise, drank herself to a Smirnoff death; and her older brother, Darnell, was shot to death by a seventeen-year-old Nutty Blocc Compton Crip because he had on a maroon t-shirt.

Rather than melt into the city's sidewalks, Debra Sady, then twenty-two, was fervently determined to make something of her life. She worked hard. Before her night shift as a stock clerk at the Food4Less on Slauson and Western, she attended bus-driving school. Her goal was, after two months on the bus gig, to move out of her apartment on Brynhurst Avenue, a mid-size city's worth of urban nightmares squished into six narrow blocks.

The day before she was to start driving kids to school for Laidlaw Bus Company, Debra went to her cousin's house in Lynwood, a suburb on the relatively right side of the Alameda tracks. To her tearful surprise, a dozen family members and friends had gathered to celebrate her graduation and her new job. It was one of the great times of her life. Never had Debra Sady felt prouder, never had she felt more in love with life.

About the time Debra was singing along to Junior Walker and the All Stars's "What Does It Take (To Win Your Love)," there was a shooting several miles to the west near the Harbor Freeway.

The Hotel Mary on Vermont near 75th had recently undergone a $680 renovation that included a new mop and bucket, a rug cleaning, a Bissell vacuum cleaner, and painting of the front awnings green, and the front and side walls hot pink, a popular color in these parts. It was called a hotel, but it was just a flophouse where the rooms rent for eighty-five dollars a week, the air never moved, and the hallways reeked like a Figueroa Street whore who hasn't paid her hot water bill since summer began.

In a second-floor room, a drug deal had gone wrong. A Seven-Four Hoover Criminal had been shot in the shoulder and robbed of his stash, about three hundred dollars in rocks. The wounded twenty-year-old recognized his assailant, a rival from the Rollin Sixties Crips, their decades-long mortal enemies. As his homies drove him to the hospital, he told them who the shooter was. No one waited for the paramedics on the Southside of L.A. In the emergency room of Harbor/UCLA Medical Center on Carson Street in Torrance, police questioned the victim, who told them he had no idea who had shot him and that it wasn't much of a shooting anyway.

As police interviewed the wounded man, three of his boys from Hoover, a gang admired for their quick payback shootings, were already searching for the shooter. They knew him to be staying with a cousin on Brynhurst Avenue in Hyde Park. Hoovers also had good intel. About fifteen minutes earlier, Debra Sady had gotten her hugs and well-wishes and said her goodbyes and was headed back to her apartment complex on Brynhurst.

In Southwest Los Angeles, in the area west of Crenshaw and both south and north of Slauson Avenue, amidst the fragrant cloud of Woody's BBQ, is the neighborhood of Hyde Park.

If you took a corner boy from, say, 25th and Diamond in North Philly, he'd drool over the neat two- and three-bedroom Spanish tile-roofed homes with their sweet-smelling red Mister Lincoln rose-bushes and Purple Queen bougainvillea that line the streets.

But, that corner boy would be surprised to learn that this neighborhood was the domain of one of the deadliest black street gangs in the United States—The Rollin Sixties Crips, often both affectionately and dreadfully referred to as "Six-Oh." As in "'Dem niggas from Six-Oh just shot your grandma."

The guts of Six-Oh turf is Brynhurst Avenue, a place to be caught dead. The blocks along Brynhurst are lined with cramped two-story apartment buildings and courtyard bungalows. Many of the twelve-hundred-strong Rollin Sixties lived on Brynhurst, thugs with names like Tiny Creepy, Hammerhands, Felony Fred, Scatterbrain, Papa Loc, Peedee Wac, and Wild Cat.

As Debra Sady drove her blue-green 2001 Nissan Sentra toward her Brynhurst rental, she was singing still, now to Marvin and Tammy's "Ain't Nothing Like the Real Thing."

The real thing would start tomorrow for Debra Sady: a bus driving job with real benefits and a 401K savings plan. Seconds after she turned off 63rd Street and onto Brynhurst, so did a carload of Hoover Criminals looking to avenge. As she exited her Sentra, carrying a plate of smothered pork chops from her cousin's house, down rolled the window of a brown Ford Bronco driven by one Lyles Davis aka "Tiny Trouble." Another Hoover screamed "Hoo-va" and speed triggered a Glock 19 at the suspected shooter of their homie. Near him were two other men, two women, and two boys, one of them doing circles in a blue on red Big Wheel. Before the "va" came out of his mouth, targets were running for cover. None of them, including the target, were hit. Not unusual. If gang members were good shots, L.A. would have one of the highest homicide rates in the world.

But, as Debra Sady stepped from her Nissan, she heard the shots and a bullet struck her back, just piercing a kidney. The plate of pork chops went flying as she reeled for two spastic steps before tumbling to the concrete driveway of her apartment complex. The plate of food shattered near her head. Debra Sady lay oozing blood and dreams.

CHAPTER 9

The most mundane element of being a crime reporter is making the dreaded "cop calls." Cop calls are when a reporter calls every police and sheriff's station in the city and county to check if there is any fast-breaking news. Fire departments, too.

It's almost always an exercise in futility. Having made thousands of cop calls over the years, Michael had found that they generated a story—mostly briefs—at a ratio of maybe one in five hundred calls at best.

Still, cop calls are required. Especially on night cops. Sometimes reporters get lazy—Michael was no exception—and they just call the main public-information numbers of the LAPD and the Los Angeles County Sheriff's. The problem with that is that sometimes even the headquarters isn't up on the latest breaking crimes. The sheriff's are okay, but it is hit-and-miss with LAPD press relations. One of the LAPD public information officers, Sergeant Chris Feldmeier, always had the same report: "All quiet in the city tonight." Always. No matter what. A dirty bomb could have been unleashed on the stadium during a Dodgers/Giants game, and Feldmeier would give his "All quiet" reply.

Some of the LAPD PIOs, Public Information Officers, are engaging. Mike would often flirt with one of them, Lucy Sanchez, whose voice was sweet as butterscotch budino. About ten years ago, he even took Lucy out for drinks and oysters one lovely night.

The proper way to do cop calls is to call every police station, every fire station in L.A. County. You might call the Redondo Beach watch command 755 times and get nothing. But, one of the cop reporter's nightmares is that the night you don't call, there'll be a double homicide at the Redondo Pier.

On that Sunday when Debra Sady was shot, Hector Salazar was the night cops reporter. When he called the 77th Street Station and asked what was going on, he was told there'd been a nonfatal shooting on Brynhurst near 64th Street. Salazar, raised in Boyle Heights, a graduate of Roosevelt High and Cal State-L.A., was not stunned by this, knowing the address was Rollin Sixties turf and shootings there are as rare as sunsets. He thanked the cops and told the night editor nothing was going on.

About an hour later, the night editor, Marcy Duval, e-mailed him that they could use a brief or two to fill out the section. Hector e-mailed back quickly in the style of many reporters and even editors, not bothering to check the spelling. "got a shhooting on 64 street womanwounded"

Marcy e-replied: "64 and what?"

Hector: "Brynhurst"

Marcy: "Thats not news"

Monday morning, a week after he was shot, Michael was released from the hospital. His sister, Jeanine, all smiles and tears, picked him up. They drove by the Los Angeles County Coroner Building and Michael pointed it out to her.

"I just thank God you didn't end up there. I love you, Michael."

"I love you, too."

She drove him to her St. Andrews Place home in Gardena, aka G-Town, where they grew up and where she now lived with her two kids. Her husband, Ralph, having died unexpectedly four years ago from a stroke.

Dr. Wang had told Michael he should not be alone the first few days and since Francesca was in San Francisco for a charity food event, he decided to stay with his sister for a night. He headed to his nephew's room that used to be his and took to the bed. It felt good to be in this bed and he slept for seven hours.

On his cell phone he had nine messages, eight from well-wishers and one of much interest. It was from a street source about a shooting on Brynhurst. Some saint got strayed. Sounded like a good story. He couldn't do the story, so that evening he called Hector Salazar.

After hearing from Michael Lyons, Salazar felt the rush, knowing he had a powerful story on his hands. All he had to do now was convince his editors the bus driver-to-be was indeed a great story. It would seem on the surface to be a natural. But, assistant city editors at the *Times* were, for the most part, a cautious group, the type whose main concern was to not make waves and to continue to get their $2,000-$2,500 a week.

Salazar approached night editor, Marcy Duval, and pitched her the story of Debra Sady Griffen. The night before she had dismissed the story as just another nonfatal shooting in Rollin Sixties 'hood. But, now Salazar was armed with a hard-luck, against-all-odds tragedy. Salazar's worrying was for naught as Marcy said, "That's a good story. Let's get the background, interview folks, the cops, bus people. Get me a sked. Say twenty to twenty-two inches. We need art of her. Let's shoot for Wednesday, even Thursday."

Hector nodded and headed back to his desk. Marcy sent Hector an e-mail: "Maybe we can tie it into the Mike shooting—another big shooting and they get away with it. Where's the LAPD?"

Hector, energized by visions of the front page, fired off a "sonds goood ill get onit."

Two days later, Michael got out of Francesca Golden's bed. Francesca was already on her daily morning exercise walk, three miles, always the same route in her tree-lined neighborhood—Van Ness to Clinton to Wilcox to Rosewood, back to Van Ness. That course never varied.

On the LATEXTRA front page he read Hector Salazar's article entitled "SAINT OF OUR GUTTERS GUNNED DOWN." Lyons muttered to himself, "Gunned down?" To him that meant dead.

And on it went, extolling Debra Sady's virtues and decrying the random gunfire. The local media had another field day. The LAPD looked bad again. So did the headline writer. Lyons thought Debra sounded like a good woman, but Mother Teresa?

On most gang shootings, the chances that the cops will get any cooperation from residents are criminally slim. Witnesses fear for their lives. It's that simple. But, Wednesday, one witness came forward for Debra Sady.

As the gunfire that laid out Debra Sady briefly drowned out her television, seventeen-year-old Cardella Jackson calmly laid low in her bedroom.

As the squeal of the tires was heard, she peeked out her bedroom window, got a good look at the Bronco and its rather easy-to-remember license plate, 069TDY. She laughed. The first—and last—time she ever tried 69ing was with a high school point guard named Teddy Jones who twisted and sprained his neck during the act and had to miss his Crenshaw High School basketball game vs. arch rival Dorsey. Dorsey won by four points. Anyway, she wrote it down, just in case.

When Cardella heard that Debra Sady was the victim, she was torn. She liked Debra Sady a lot. Debra had on more than a few occasions brought over some "Sock It To Me" cake that was her specialty. She was quick with a sincere, kind word of encouragement. Debra had always treated Cardella with respect and when you don't have anything and someone gives you respect, well, that's one of the most precious gifts you can give in the ghetto, ranked not far behind giving up some of that cash.

Consequently, Cardella was numbed by the shooting but scared to her core to go to the police, even with their promise of anonymity. Yeah, they say no names, but what about if and when the trial comes? They'll pressure the shit out of you to testify in open court. She remembered her second cousin, Jermaine, who was set to testify against a gang leader a few years ago. From prison, the leader, Big Evil, ordered him dead, and dead he was in a week.

Cardella prayed on it, then drove three miles to Gardena and punched 911 at a phone booth that had one window shot out and G-13 graffiti scrawled inside and out. Shit, she thought, you can't go anywhere in this fucked-up city without some gang screwing things up. She asked to speak with a detective and she was trembling. She put her hand over her mouth and mumbled into the mouthpiece. The detective couldn't understand her. She moved her hand away. "That shooting on Brynhurst. The one where Debra Sady got shot."

CHAPTER 10

Two hours later, Tiny Trouble of Seven-Four Hoover was in an interview room at the notorious 77th Street Division police station drinking a Dr Pepper in the shadow of the intimidating Detective Mo Batts, six foot five, 275, and Sandra Core, a very attractive dirty blond deputy district attorney from the Hard-Core Gang unit.

Batts pulled his chair close to Trouble. "Let's get down to business. Brynhurst. You know Brynhurst?"

"Never met the man."

Batts slapped the top of Trouble's head. Deputy D.A. Core shot him a look that said, "Don't overdo it."

Batts resumed. "Are you familiar with a street in the Hyde Park area of Los Angeles called Brynhurst?"

"Yeah, that's the street where the Rollin sissies hang out. Or so I heard. Towards myself, I ain't never even been there. Too many faggots there for me. Me, I likes me some pussy. Some white sugar." He leered at Sandra Core. She rolled her eyes.

"Who you rollin' your eyes at, bitch?"

This time, Batts smacked Tiny Trouble upside the head. Hard. For Los Angeles gang members, rolling your eyes at them is a disrespect of the lowest order, a step from putting down your mother even if your mother was sprung and just a few steps away from putting down your saintly grandmother.

"Look, here's the situation," said Batts. "We got several witnesses who saw you driving a Bronco on Brynhurst the night Debra Sady Griffen, the bus driver lady, was shot. They can point you out and identify the car as being the shooting vehicle. Do you think we just came up on you out of the blue?"

"Fuck blue. This is Hoova. Hoova is orange."

"Enough with the colors bullshit," said Core. "Didn't that go out in the eighties? Wake up, boy."

"Who you callin' boy, slut?"

Batts slammed his fist into the wall. "Motherfucker. One thing I hate is for a lady to be disrespected in front of me. You know why, bitch? Because it's disrespectful to me. Miss Core, can you let me alone with him for a few minutes? Wanna teach him some manners."

Core hesitated, but left. The hulking Mo Batts moved in close.

"Get away from me," Trouble said. "This ain't *Zero Dark Thirty*. No torture. Back the fuck off."

"Too late for that. You dissed me. And now you're going to be my punching bag." He started throwing jabs that came close to Trouble. Trouble started to get up, but Batts, with one mighty paw, put a vise grip on his neck and ground him back down into the seat.

"I'm gonna start yelling, you don't back up."

"Go ahead. Yell. Scream like a bitch. Like the bitch you really are. You know what? I just came up with a better plan for you. Why bruise my hands? We need to give you a full-body cavity search."

At that, Batts pulled out his big nightstick. "Maybe I'll get that pretty district attorney in here to watch to make sure I do this by the book."

"No! No!" It was like a sweat spigot opened over Trouble's whole body. Then his bowels started to loosen. He was about to smear his shorts. *Damn*, he thought, *why'd I go to Popeye's?* He tried to squeeze his insides together. That seemed to work. A foul smell emitted, but the brown tide scare receded. He took a deep breath. More sweat came off of him in rivulets. But nothing else. "Okay. Okay, I was there. I was on Brynhurst. I didn't do no shooting. Leave me alone. I din't even know there was a gun in the sled."

Batts stepped back, put his nightstick away, opened the door, and Sandra Core came back in and closed the door. She sniffed the polluted air. Batts said, "Our tough Hoover here just had a close encounter of the turd kind." He laughed heartily. Core reopened the door and, with exaggerated, frantic hand movement, attempted to scoop fresh air into the room. She looked at Batts and started laughing too.

Never had Trouble felt lower. He thought his life had bottomed out three years ago when he'd seen his mother sucking off one of his homies for a rock behind the Bethel A.M.E. Church on Fig, but, this bottomed that. Does life even have a bottom? How low does the basement go? How many floors down? Sad thing is for fellas to be in the basement, say on like negative level four and they be happy as shit 'cause they ain't on basement level negative eleven. Ain't even on the ground floor and they cool with the view. Damn, but to almost shit myself. And I know these exaggerating motherfuckers gonna tell everyone I did. Fuck, I'm gonna play my wild card today. Get me to the lobby and get out this building. A touch of his bravado came back. He'd play his ace.

"Look," said Trouble, "you wanna make me a deal? We can deal."

"Deal?" said Core. "You were in the car with people that shot an innocent lady. A saint, from what I hear. How the hell you going to deal?"

"I know the Brynhurst shooting is big to y'all. But, the real big case is that reporter from the *Times* who got hit downtown. Am I right or am I right?"

"What about it?" Batts said, trying to hide his interest. "You shoot him, too?"

"Nah. But, I heard some very interesting information about that. That case been on like CNN and HBO and shit. Channel seven."

"Go on."

"I need to get a deal before I be sayin' any goddamn thing."

"Say something interesting and maybe we can talk," said Core.

"But, you are not walking anywhere. You can give me the new pope from Argentina as the reporter's shooter and you still gonna do something for the lady on Brynhurst. Maybe we can work something out, though. What do you have, Mr. Trouble?"

"I like that. You calling me Mr. Trouble," he said, eyes darting cautiously toward Batts. "Look, I ain't actually heard it myself, but one of my g's told me 'bout a tape floatin' around that talks about the reporter's shooting."

"A tape?" Core said. "Like a videotape of the shooting?"

"Nah, nah. Not a video, a tape, you know just a sound tape."

"An audiotape?" said Core.

"There you go. An audiotape."

"What's on this tape?"

"That reporter Lyons. He on the tape. Talking."

"So what's so important on the tape?" asked Batts.

"The reporter is on the tape planning his own shooting."

CHAPTER 11

An hour later, LaBarbera and Hart walked into the 77th Street squad room and spent a minute bullshitting with detectives before getting serious with Batts. "Kuwahara told us what this guy said," said LaBarbera. "It's hard to believe. I've known Lyons for over ten years. I can't see it."

"Well, let's go talk to our boy here," said Batts. "After he said that, we didn't go too hard, though I gave him a good scare."

"You'd scare just about anybody, including me," said Hart.

"No. A stinky scare," said Batts who fanned his hand in front of his nose.

"No shit?" said Hart.

"Yes, shit. A trouser tragedy."

"You are one sick fuck, Mo," said Hart. "But, I'm glad you're on our team."

In the interview room with Sandra Core, LaBarbera sat near Tiny Trouble. Hart pinched his own nose and looked at Mo Batts who nodded proudly.

"I'm Detective LaBarbera. This is Detective Hart. We hear you have information regarding the shooting of Michael Lyons. What's the story with this audiotape?"

"See, I ain't like actually heard the actual tape. My dawg Mayhem from Seven-Fo' heard it. He say the reporter is saying like 'shoot me 'cause then I can be a hero.' Some shit like that. Serious. He sounds serious."

"I thought you just said you didn't hear the tape. So how can you say he sounds serious?" said Hart. "You better not be wasting our time. I'll put your ass in the Rollin Sixties module at Men's Central. Now, did you hear it or what?"

"Nah, man, nah. I didn't hear it. I'm just relaying what my boy told me. You want me to start every fuckin' sentence with, 'this is what my boy told me'? Or you want it more real? My boy said that reporter sounded like he meant it."

"How'd did your boy get the reporter's tape?" asked Core. "And why would Lyons tape himself saying that? Doesn't make sense."

"It wasn't the reporter's tape. It's my uncle's tape. My boy said my uncle was taping the reporter for like, backup. To play it safe, you feel me? Ya know, like if he makes up something we didn't say, we got proof we didn't say it. What they call being misquoted."

"Where's your boy Mayhem with the tape? Call him," Hart said.

"He don't have the tape. I told you. It ain't his. He just heard it. My uncle, his shot caller, got the tape."

"The shot caller for Seven-Four Hoover?" asked Hart. "He's your uncle?"

"Yeah. You know who he is?"

At the same time, Hart, LaBarbera, and Batts said, "King Funeral."

CHAPTER 12

One hour later, LaBarbera, Hart, and Trevon "Li'l Mayhem" Browning, eighteen, from Seven-Four Hoover, were driving to the home of Thomas Barrow, aka King Funeral, a menacing, muscular five-foot-nine thug, reputed, with his crazy young homies, to be responsible for keeping at least two Southside mortuaries in business.

King Funeral's only sister, Bonnie, four years his elder, had once saved his life when she stepped in front of Eight Trey Gangster Crips who were about to shotgun her brother in an alley off 83rd and Denker. Bonnie had dated an Eight Trey shot caller and they honored her request to spare her brother. After, she asked Funeral one thing. Like a black female Don Corleone, she told him, "One day I'm ask you for a favor." This favor would be to help her son Lyles "Tiny Trouble" Davis, stay out of prison. Bonnie had already lost her oldest son to Corcoran. At the precinct, Lyles had called his mom and she had called her brother to cash in that long-ago earned favor. King Funeral had no choice but to help the sister that saved his life.

Funeral kept the two-room dump right on 74th and Hoover where he came of age, but lived in a four-bedroom home in Palmdale, fifty miles from the city. Hart was at the wheel, LaBarbera shotgun, and Li'l Mayhem in the back, uncuffed after a vigorous frisking. The road peeled away in fast-forward mode, and Hart was relentless on the gas pedal. Just fifteen minutes into the hour drive, Browning started complaining.

"I'm hungry." The cops agreed, and five minutes later they were at the drive-in window of the In-N-Out Burger in Sylmar. Li'l Mayhem leaned up to Hart and said, "Gimme two double-doubles."

Hart turned and looked at the criminal.

"Oh, yeah. Please," added Mayhem.

Hart placed the order, four double-doubles, three fries, three large sodas, two Dad's root beers, one orange Crush. "How do you know about double-doubles? Not an In-N-Out Burger anywhere near the Southside."

"Man, don't you know where the juvenile hall is? In Sylmar. Every time I got out, my boys used to take me here for a celebration. You feel me? I even know the burgers not on the menu. Animal style, protein style, four by fours. Just 'cause I'm from Hoova, don't mean I ain't worldly. I know plenty about the world. Geography and shit. You cops just think we stupid. We just temporarily trapped is all. I'm getting out and seeing the world. Seeing all the capitals. I bet I know more world capitals than you, cop Hart. That used to be my specialty in geography class."

"It's Detective Hart. But, all right, my Hoova," mocked Hart. "What's the capital of California?"

"Come on. Do I even have to answer that? Shit, Sacramento. Okay, wise man. How 'bout Libya?"

"Libya? Libya. Man, Libya's capital is Tripoli. Okay, let's go to Columbia."

"Bogotá."

"Well, I guess you should know that one since you're doing business with those dudes," said Hart. Once their food arrived, they drove away and Hart continued, "Okay. Now, where were we? How about Russia?"

"Man, it ain't even my turn," said Mayhem as he wiped cheeseburger juice off his mouth with his hand and smeared it on the rear seat. "But, if that's the best you can come up with, then Moscow."

Hart smirked. "You know, Sal. It's kinda sad the kid here thinks he knows capitals because he knows three or four. Like, he knows

Moscow and that makes him kinda smart for just knowing Moscow is the capital of Russia. You know what I mean? The sad thing is, he's right. He is smart compared to his partners. At Fremont or Manual Arts or Gardena? Knowing that Moscow is the capital of Russia gets you put in the advanced class."

Hart continued, talking like it was just the two of them in the car. "It ain't their fault. It's the parents. It's the teachers who don't care. It's the decrepit classrooms with seventy kids in them." Hart looked in the rearview mirror at Li'l Mayhem. "Don't get me wrong. I think it's good you know places like Bogotá and Tripoli and Moscow. Seriously."

"Gee, thanks. I'm so glad I got your approval of my brain. But, maybe we oughta play for a few ducats. A Benjamin or something. You're so smart. Putting everyone down in my 'hood. Let's play the capital contest for some cash."

"I don't want your money. Plus, you probably don't have but two dollars in quarters and dimes on you anyway."

Mayhem reached into his pockets, and LaBarbera suddenly turned around, his right hand on his Glock 40, his left hand over the seat about to grab the Hoover's throat, even though they had thoroughly patted him down earlier. "I'm cool, I'm cool. You already done frisked me."

Mayhem slowly pulled out a tattered wallet and some cash. He had fifty-four dollars. "Let's go for fifty. I even let your boss hold the green." He handed LaBarbera fifty dollars.

Hart looked pissed off. Sal laughed. "Johnny, he's calling you out." Hart reached into his sport coat chest pocket and checked his cash. He had sixty-five dollars.

"Lebanon." Hart said.

"Beirut. Madagascar?"

"Madagascar. Damn. Madagascar. Madagascar."

Mayhem smiled. "Saying it over and over ain't gonna help you, my detective. First round knockout. Give it up, Smarty Jones."

Hart was getting a bit red. His foot was getting even heavier as the Vasquez Rocks slipped by on the left. The Ford hit 105. "Slow it down, A.J.," Sal said. "Funeral ain't goin' nowhere."

"All right. I don't know. What is it?"

"Capital of Madagascar is Antananarivo. Pay up."

"First of all, even if that is right, this isn't a sudden-death game. It's just one strike."

"You didn't say that."

"I'm saying it now. No game ends with one strike. We are doing three strikes, then you're out."

"Figured you like that three strikes rule. I got a homie in Pelican Bay on three strikes doing life because he swiped some lasagna. Believe that shit? Your whole life for some lasagna. Three strikes sucks."

"Well," said Hart, "Here's your first strike. Liberia."

Mayhem crossed his thin, but hard arms, sat down lower in the seat, and smugly said, "Monrovia. Named after President James Monroe. Just happens to be the only non-American capital city named after a U.S. President. How's that for a dummy from the Southside? And for you, my cop, I wonder if you know the cap of Pakistan."

Hart, after some serious brain searching, got Islamabad, but he stumbled soon after losing on Mongolia—Ulan Bator—and North Korea—Pyongyang—while Mayhem scored with correct answers to Finland—Helsinki—and Uruguay—Montevideo.

"Fuck," said Hart.

Li'l Mayhem silently stuck his hand toward Sal who handed him his fifty back. Hart handed over fifty. "Don't say a word, scum. I'll pull this car off this lonely desert road here. Got me a shovel in the trunk. You'll never be found."

Mayhem didn't say a word, probably figuring that was not out of the question. They sped in silence out of the craggy hills and into the suburban desert pot marked with cookie-cutter homes. This was once considered the promised land for middle- and lower-middle-class whites and blacks, a place where you could get away from crime and smog. But some of Utopia had turned into a desert nightmare. Sections of it were a lightweight version of Los Angeles, complete with gangs and drugs and bored teenagers whose virginity was long gone by fourteen.

"Take that next off ramp. Freeman Street," Mayhem said. "Then go left like two miles and turn right on Daisy Hill Lane. That's where he lives. I forgot the number, but I know the house."

"Daisy Hill Lane?" said Hart, breaking his silence. "What a fuckin' pussy name for a street. Why don't they just call it Pussy Street? His wife must be in charge. I always knew he was a punk. How else would a man live on Daisy Mae Lane?"

"Daisy Hill Lane."

"Daisy Hill. Daisy Mae. Same thing. You think this asshole who used to shout 'I'm from Hoover Street, this is Hoover here.' You think he's bragging, claiming 'I'm from Daisy Mae Lane.'"

Mayhem knew better than to correct. A minute later they turned into King Funeral's driveway.

CHAPTER 13

Detective Sal LaBarbera, the purported inventor of the "One Knock" policy, rapped his punched-through-many-a-wall knuckles on the black metal security door, rattling it like a gigantic tuning fork. Five seconds later, King Funeral, all 220 rock-hard pounds of him, opened the door and shook his shaved head. "I'd know that knock anywhere."

"Damn, Fune, I figured you'd have a butler opening and slamming doors for you by now."

"Cut the shit, Sal. You know I can't trust no one. No one but the police and my rivals. One to lock me up, one to shoot me. Least I know where they coming from. Everyone else, you gotta be leery."

"Thomas, we ain't coming to lock you up," said Hart. "Been there often, often done that."

"Don't remind me. C'mon, c'mon in. I don't want my neighbors to see me associating with riffraff."

Funeral was dressed casual nice, loose-fitting black slacks, a green-and-orange silk short sleeve and orange Nike Air Jordan 3 Joker sneaks. "Nice wheels, boss," said Li'l Mayhem. "The Jokers are sweet."

Funeral ignored him and led the cops into his living room, offering them a seat on a cushy seven-foot orange leather couch. A rust-colored carpet was strewn with big pillows and a chrome coffee table displayed two big books—one about Rome, one on Muhammad Ali. Li'l Mayhem pointed to the Rome tome and said to Hart, "Capital of Italy."

"Fuck you, asshole."

"Hey, King," said Mayhem, "did you know that Muhammad Ali won his Olympic Gold medal in Rome, or is that why you put them books out together?"

Funeral shook his head and looked at Hart and LaBarbera. "Almost nothing more annoying than a young brother who thinks he can educate a man. Maybe, I should tell you to wait outside with my rotty-shep or go wash my Escalade or clean my gutters, but just go in the den there and get us something to drink. You know what a den is, right? It's a nice room."

"I know what a den is, boss," said Mayhem. "I even know what it stands for. D.E.N. Decorated extra nice. Maybe you didn't even know that."

"Your boy is one annoying piece of a shit," said Hart to Funeral. "What I don't understand is how you haven't had him shot yet."

"It is a mystery," said Funeral. "Now, boy, spare us your bullshit and get me a drink before I decorate your face extra ugly. Get one for yourself, too. Then shut the fuck up. Detectives, how about some con yak? Relax for a minute with an old enemy."

Hart glanced over at Sal who just shook his head once.

"Get the Rémy, youngin'. The fancy bottle."

"Not a bad place," said Sal.

"Compared to what? My old dump my momma raised us on 74th? Yeah, it's a long way from there. But I ain't forgot my peeps."

"We know."

Li'l Mayhem returned with Rémy XO and two snifters that he set on the coffee table and poured two deep drinks.

Funeral lifted his glass. "To all the guys, mine and yours, who didn't make it through their tours." The detectives nodded. Funeral poured a smidgen on the glass-topped chrome coffee table. It pooled up like balsamic on extra virgin, settling into a small glowing amber pool.

Hart surveyed the room. Sony eighty-inch HD TV. Bose sound system. Some framed photos, including one of King Funeral in an orange tux next to a gold Lamborghini Aventador J roadster. "Gangster life has been good to you," said Hart. "Anyway, you know why we're here. Get the tape. Let's hear it."

Funeral took his nose out of the snifter. "This some sweet stuff. I remember when you was at the Seventy-Seventh, Sal. I always had my forty of Olde English whenever you came by. 'Member that one time I talked you into taking a swig?"

"Stuff was nasty," said LaBarbera. That was ten years ago, and the stale taste of the warm malt liquor still registered on his taste buds' memory.

"But, I gotta tell you, you showed my Hoovas that a cop could be a human," said Funeral. "I'm serious. For a lot my niggas, that was the first time they saw a cop be kinda cool. They used to them uniformed motherfuckin' robots. Anyway, I always kinda appreciated that in a strange way."

"Great," said Sal. "Get the tape."

"Hold on, Sal," said Funeral. "I'm gonna get it in a minute. I even made a copy for you, but I'd like to know what kind of goodwill is comin' my way offa this. I know this is big-time important for y'all. I've been reading the *Times* stories. I see the TV news. I know y'all under a whole lotta pressure. I need serious credit here. Look, I know where we stand. I know I done a lot of wrong in my life, but I been trying to go legit. But I still have some boys to consider like Tiny Trouble. He's my sister's boy. So I'm just going to ask you two, you gonna forget how you got this tape?"

"No," said Sal. "You been up front with me and I appreciate it."

Hart shot the senior detective a look.

Funeral continued, "On the other hand, I can't have it out there that I gave up this tape. Can't have the streets know where you got it from. Just say police have discovered in a search or something, but you cannot say I gave it to you. Even if it is just to nab a journalist. Any cooperation at all with the police and well, ya know, the boys, young-and-old school, don't approve of that. A man could get shot offa this. Even me. I'm only doing this, and I want you to understand this, I'm only doing this to score some points for my sister's kid and maybe get a little grace in the future. Plus, I really don't give a fuck about Lyons. He been making a career writing about our misery and he try to come off like a brother, like he down with us. Now he trying to be a hero, when he ain't nothing but a fuckup. If this tape was some Sixty confessing he kilt Jesus Christ, I would not give it up. You feel me? But the reporter, shit."

"Jesus. Play the fuckin' tape, Thomas." said Hart. Funeral shot him a look but pushed the remote's play button. Silence in the house. The tape rolled.

CHAPTER 14

The voice of King Funeral: So why you want to do a story on the Hoovers? We been cool lately. It's them Sixties niggas and them Grape Streets, they be the ones starting shit. The fuckin' Mexicans, too. F-Thirteen. Florencia. Do something about them, fool.

Mike Lyons: I had a big story on the Rollin Sixties already. About Wild Cat. You know him?

Funeral: I know him. We cool. We was at the SHU in Corcoran together.

Mike: I didn't know that.

Funeral: You don't know a lot of shit. You just think you do. You just think because you know ten percent and all them other reporters at the *Times* only know one percent that you the gang man, the expert, but you don't know what the fuck is going on.

Mike: Educate me, then.

Funeral: I'm not your teacher.

Mike: Look, first of all, you don't know anything about me and my past.

Funeral: I don't need to.

Mike: I lived in South Bronx slums and East St. Louis. Where I lived makes the worst blocks on Hoover Street look like Disneyland.

Funeral: Fuck you. New York is old, motherfucker. Them's the old days. John Corleone times. This is today. We got sets all over the country. Even the Bloods are setting up, taking over in New York. Even in the Bronx. L.A. gangs is the takeover crews. You feel me? Invaders. Marauders. Just because we got some flowers on some blocks don't mean shit. We also have the firepower. So don't try and impress me with your badness. Please.

Mike: All I'm saying is, you know what, forget it. You probably ain't never been out of California and you know everything.

Funeral: Oh, so you gonna come down to my crib and disrespect me.

Mike: I ain't disrespecting you. I wouldn't do that. I'm just tryin' to get the true story. We going to do a story on you guys, you're a famous set, you know that.

Funeral: We ain't no damn set. We a straight-out cartel.

Mike: Okay, but the other reporters and the editors they're fine with just talking to the cops and shit and writing and publishing the story about the Hoovers that way. I'm the only one reaching out and trying to get the story from you guys.

Funeral: Reason no reporters come down here is they liable to get their ass shot.

Mike: Worse things can happen.

Funeral: Like what? What, you don't care? Is that right? You that much a badass reporter you don't care if you get shot? Nigga, please. I oughta shoot you myself. And I might just do that, but I know you put out a safety net, prob'ly told everyone at the paper where you were going. Probly bragging to everyone, too. "I got me an interview with King Funeral." Am I right? Tell me.

Mike: Yeah, I ain't gonna lie. I did tell my editor I was gonna interview you, but only because I needed an excuse to get out the office early and go to my bar.

Funeral: I can smell it. You wanna drink? Hoovers got hospitality. Give you a drink, then shoot your ass.

Mike: Well, I'd hate to get shot sober.

Pause. Some liquid noise.

Mike: To the boys who couldn't be here.

Funeral: That's cool. I don't know. I don't trust reporters. Maybe you ah'ight for a reporter. Compared to what, though?

Mike: Eddie Harris, Les McCain.

Funeral: Got that right. I do gotta say I ain't never seen a reporter anywhere 'round the 'hood 'cept when there's a shootin' and all the police is here. All the TV crews. But that don't even happen that much anymore. Guess shooting on Hoover ain't news anymore. But no one, not a one, ever comes here when nothin's going on. 'Specially at night.

Mike: I'm here and nothin's going on. And it's night.

Funeral: Yeah, I guess you are. Now let me ask you a question. What you just said. You just talking tough or trying to impress me? 'Cause if you are, you wasting your time and mine. But, what you said, "There's worse things than getting shot." What you mean?

Mike: I'm just sayin' there's worse things than getting shot.

Funeral: Like what?

Mike: Getting tortured. For one. Like being punked out and having to live with it.

Funeral: You been punked out?

Mike: No. I ain't never been punked out, you know, jail-style, that's what you mean. No. Fuck no. But, I've done some things. Or not done some things that kinda were, I don't know, like backing down and regretting it. You know what I mean?

Funeral: I ain't never backed down.

Mike: Well, it's like, like there was this time way back in the, I think it was the tenth grade. Over at Gardena High.

Funeral: Gardena High? You went there?

Mike : Yeah, for a year.

Funeral: Nigga, I thought you from East St. Louis or the South Bronx. Come to find out, you a lyin' motherfucker.

Mike: I ain't lyin'. I was born here, went to school here, then moved to New York. To the South Bronx. Chicago. East St. Louis, Illinois. Baltimore, too.

Funeral: One of my niggas is from the South Bronx. Mad Bone. I should get him and test your ass.

Mike: Go ahead. Get him. I probably kicked his ass back there anyway. I'll do it again. Most of them fools from the day. Now, twenty years later, they let themselves go. Got fat. Don't work out. Me, I'm still strong.

Funeral (laughing): Nigga, you a crazy drunk ass motherfucker. Talkin' all this shit. Yeah, you might be ah'ight for a white boy.

Mike: I ain't no white boy. I'm an Armenian man.

Funeral: Sure look white to me. But, you a trip, fool. Go ahead, Armenian man. I want to hear this tenth grade story now. Though it's probably some bullshit, too. Here, have 'nother sip a cognac. Good stuff. Courvoisier. Usually, I have me some Rémy, some XO.

Mike: It's pretty smooth. I'll bring you some Armenian cognac, Armenian brandy called Ararat one of these days.

Funeral: Yeah, if you make it out of here alive. Go ahead, nigga.

Mike: Where was I? Oh, yeah. Anyway, this guy, this muscular Mexican guy, he was really no bigger than me, a gangster from G-Thirteen. Gardena-Thirteen. Anyways, I bumped into him one day accidentally and he just like stared at me and I walked on. Right? So the next day, at the very same place near the lockers, there's a lot of people, big crowd just walking to another class, right? So we're walking toward each other and he goes out of his way to bump into me, hard. You know, shoulder-rams me and just stops and stares me down. And I'm thinkin', ah shit. But anyway, he just looking at me like "What you going to do?"

Funeral: Whadd'ya do? Don't tell me.

Mike: I walked away.

Funeral: Bitch.

Mike: Yeah, I guess. The rest of that day I just felt like shit, like such a coward. And I got to thinking the ass whopping that Mexican might have given me had to be a whole lot better than the mind whopping I was giving myself. I was beating my own self down over it. Way down.

Funeral: So what happened the next day or was that it?

Mike: Well, the next day, I'm thinking about it all morning because I know we're gonna meet up again and I just can't go through with this torment I put myself through for backing down. So couple hours later, we're walking toward each other, same place, by the lockers. Then, outta nowhere, my neighbor, Blinky, this Samoan guy, the baddest street fighter I have ever known in my life, he comes over to me and hits me on the shoulder and says like, "Let's get a football game going on St. Andrews after school." I say, "For sure." We lived on St. Andrews Place. So anyway, the Mexican sees that Blinky is my friend and from that day on, he avoids me. Like the bubonic. Still, ever since then, I get pushed, I push back and hard. Even if I know I'm the underdog.

A pause for several seconds.

Funeral: So what's the point? Getting shot is better than getting punked?

Mike: Getting shot isn't better than getting punked if you die in the shooting. But, if you just get wounded, you know, wounded, but not left crippled, that has its benefits.

Funeral: How? You mean you can brag about it? That what you mean?

Mike: In a way. I know it's sick, but that's just the way it is. Even in the Army or Marines in Iraq, Afghanistan. Like the guy that gets shot, you know, shot not too badly, but shot and then he returns to the unit. That guy? That guy gets respect. Instant respect. The other Marines are envious of him. Damn, Smith got shot. He's a man. He took the ultimate test and made it back. You see what I'm saying? Walked right up to death's door, knocked, and came out all right. People envy that. That's just the facts.

Funeral: Yeah. But I ain't never been shot. Been out here twenty-five, thirty years and never took a hit. Been shot at fifty times, never took one bullet. And I'm cool with that. And believe me, I get my respect.

Mike: I know you do. That's why I'm here, man. I respect you. But, I'm just saying getting shot has some good points.

Slight pause, then the soft sound of liquid pouring is heard.

Mike: Thanks. I'm used to Early Times or Jack Daniel's. This stuff is smooth.

Funeral: Look, if you want, as a favor, I can have one of my boys shoot you.

They both laugh.

Mike: For how much? Yeah, set it up. Little wounding. Not a graze. Something kind of serious. Like a shot in the side. So it can be like, "Where did Mike get shot? The torso. Ah, man. He gonna make it? I don't know, man. Took two in the torso."

On the couch, a rapt Hart and LaBarbera look at each other. "That's what he got, two in the torso," said Hart.

Funeral: Come back to work, big hero.

Mike: Yeah, walk in the newsroom, greeted royally.

Funeral: Big time hero.

Mike: All because a couple little pieces of hot metal went though some fatty part of my body. Not in any organs. I'd plan it out. Study the body.

Funeral: Sounds like you've been giving this some thought.

Mike: I think about a lot of things. So when we going to do this? Just my luck. We'll set it up and your boy turns out to be a bad shot.

Laughter.

Back in the living room, King Funeral thumbed the remote. "That's it."

"So?" asked Hart. "So, did you have Lyons shot?"

"You think I'm stupid? Just thought you might wanna hear that."

CHAPTER 15

The next day, as a hard, slanting rain lashed the city, Detectives LaBarbera and Hart, Captain Tatreau, South Bureau Commander Lester Kuwahara, and Lieutenant Lucy Sanchez of press relations gathered around the mahogany desk of LAPD Chief Charlie Miller.

"This is awesome," said the chief as he gazed out his sixth-floor window through the deluge to the *Times* building across the street. How appropriate this downpour, he thought. How gloomy the *Times* building looked. How gloomy it would soon be inside. "This tape is awesome. After those assholes at the *Times* put all the bullshit pressure on us, and now this? I believe in miracles." The last four words were uttered in sort of a sing-along to the hit song "You Sexy Thing." The others winced as if stung by yellow jackets.

Lucy Sanchez wasn't even paying attention at this point. She was that stunned and disturbed by the tape. She liked Mike. She often talked to him. When he called the LAPD press office, he would usually ask for her. She had even made out with him at the Water Grill bar years and years ago. There were martinis involved and Hama Hama and Kumamoto oysters, too. She enjoyed the lingering kisses and more.

"This is almost too good to believe," continued Chief Miller. "How sure are we that it is real?"

Lucy snapped out of her daze.

"It's real, Chief. We checked it," said Tatreau.

"Sal and Johnny here talked to Lyons last night. They went and paid him a visit. They had a recorder with them."

"Did he know?"

"No," said LaBarbera, who was not proud of what he did, just following orders. "We weren't looking for evidence. We just wanted his voice. We checked with Legal before we went to him. He's doing really good, by the way. All things considered."

"Yeah, he's home, ya know," said Hart. "Doing good, like Sal says."

"He could drop dead for all I care. Now gimme what you got. Get to the damn point."

Hart and LaBarbera looked at Tatreau who took over. "They recorded him and took it to the lab. Three of our tech guys heard the tape. They compared it to the tape you just heard. It's the same guy."

"Is this gonna come back to haunt me? Will you stake your rep, your job on it, Jimmy?"

"Yes, Chief. Sir, that voice is the voice of Michael Lyons," Tatreau said firmly.

"Okay, then that's good enough for me. We're going public today. Five o'clock news. No. No. Six o'clock news."

"Chief," LaBarbera said, "I just gotta say something. We know it's Lyons on the tape. But, we don't know the context. I know Lyons and Johnny knows him well, too. You could even say we're friends."

"Point?"

"Point is we both find it kind of hard to believe he is serious."

The chief kicked his black Johnston & Murphy wingtips on his sturdy desk near a 1977 picture of him in uniform walking a beat on 25th and Diamond Street in North Philly. "He's telling a known thug, a killer, a prison rapist from what I've gathered, that he wants to be shot. It doesn't sound like a joke to me. That's not a guy you joke with."

"I know. But, Mike is a street reporter. He lived in the South Bronx back when they called it Fort Apache. He hangs out in Watts, Green Meadows, and Compton. He could be just joking or talking smack, trying to act tough."

Hart jumped in. "Trying to impress the guy. I can't see him wanting to get shot. He sure seems to get a lot of fun out of life."

"Our point is simply this," said LaBarbera. "Play the tape if you must, but give out that warning."

Miller didn't like this. He wanted to lay the whole culpability for the shooting of Lyons on Lyons himself. Even more so, he wanted the *Times* to look like the shit they tried to smear on the LAPD. He wanted the *Times* to be held responsible for this shooting and for the panic they'd tried to create. He absolutely loathed the *Times*, to the point his shoulders knotted when he thought about the paper. He wanted the *Times* to be blamed for everything wrong about Los Angeles. For the smog, for the traffic, for the drive-by shootings, for there being no NFL team here, for the 1992 riots, the 1994 Northridge earthquake, the deadly 2008 Metrolink crash in Chatsworth, the overdose of Marilyn Monroe, the motel shooting of Sam Cooke, the deadly drunken fall of William Holden, the drowning of Natalie Wood, the arthritis of Sandy Koufax, the birth of the mini mall, and the closing of Larchmont Hardware and Henry's Tacos.

"Look, here's what is going to happen," the Chief declared in his most pompous voice, a voice to annoy a Cambridge English professor, a tone to make Cicero cringe. "I and I alone will make an announcement that there has been a significant development in this most curious of cases. A most perplexing case, indeed. There have been no arrests in this case, but a major new lead has been discovered by our detectives. Then I will play the tape, announcing beforehand that the voice is Michael Lyons, the famed glory asshole gang-loving reporter who was shot downtown last week. That's it. Come what may. Let the public reach their own conclusions."

"Okay, but we have to make—" began Hart.

"Okay?" mocked the chief. "Well, it's so comforting, Detective Hart, that I have your okay. That makes me feel very good. Very good, indeed."

Hart swallowed, then continued. "Chief, I was just going to say we need to make sure that the other voice is not identified. That was part of the deal. I know Commander Kuwahara spoke to you about this, but I just needed to say it again."

Miller took a long, slow inhale. "Kuwahara already mentioned the deal with this Hoover, as you just stated, but you felt the need to, I guess, what, remind me? Once wasn't enough? Do you think, young Hart, that I am an old, dense geezer and that is why I need to be told repeatedly about something?"

Silence in the room. Finally, Hart said, "I'm sorry, sir."

"So, how are we going to play it?" Lucy asked. "Should I get the word out that there'll be a news conference here at six?"

"Yes, Lucy," said Miller. "But, absolutely no leaks. I want this to be a bombshell. A goddamn improvised explosive device set off in the *Times* newsroom. Announce a news conference at six regarding the Lyons shooting. I think you should say the conference is not to announce an arrest. I don't want any let downs. Just say, at first, it is to give a update. Then around five, start leaking that this is going to be a shocking announcement. Okay, Luce? Lucy?"

Lucy's thoughts had once again strayed back to the Water Grill where Lyons got her as wet as the Hama Hamas they were slurping, slithered in two fingers, then pulled them out, sucked one of them and gave her the other. How she went down on his drenched middle finger. How she rubbed him through his slacks.

"Lucy?" said the chief. "Lucy?"

"Yes, Chief, yes, sorry," she said snapping out of it.

CHAPTER 16

As the LAPD strategized, a man named Eddie Sims returned to his modest three-bedroom home in Los Angeles on 89th Street just east of Central Avenue. The neighborhood known as "The Kitchen" after the name of a liquor store and the heat of its streets. Turf of the Kitchen Crips, it was one of the three Crip gangs that surrounded Eighty-Nine Family Bloods territory just west of Central.

Sims had vamoosed out of town after he shot Michael Lyons as the reporter exited the Redwood Saloon. He had emptied his nine-shot Smith & Wesson 9mm with hands as still as an alcoholic four hours without a drink. It was shocking to him that he hit Lyons at all. Sims then dashed to his idling Cutlass, sped off, and was on the freeway, gun under the driver's seat, less than a minute after he torso-shot Lyons two times.

He managed to keep the Olds under seventy miles per hour as he maneuvered onto the 10 and headed toward Las Vegas. For the first five miles, he was shaking like Tina Turner in her prime, his foot lightly Bo Jangling on the accelerator. But, he chilled soon enough and four hours later, while Lyons was being mended, Sims was checking into a forty-nine dollar room at the Best Western Mc-Carran Inn on Paradise Road near the airport and the strip.

That night he stayed in his room and watched the news. There was nothing of interest. He finally fell asleep around three in the neon morning, his reloaded S&W in the nightstand drawer atop the Gideon Bible.

After four hours of sleep, he'd woke disoriented, but, soon, exhilaration took over. He felt alive, juiced, electric. He tuned to CNN. Nothing. *Today* show, nothing. Same for the local channels. No news of Lyons.

He went to the lobby and got a *USA Today* and the *Las Vegas Sun*. Nothing about the reporter. He knew the *Los Angeles Times* would have something, but the *Times* wasn't available, and Sims was computer illiterate.

Still, he figured the reporter was alive or he would have heard something. He had a couple casual friends and distant family in Los Angeles, but he didn't want to risk a call. So he went slotting and free drinking that morning.

He wanted to tell Jennette, his wife, whom he hadn't seen or spoken to since their son was murdered years ago. She'd probably bitch anyway if she knew, he thought. Say something like "You couldn't even kill the reporter, the easy one. Loser, how you gonna do with the others?"

Now Sims was back home and ready to shoot again. This time to kill.

Lyons w*ould* be the easy one, the others would be daunting. At least now he had some experience in firing a bullet into a body. The first shot was the hardest.

He wasn't done with Lyons. He'd come back and kill him, finish the job if he wasn't already dead. He'd really like to walk up to him and shoot him in the head, just like Denzel did in Harlem with all them people around and calmly walk away. But, that was the movies. That was Hollywood. This is Los Angeles.

Up the hill on Landa Street, overlooking the Silver Lake Reservoir, I lay on my bed in my one-bedroom cottage. I was feeling stronger. I'd been going to physical therapy twice a week and the doctor once a week. But, I felt pretty good, all things considered. I could deal with the occasional stabbing sensation the way one becomes accustomed to life's discomforts.

My life began in Chinatown at the French Hospital, a few blocks from downtown Los Angeles. My dad, Tony Lyons, a white Heinz 57 mix, was from Oakland. He was one of those rare individuals who may have been saved by the Vietnam War. He was big time into motorcycles, a good rider, a better mechanic. Many Oakland Hells Angels, even legendary leader Sonny Barger, would take their Harleys to him when they couldn't fix their own bikes or wanted them souped up. He and Sonny had gotten to be friends and my dad was given the opportunity to "prospect" or try out to be a Hells Angel. Most parents dread their sons getting the draft notice, but my grandparents were apparently thrilled when their son got his. In Vietnam, as horrific as it was, there was a chance to get out. Back then, being an Oakland Hells Angel was just a surefire ticket to Folsom or the graveyard.

My mom, Rose Mahtesian, grew up in West Pullman, the Armenian quarter of the South Side of Chicago and her family moved out to Los Angeles in 1965, just one week before the Watts riots erupted. She used to tell me my grandma would often chide my grandpa. "Nahabed, you picked excellent time to move to Los Angeles, California."

After coming home, my dad, figuring he'd seen enough action in Vietnam, decided he didn't want to risk the temptation of the Hells Angels, so he moved to Los Angeles. At a gas station on 90th and Normandie he met Rose and their courtship began. Two years later they were married and living in South Central on 39th and Broadway.

Eventually, we moved to Gardena, a little city neighboring south L.A., the mostly black Compton, and the mostly white Torrance. We lived in a nice thousand-square-foot, three bedroom home on St. Andrews Place in a racially mixed middle-class neighborhood that could only be found in Los Angeles County. There were Japanese, Samoans, Filipinos, Mexicans, whites, blacks, and one half-Armenian family. There were Jews, too, but we figured them for white people. The only way I knew they were Jews, whatever that meant, was when

I asked my dad why Lance Greenberg and Lenny Weingart's houses had all blue Christmas lights. He told me, "Jewish people like blue lights." Somehow, everybody got along. I think maybe we, the kids of St. Andrews Place, that is, just thought this was how it was all over. We played football and baseball in the street almost every day and evening. We boxed and wrestled, too. We lifted weights, at first large Yuban coffee cans filled with cement, then fifty-pound white rocks our neighbors used for landscaping that we hoisted, pretending to be Hercules, and then, eventually, an actual Joe Weider two hundred-pound barbell set we all pitched in to buy. We had fun. We had tough car clubs in Gardena—the Barons and the Bedouins—and street gangs—Gardena 13, Payback Crips and Shotgun Crips—but no one messed with our block because Blinky, my Samoan neighbor, was there to protect us. No one messed with Blinky.

I called Sal. He had no news on my shooting.

I cleaned up, dressed in black, and headed out. In fifteen minutes, me and my 1995 Lexus SC400 were motoring down the Harbor Freeway. My coupe was in need of a paint job—had once been bright gold, was pale beige now—and some minor bodywork. When someone asked me why I didn't get it fixed and painted, I usually replied that I didn't want my car looking too tempting considering the neighborhoods I toured. A more accurate answer would have been that I couldn't afford it.

If the police couldn't find out who shot me, then I would. I couldn't stand knowing that whoever shot me may be planning to come back. I had done too many stories about gang members wounded and in the hospital when they got a second "visit." Often that visitor had a knife.

I had a knife and a gun, too. A .380 Beretta Model 84, thirteen shots. Nice gun, for a gun. I almost never wore it on the job for a few reasons. First, it was illegal for me to carry a weapon. Second, if I had it, I might use it and hurt someone. Third, it was much more exciting to go into a dangerous neighborhood unarmed. I did carry it, long before I was a reporter, during the 1992 riots, or "uprising" at it was known on the Southside.

I wasn't going to take the gun or the knife this time. Last thing I needed was to get pulled over with a gun or even a knife. The knife I had was illegal and, no, it was not a switchblade. I wanted to hurt this guy, but more than that, I wanted to find out why he shot me. The way he came at me was not random.

My first stop would be Jordan Downs, domain of the Grape Street Crips, the color purple. I didn't think the shooter was a for-real Grape, just had the scarf, but I had to start somewhere and at least I could eliminate them for sure. Sal and Johnny had ruled them out, but they hadn't ruled anybody in. Maybe someone I knew, and I knew a few, could point me.

My first stop would be the home of a seventy-year-old woman, Betty Day, the godmother of Jordan Downs. Betty lived on Grape Street in a house three blocks from the projects. I'd known Betty for more than a decade and I know she don't take shit from anyone. She'd call the mayor and the chief of police a motherfucker in a heartbeat if she thought they were bullshitting. I'd seen her do it, twice.

Part of the respect she gets, aside for knowing everyone and having an open-door policy, was that her son, "Honcho," was once the shot caller for Grape Street. The feds eventually got to him, and he did twelve years at Marion in Illinois, one of the toughest federal joints. He was recently paroled, but trying to stay out of the old life.

"Come on in, you crazy black Armenian. How you feeling, Mike? I knew when I heard about you on the news, you was gonna be fine. But, boy, you had me a tad worried."

I hugged Betty and entered her neat, small three-bedroom home. Before I could even say a word, she was reaching for a bottle of Beefeater gin. "Betty, none for me. How you do?"

"I'm fine. Come on. Have one to celebrate your health."

We did. Betty wasn't a big drinker, but if she could find a reason to toast, she was all there. After some bullshitting, I got down to it.

"You know the shooter, my shooter, he had on a purple rag around his head."

"Negro, what you tryin' to say?"

"Betty, I'm just telling you what he was wearing."

I described him as best I could, which was rather vague, the key point being he was older, like I said, maybe forty-five, fifty. Betty dialed her cell.

"Wayne, where you at? Come over the house." She took a sip. "You know Sal and Johnny already been here."

Ten minutes later, Honcho was having a gin on the rocks with us. I had known him before the feds got to him, when he ruled the crack empire in Jordan Downs. The FBI once called him the "Godfather of Watts." He once had a house in Las Vegas and a Wilshire Boulevard condo, but he lived mainly in the projects. He was forty-nine years old, five foot nine, and solid as Half Dome.

"Man, Lyons, whoever shot you, if he was anywhere between thirty and sixty, he was not from Grape. I can tell you that for a fact."

"Have you heard anything? Anything at all about my shooting?"

"Not a word of fact. Just guesses."

"Like what?"

"Eighty-Nine Family."

"Why Eighty-Nine?"

"I might been locked up, but I kept up, you feel me? I had heard about that, ugh, what you call it, that uh, not a biography, a . . . a . . ."

"A what?"

"You know when you write about someone and their life."

"A profile," Betty cut in.

"Yeah, yeah, a profile. That profile you did on Big Evil."

"Evil loved that story," I said.

Betty Day burst into laughter. "Only you, Mike. Only you could write a story Big Evil would like." She took a healthy sip. So did I.

"I don't know, man," said Honcho. "Then maybe it was someone who didn't like the story. Maybe one of Eighty-Nine rivals. Got pissed he got all the press. Became a legend."

A few minutes later I left, having gotten no closer to a suspect than I was before I got here. The only thing I did, besides get a gin buzz, was rule out one of the largest gangs in the city, something LaBarbera and Hart had already done.

Twenty minutes later, I walked into the *Times*'s lobby at 2nd and Spring Streets for the first time since my shooting. No longer was entering though the impressive Globe Lobby on First Street an option for employees or guests. Budget cuts. A sign of the times, of the *Times*.

I took the stairs to the third floor, the editorial heart of the paper. I didn't want to chance being stuck in an elevator with editor Harriet Tinder or her kiss-ass bitch boy Ted Doot. As I strolled down the seventy-yard-long corridor that led to the newsroom, the hallway where I would sometimes sprint to catch a breaking story, I was glad no one was in sight. I reached the end of the corridor and took a deep breath as I stood near the entrance to the newsroom. I hate to admit it, but I was nervous, a feeling rare to me. I could confront five stranger Bounty Hunter Bloods in a midnight parking lot so tough it was called the Folsom Lot and be calmer than I was right then. I took a step back and thought it wasn't too late to back off. No one had seen me.

But damn, the two people in the whole building I least wanted to see were now heading toward me, face-to-face like a game of car chicken in a James Dean movie, like medieval lancers on horseback heading toward each other in slow motion. Tinder and Doot.

There were several doors along the long corridor, two leading to what they call Baja Metro, one to the photo lab, one to the test kitchen. I took the photo lab door more than any other reporter at the paper. Two of my best friends at the paper were photojournalists, Carolyn Cole and Clarence Williams, both Pulitzer Prize winners.

Forty yards away now. But, damn if I was gonna meek out and take the photo door now. And damn if I was gonna speak first when I came upon these two dimwits and say something pleasant like, "How you doing, Harriet, Ted."

Fuck that.

Thirty yards to go. Our eyes were locked on each other. At twenty yards, Tinder turned to Doot and started some conversation, hopefully meant to avoid contact with me.

At ten, they were back to looking at me. At five yards and closing fast, Doot voiced a robotic, "Hey, there." And Tinder grunted something barely audible. No idea what the sound was intended to be.

I looked right in their eyes but didn't say a word and walked right on by. That's not easy to do for me.

As I neared the entrance to Metro, I got down on one knee to retie my shoe when I heard an, "Oh, my God."

I looked up to see Carly Engstrom, my pretty Korean/Swedish former pod mate. "Michael!" She hugged me hard. I pulled away in slight pain. "Oh, I'm sorry. I forgot. It's so good to see you here. I missed you."

"Damn, Carly, you're looking fine. Hey, I'm going to the Redwood. Get a crew and meet me there. I wanna get out of here. Can you meet me?"

"You know it, honey."

After seeing Carly, knowing she'd alert the people I wanted to see, I decided I didn't need to go into Metro. I left the building and walked toward the Redwood, passing the 2nd Street sidewalk where just a few weeks earlier I lay leaking onto the grimy concrete. I looked down on that spot I was pretty sure was it, but didn't even break stride.

My cell phone rang. It was Morty Goldstein.

"Mike, there's some kind of break in your case."

"What kind of break? They found who shot me?"

"I don't know. They are being super tight-lipped about it. I called everybody, and they are not giving up anything."

"That's strange. I wonder why Sal or Johnny haven't called."

"All they are saying is the *Times* and Lyons are going to look like shit."

"The *Times* and me are gonna look like shit?"

"That's what the chief told me, and he added—and this is a quote—'Your boy Lyons is through.'"

"What? What the hell does that mean?"

"I don't know, but that's what he said. There's a news conference coming up. I'm heading there now."

"All right. Thanks, Morty."

As I entered the warming darkness of the Redwood, I heard the greeting. "Hit 'n' Run!"

In all the years I've been coming to the Redwood, I had never seen Danny come from behind the shelter of his bar unless it was time for him to leave. Never, until today. Danny saw me, yelled out his greeting, and quickly walked around the bar and up to me and firmly shook my hand.

"How the hell are you, Michael? Jesus, you had us worried out of our minds."

"I'm feeling all right, all things considered," I said. "But, Danny, I'm still Jack around here, ain't I?"

"Of course, of course, Jack. Jesus Christ, Jack. I don't think you know it, but Jack and I, I mean Sharky and I, we heard the shots and we came running out, like damn fools. We were the first to get to you. You don't remember, but you looked up at us."

"Nah, I don't remember much. But, I sure could use a Jack. A big one."

"You got it, Jack. And this one's on me."

The first sip of Tennessee sour mash made me wince as it often does. But, it quickly started to work its magic. By the time I finished the second drink, the mixture of blood and alcohol was getting right. I was feeling pretty good. I wasn't overly concerned about what Goldstein had said about the chief saying I'd look like shit. He was just *talkin'* shit.

The television stations started flooding the late afternoon screen with teasers. Channel 4 came in with "Big break in *Times* reporter shooting." Channel 7 Eyewitness News announced, "Breaking

News. Is there an arrest? LAPD to hold news conference on the crime against crime reporter." I laughed and told Danny, "I think breaking news is when something is happening, not to announce that something will be happening."

As Danny set my third JD before me, the front door creaked again and Carly Engstrom, Nona Yates, and my cousin Greg filed in. They ordered two martinis and a tonic water for Nona. They sat in a booth. I joined them, saddling up between Nona and Carly, whose white skirt glided up her leg as she sat in the booth. As when she was my pod mate, I made a feeble attempt not to look down. I was true to my girl, Francesca, never cheated once, but I looked. A lot.

The local news went "live" to the PAB. By now, the Redwood was packed, twelve people at the bar, another twenty at booths and stand-up tables. Danny turned up the volume. My table grew silent. Other tables followed suit. Soon, the only sound in the old saloon was that of ice cracking.

Chief Miller came to the microphone surrounded by his brass, Kuwahara and Tatreau and Detectives LaBarbera and Hart who looked uncomfortable.

"As you know," Miller began, "*Los Angeles Times* reporter Michael Lyons was shot nearly three weeks ago while walking along 2nd Street near Broadway. I'm glad to inform those of you who don't know, Lyons has been released from the hospital and is said to be doing very well."

Miller continued. "As I'm sure many of you know, the *Times* has been relentless in their criticism of the Los Angeles Police Department, the finest police department in the world. They questioned our ability to solve crimes. They brought an element of fear to the downtown area."

"What's his point?" said Greg.

I was beginning to squirm. I took a swig of the whiskey and wished I had another full glass. Too bad we weren't at the bar. I could just nod at Danny then look at my glass.

Miller went on. "During the course of our exhaustive investigation, our detectives have come up with a striking piece of this puzzle. It is a taped conversation between Michael Lyons and a known gang member. We cannot at this time reveal the name of the gang member, but the tape is definitely the voice of Michael Lyons. Three of our lab technicians have verified that."

"What is this?" I mumbled.

"I have the tape here and will play it. But first, I want to say that to protect the other person on the tape, his voice has been altered. Also, a couple short snippets of the tape have been edited out to protect that same individual. I have to warn the public and the media the tape does contain vulgar language, so bleep away if you want. We will play the tape momentarily."

Then Miller went off script. "I want to say up front that this tape appears to indicate that Michael Lyons paid for and ordered his own shooting. Play the tape."

In the bar there was a gasp. My body released a cold sweat. I grimaced in agony like the moment when I was shot. Everyone in the bar shot me a look.

The tape played. Closed captions of the conversation took up the screen with a small insert of a photo of me.

Unidentified altered voice of King Funeral: So, what's the point? Getting shot is better than getting punked?

Lyons: Getting shot isn't better than getting punked out if you die in the shooting. But, if you just get wounded, you know, wounded, but not left crippled, that has its benefits.

Funeral: How? You mean you can brag about it? That what you mean?

Lyons: In a way. I know it's sick, but that's just the way it is. Even in the Army or Marines in Iraq. Like the guy that gets shot, you know, shot not too badly, but shot, and then he returns to the unit. That guy? That guy gets respect. Instant respect. The other marines are envious of him. Damn, Smith got shot. He's a man. He took the ultimate test and made it back. You see what I'm saying? Walked right up to death's door, knocked, and came out all right. People envy that. That's just the facts.

More of the tape played.

Funeral: Look, if you want, as a favor, I can have one of my boys shoot you.

They both laugh.

Lyons: For how much? Yeah, set it up. Little wounding. Not a graze. Something kind of serious. Like a shot in the side. So it can like, "Where did Mike get shot? Oh, the torso, man. Ah, man. He gonna make it? I don't know, man. Took two in the torso."

Funeral: Come back to work, big hero.

Chief Miller came back to the microphones. "That's all we can release for now. But that's an incredible tape. Just a reminder. On the tape Lyons is heard to say 'two in the torso.' Michael Lyons was shot two times in the torso. I'll take a few questions."

The scene exploded with reporters yelling questions. Even Howitzer Hal Hansen was drowned out.

At the Redwood, my table was silent. They all were looking at me. Even among this group, though no one said so, doubt was prying. Then Nona asked, "You were joking with that guy, right?"

"Of course, he was," said Carly, rubbing my suddenly tight neck and shoulders. "Right?"

I finished off my drink. "I gotta go. This sucks."

Nona kissed my cheek. Greg touched my arm. "I think maybe you should go back to the office and explain this. They're gonna want to talk to you. It's a big story. This is not good. Not good at all."

"Yeah, Michael, you know Duke and Ted and Harriet are going to want to have a quote from you and want to talk to you," said Carly.

"I can't go back there now. Plus, I had some drinks."

"He's right, Greg," said Nona. "They're going to sniff booze on him and that's the last thing he needs." The others agreed.

"Well, go home. Can you drive okay?" asked Greg.

"Want me to drive you home?" asked Carly.

"No. No. I'm okay, I need to go," I managed. "This is surreal. I just got shot. I don't have a clue by whom. He might come back and try to do it again for all I know, and now I got this bullshit to deal with. I gotta find that shooter if the cops can't."

"Not tonight, please," Greg said. "Just go straight home or to Francesca's, and I'll call you. I'll tell them I'll get a quote from you for the story tomorrow. You have to say something."

I stood up and said, "Good-bye." I never said good-bye. I hated that word.

CHAPTER 17

Eddie Sims had four, maybe five, more people to shoot. This time he was gonna kill, not wound. Not let them live, as Lyons had. He'd take another shot at Lyons. This time kill him. But next on the to-do list was Terminal.

After his trip to Vegas, after he had shot Lyons, after he felt the heat of the investigation was lessening as it always did after the initial swarm, Sims had returned to his routine in Los Angeles, in the Kitchen, working on cars, drinking, and sleeping. He was a loner now, a man who said a polite hello to his next door neighbors, but that was it.

He hadn't always been that way. He had been a friendly, hard-working man who raised his one son with love and affection. That ended on August 12, 2004 when Cleamon "Big Evil" Desmond ordered Darnell "Poison Rat" Jackson to "serve" two men at a carwash at Central Avenue and 89th Street. The two men, both not gang members, were Marcus Washington and Payton Sims, his son.

Prosecutors contended that Evil gave Poison Rat an Uzi and ordered Rat to kill the two so he could earn his stripes for Eighty-Nine Family Bloods. The two were arrested. While in custody, Evil was a trustee at the Men's Central Jail and had extraordinary access inside the jail. In return, he ran the huge Bloods module at the jail and kept things relatively quiet for the sheriffs. He had a job, too, as a food server. He once told Lyons in an interview that "No one complains about the service. That would be stupid."

Eventually, the case against Evil fell apart after he successfully ordered the killing of two witnesses from behind bars. After that, the other witnesses got amnesia. Or moved out of state.

It took a joint task force involving the FBI, LAPD, L.A. County Sheriffs, U.S. Marshals and DEA, to eventually bring Evil down seven years later. One witness was so scared to testify that his face was covered, and he dressed in so much clothing that an FBI agent said, "the guy looked like the Michelin Man."

But, because of the weak main witnesses against Evil—one Freddie Gelson who saved his own ass by testifying—and the tendency for juries in California to shy away from the death penalty, the prosecutor, Deputy District Attorney Leslie Harrington, decided to play it safe and not go for the death penalty. Even the judge in the case, the verbose Harold Reese, let it be known in open court that he thought that was the right call. Evil was convicted and sentenced to LWOP, life without the possibility of parole.

This had infuriated Eddie Sims. Big Evil would be in prison all his life, but he would be the big shot in a world where he was comfortable. Gambling with the lesser Poison Rat, the actual triggerman, prosecutors went for the needle and got it. Rat was now on San Quentin's death row.

But the cataclysmic event that would send Eddie Sims on his revenge quest was a television program on the cable show CNBC called *Lockdown—Pelican Bay* that aired five weeks before Michael Lyons was shot.

CNBC was running a miniseries called *Lockdown*, and each episode featured a notorious American prison. They had done San Quentin, Folsom, and Corcoran already. They had done Angola in Louisiana, Joliet in Illinois, Huntsville in Texas, the supermax federal prisons at Florence, Colorado, and Marion, Illinois. This one was on Pelican Bay, the most severe prison in California. Sims had been flipping channels on his remote when he stumbled across the program. Knowing that was where Big Evil had been sent, he decided to watch the show.

He poured himself a glass of cognac on ice and sat down to watch. What he saw in the next five minutes changed his life and gave birth to the Revenge. At first, he could not believe what he was seeing and thought he was just imagining what he was seeing on his television. And then slowly, the sickening reality crept into his pores.

There, in the prison known for breaking inmates by keeping them in their cells twenty-three and a half to twenty-four hours a day, was Big Evil playing basketball on the yard. He was playing with four other inmates in a game against the guards. Evil made a rebound and then muscled in for a hard two-handed dunk, smiling his big-ass smile. Evil, the man who killed his son and at least twenty-four other sons, was having fun in prison on the California-Oregon border. Sims was dumbfounded.

"As one can clearly see, not every inmate at Pelican Bay is locked down all day in his tiny, gloomy cell," said the narrator. "Certain inmates, known as 'super trustees' are allowed to go outside their cells for hours at a time."

The camera zoomed in on Big Evil playing defense. "This man was the leader of a small, but extremely deadly, street gang in Green Meadows, Los Angeles. The LAPD had called him the deadliest gang member in the city before he was convicted of a double murder. The *Los Angeles Times* made him the cover story years ago in a Sunday magazine profile that sealed his infamy. Yet, his very power has earned him a greater degree of mobility inside Pelican Bay."

They cut to a guard being interviewed. "There are some inmates, like Desmond here, who get certain privileges because they are super trustees, and we rely on him and a few others to keep the peace inside the prison, particularly when inmates gather at food service periods. While inmates in the security housing unit do not mingle, there are more than a thousand inmates here at Pelican Bay who do get out of their cells for meals, and Desmond and others make sure these gatherings are not violent. In return, he gets more time out of his cell than most inmates serving a sentence of life without the possibility of parole."

They cut one more time to the smiling Desmond before they cut away to a commercial. Sims was nearly in medical shock.

He walked, dazed, around his front room. Evil, the man who killed his cherished son, was enjoying himself playing basketball and would be alive for decades. Sims's blood boiled. The Revenge was born. He would have revenge if it was the last thing he ever did. He knew he couldn't get to Evil directly, so his family and the people responsible for his not getting the death penalty and allowing him to live his life out were the next best thing.

So now, it was six weeks since he had hatched his revenge mission and it was one down—or partly down—several more to go. Next up was Terminal, aka Bobby Desmond, Big Evil's younger brother. After that, he'd make sure Evil's mother would join her son in hell. He felt no remorse about this. He wanted revenge for his son.

Terminal himself had beat three murder raps already and was known to be almost as deadly as his big brother. Well, maybe not almost, but still a cold-blooded killer. Bobby stayed with his girlfriend in 79 Swans, another Blood 'hood less than a mile away, but he was often at his parents' home on 89th Street just on the other side of Central from Sims. The Desmond and Sims homes were less than 150 yards apart.

Sims had bought a high-powered telescope from Big Five. He set it in his front room, zeroed in on the Desmond family porch. At first, Sims spent hours at the scope. He'd have the TV on, a meal and a cognac at his side. This was a man determined. Still, even the most determined man, unless he is Stalingrad sniper Vasily Zaitsev, the most famous sniper of them all, had his limits. And after a few days, Sims's telescopic time lessened, though his desire to kill Big Evil's family did not.

Two weeks after he returned from Vegas, Sims was ready. He knew the smart move would have been to get rid of the Smith &

Wesson 9mm he'd used on Lyons, but he didn't. At some point you just don't care. He was thinking of himself as already dead. His wife had left him. He had shot a reporter with the sun shining and L.A. traffic all about him. He just didn't care. He needed help. That help, he realized after he shot Lyons, came from revenge. God, he loved that word. His whole life now was fueled by that word. Revenge.

His estranged wife, Jennette, had once been a God-fearing, churchgoing woman. Sims thought that was absurd. Praying to a God that didn't exist. He was proud of his black roots, but felt the way black people turned to God when death came to their young, the way they'd said at his son's funeral "Payton is with Jesus now," or "Payton is walking on streets paved with gold" was maddening. "Payton is in a better place now," they said. A better place? Even South Central and Watts were better than being boxed in the Inglewood Cemetery dirt.

At night, Sims loaded up, and walked down the street to the corner of Central. He stared at the Desmond house. The lights were on. He started to cross the street, then abruptly turned around. He came home, got his Cutlass, and parked it in the alley across Central, bordering the side of the Desmond household.

As he got out of the car and walked to the 89th Street sidewalk, he couldn't look into the house because the alley-side windows had been cemented up. Probably to prevent drive-bys, Sims thought.

He opened the waist-high metal gate of the fence that surrounded the unassuming front yard. He knocked on the door of the oddly royal-blue two-bedroom home. What kind of Blood family paints their house blue?

It was dark out, a little after eight. From inside came a cautious, "Who is it?" from Betty Desmond, Evil's mother. She was home alone, an elegant dark-skinned woman of sixty-two, dressed neatly in a knee-length green plaid skirt, a yellow sweater, small gold hoop earrings, and Nike running shoes. From the living room Sarah Vaughn was singing "In the Wee Small Hours of the Morning" and vowing to never, ever think about counting sheep. Sims knew the song and thought it a sweet counterpoint to the savagery he was about to inflict. He was planning on taking out Terminal first, so the mom could suffer that agony, but he wasn't rigid in his plan. If she had to go first, so be it.

There was a heavy black steel security door and a thick, sturdy brown wooden door with a little two-inch peep window. "Who is it?" she repeated.

Suddenly, in the cool night air, Sims realized he wasn't the cold-hearted killer he aspired to be. At least not yet. He started to sweat, to get a little nauseous. His mind raced. It was stuck in neutral. Nothing came to him. Then, from behind, he heard the small metal chain-link gate swing open.

"Who the fuck are you?"

Sims was standing on the first step of the small two-step porch. He turned to look eye-to-eye at Terminal.

"Fuck you want here at night? The fuck you doing at my mom's house?" said Terminal, wearing a mid-thigh-length black leather coat over a red Fresno State Bulldogs sweatshirt and baggy Levis.

If Sims had somehow just emerged from the Eurasian Basin of the Arctic Ocean, he couldn't have been more chilled. He tried to talk, to think. His clutch wasn't working, his brain just spinning uselessly.

Terminal violently two-hand pushed him up against the door. He grabbed Sims by his ear and shoulder and spun him around, forcing his face into the cold steel security door.

"Answer me, bitch, before I go violent on your ig-nent ass." Terminal was leaning hard into Sims. With his left hand he patted the intruder down. He felt it in two seconds, tucked in his waistband. "What the fuck? Cunt, you just ruined your life."

Bobby grabbed the S & W 9mm from Sims's gut and bashed him on the side of his face. Blood drizzled down his temple over his eye. He wished he had passed out. He didn't. "Moms, open the door."

• • •

This much I knew. That was King Funeral from the Hoover Criminals on the tape just days before I got shot. The interview was not a formal one, but rather just a get-to-know-you session. I was on my way to the formal interview when I got shot. I found it hard to believe Funeral would just cooperate with the police and give up some tape.

That part I didn't get. Maybe Funeral got in a jam and played his get-out-of-jail card. I was going to take him out if this caused my downfall. I was. I wasn't going to let him punk me out. I'd push back and hard.

I finally made it home and took a long shower. Any trace of a booze buzz was washed down the drain. I felt clean. Ready for a fight. I had to be on my toes. It was time to defend myself. I had been in the position of defending myself many times. As I showered, I kept wondering how bizarre it was that it seemed someone was trying to frame me for my own shooting.

After that shower, I sat on the couch, phone in front of me, a list of contacts, a notebook, a cold bottle of water, and a small bag of Fritos, the original kind. Who should I call first, the cops or the streets? I dialed Sal's numbers, got him on his cell.

"Sal, you hear that news conference?"

"Hear it? I was there."

"Oh, yeah. I saw you and Johnny. Do you believe that shit? Do you actually believe I would have someone shoot me?"

"Lyons, look. This is off the record, right?"

"Jesus, Sal, I'm not writing a story about myself. I just need to know how much damage this fuckin' tape is gonna cause me. I mean, if you believe it, then I am done."

"Do I believe that is you on the tape? Yes. Do I believe you are talking to a gang leader, who I know is King Funeral from the Hoovers, and telling him to set up a shooting of yourself? Yes. Do I believe you are serious? Hell, no. You're a crazy, tough street reporter. You'll go places unarmed, where I wouldn't go armed. But you're not insane. Of course, I don't believe it. That's just how you talk. Unfortunately for you, lot of people are not going to understand that kind of talk."

"Shit. I just got shot and now I gotta deal with the editors. I don't know what's worse, dealing with gang leaders or editors. No, I do know what's worse. Hey, forget this. I'm sick of this already. All this bullshit for jokin' around. Sal, what's the latest on my shooting? Anything at all? Anything."

"Not in the way of suspects. Just in the way of eliminating people and certain gangs. Like I told you, the Sixties didn't do it. Grape Street, they didn't do it."

"I know."

"The Bounty Hunters seem to think you're aces, so they didn't do it. The Hoovers, they didn't do it."

"Sal, I know for sure the Hoovers didn't do it. Funeral is a smart guy. He wouldn't give up that tape if he had had me shot. That's absurd, and Funeral knew I was joking. But why did Funeral give up the tape?"

"I can't say. You can guess, but I can't say."

"Get-out-of-jail card for one of his homies? Got to be."

"I can't say. So Johnny and I, the more we work the case, the more it seems that it is not gang related after all."

"You mean to tell me there are nongang members, regular people who don't like me? Just keep me posted on anything. Sal, I am desperate at this point to find that shooter. It's the key to my redemption. Maybe even to saving my job."

"Michael, we are on it, and I'll keep you posted, but knowing how the chief feels about the *Times*, I have a feeling Johnny and I are not going to be on it exclusively like we were. We're still on it, but I'm sure they will give us other assignments in light of the tape. I'll keep you posted."

"Thanks, man."

I made my next call. This would be a tough one. I dialed Francesca's cell. I can never tell with her how she will react to something. Sometimes she is so wrapped up in the restaurant that if I told her I had just been gored by a Cape buffalo she might say, "I'll call you back later." This time she made me laugh. She had heard the news.

"Why didn't you tell me you wanted to be shot? I would have gladly done it."

"Before this is all done, I might take you up on that offer."

"So, how are you holding up, Michael?"

"I'm holding up, but I could be screwed at work. I'll find out tomorrow."

"Why? Your editors believe that tape? Are they that stupid?"

"It's more than that. You know I don't have a good relationship with some of the editors to begin with. Plus, Duke wrote those editorials blaming the LAPD. Anyway, we'll see."

"You coming in tonight?"

"I don't know. I don't think so. I'll see you at the house, though, for sure."

"Okay, I gotta go. Michael, I love you."

That nearly brought me to tears.

Before I could decide whom to call next, I heard a tinny rendition of "When the Saints Come Marching In." My cell phone. My cousin Greg.

"Well, Michael, like I told you, we're doing the story. We've been getting calls from all over. *New York Times*, the *Post*, *WSJ*, CNN, *Today* show, all the local TV stations. But, we knew that."

"Yeah, it's a good story. I just wish I was the writer, not the subject."

"I know it, cuz. But, I need to get something from you. Duke and Tinder and Doot, they are royally pissed. In a way, hate to say it, but I can't blame them. They're saying how bad you made the paper look."

"Am I guilty as charged? Don't I get a trial? I was fucking joking!"

"Slow down, man," Greg said. "This isn't the time for an attitude.

You have to understand their view. We did all those editorials and now the LAPD comes up with this. People are really upset here. You're not looking good right now. Just give me something now, and I'll go back to them. I'm here at the paper. Morty is doing the story. He's bummed that he has to do it, but that's his job. You know that. Give me something."

"You think I'm gonna get fired?"

"It's a definite possibility," Greg responded. "Wake up. If they perceive this hurts the paper, yes, I do think you might get fired. I hope not, but you need to know how serious this is. You do understand that? Right?"

"Yeah, I do. I understand it's serious. But, I didn't know joking and bullshitting were firing offenses. Shit, fuck it. They're making a bigger deal about me joking than me getting shot. I'm gonna find the motherfucker who shot me if it's the last thing I do."

"Slow down. Come on. Give me something, cuz. What is your reaction to the tape? Start small like 'It is me on the tape but—'"

"Okay. Yes, that was my voice on the tape. I was interviewing this gang leader King Funeral from Hoover. No. No. No. Just put a gang leader. Don't mention his name. Don't. Or even the Hoovers. I don't need that. Okay? I was trying to get him to open up. We were just bullshitting."

"Come on. I can't put that."

"Just say we were joking. When I said that bit about how it would be good to get shot, I was joking. Talkin' trash. There's no way in hell I would have set my own shooting. That's absurd. Come on, Greg, man, you know me better than that. I'm not going to trust anyone to shoot me 'just right.' I almost died. A couple inches here and there and I'm a dead guy or paralyzed. That's ridiculous."

"Michael, I know you didn't set up your own shooting. I know that. That's not the point. The point is that it is on that tape and people can perceive it that way. Especially people who don't have a good relationship with you, like Doot and Tinder."

"So just say I was joking. But, what I said was almost about what happened."

"Okay, how about this? 'Lyons adamantly denied setting up his own shooting and called the whole thing ridiculous.' Then that quote 'I was joking. By some freak coincidence what I said was just about what happened.'"

"Yeah, maybe that's all we need. Whaddya think, Greg?"

"Let me tune it up and I'll send this over to Morty and I'll get back to you."

"All right, Greg. Thanks. I'm sorry to put you into this. I love you."

"Hey, Mike, everything is going to be all right. But you have to be strong now. One more thing, Duke wants to see you in the office tomorrow morning at eleven."

"Great. Sounds like a blast."

If you need to find out what's going on in the streets, you don't go to the streets, you go to jail.

So, after talking to Greg, that night I was on the Hollywood Freeway heading to Men's Central Jail. Friday nights they allow visitors. I got in line, a line that can be as long as three football fields on the weekend. Nights weren't nearly as bad, but it still could be a sixty-minute wait.

I knew several people incarcerated here. I have been incarcerated here twice, a long time ago. Once for knocking out a security guard who was pounding my cousin Dave with a nightstick after he was caught shoplifting a Rolling Stones tape—I think it was "Exile on Main Street"—and another time for winning an extended bar-room brawl in Dominquez near Compton.

Anyway, after only a forty-minute wait, I filled out the visiting forms for Red Man from the Grape Street Crips and for Bat Mike from the Denver Lane Bloods.

Red Man came out first, and he was delighted to see me through the window. I know "delighted" might be too jaunty a word to be associated in any way with jail, but he really was. No one from the projects had taken the time to come to this hellhole, and he really appreciated the visit. I told him that I needed info on my shooting, but he said the jailed homies had talked about it earlier and no one had claimed it and no one knew anything about a possible shooter. It was a mystery inside the jail and out in the streets. Red Man promised he would ask around again and call me collect if anything popped up. I told him I'd leave him twenty bucks on his books.

Twenty minutes later, Bat Mike came to the pitted window and while he smiled at me and appreciated the visit, his mood was much darker than Red Man's. He had some bad news about himself. His trial for attempted murder was not going well and he faced a life sentence as this was a three-strike case. Like Red Man, he had no news for me about anyone claiming responsibility or even any rumors about who shot me.

"It's kinda strange, Mike," the Denver Lane Blood said. "Usually, up in here, you find out just about anything because everyone willing to give up that 411 to save their own ass. But on your case, nobody knows jack shit. Must notta been gangsta related."

I thanked him and said I'd put twenty bucks on the books for him, too. Guys like that, you come visit them when they're locked up and on top of it, put a few bucks on their books, they never forget that. In my line of work, that's good.

I didn't have a lot of good contacts in the L.A. County Sheriff's Department like I had in the LAPD, but I had a few. One of them was an Armenian deputy who worked at the county jail, Sarkis Sarkisian. After I put the money on the books for Red Man and Bat Mike, I went looking for Sarkis, but was told he only works days. I'd come back.

I plotted my next move. I was gonna have to hit the streets and hit them hard. I loved to do that. It made the list on that Coltrane version of "My Favorite Things."

I thought about what Honcho had said, that maybe it was someone who didn't like the story about Big Evil, didn't like Evil enough to shoot me. I know it was very far-fetched, but when you have nothing, even a far-fetched thought is something.

Evil and the Eighty-Nine Bloods had many enemies, foremost among them were the Crip sets that hemmed them in on three sides: Avalon Gardens, East Coast, and the Kitchen. To the direct north were their allies, the Swans, one of the oldest Blood gangs.

I decided to start in the Kitchen. I knew the wife of one of Big Evil and Poison Rat's victims, Marcus Washington, who still lived there. Marcus was one of the young men, along with his pal Payton Sims, who was killed at the car wash by Poison Rat on Evil's orders. The crime that put Evil away for life.

It was after eight p.m. when I knocked on the screen door on 89th Street east of Central Avenue. Yvette Washington came to the door. "Well, if it ain't Big Evil's public relations man. Why you here? You didn't glorify the killer of my husband enough. You gonna do a sequel—Big Evil Part Two?"

"Mrs. Washington, I just wrote the facts. I didn't glorify him and I apologize if you feel that way. I just wrote down what people, including the police, including you, told me."

"In that twisted world, it was a positive piece. Anyway, what do you want?"

"You may have heard, but I was shot a short while back and—"

"Yeah, I heard. Least you lived. Look healthy to me. Marcus wasn't so fortunate."

"I know and I'm still sorry about Marcus. I know he was a good, hard-working man. But, the police haven't been able to come up with any clues about my shooting and—"

"Fancy that. Even for a white boy like you, they useless. I figured they'd have the whole muthafuckin' department lookin' for whoever shot your ass. And what the fuck you doing coming to my house so late?"

"You know what, I'm sorry to take up your time." I turned about-face and headed for the sidewalk.

"Oh, shit, don't be playin' poor little me. Come on in and ask what you wanna ask. I may be heartbroken still, but I got hospitality. I can't get rid of that, either. Come on in, Lyons."

I sat on a couch. Staring directly in front of me on top of the twenty-seven-inch flat screen television were three framed photographs of Marcus Washington, one with Yvette on their wedding day. I was in a trance wondering what it musta been like, his final moments alive, walking with his friend to the car wash and then suddenly the sound of a gun and that's it. A life over. They both got hit nine times. Yvette jarred me back with, "I suppose you want a drink. I got Martell or cheap gin."

I told her I'd drink if she did. She poured me a glass of the cognac. She had a Gilbey's gin and Sprite. She wasn't lyin' about having hospitality.

I pressed her and questioned her if she had heard anything, anything at all, the tiniest lead, an atom worth of information, but she gave me nothing and I believed her. I got up to leave and, just like at Betty Day's house, ended up with nothing but a slight buzz. I turned to look once more at the pictures of Marcus and walked outside. On the porch I asked Yvette, "Didn't Marcus's friend—the one that was with him . . . um, Payton, didn't he live on this block, too?"

"Yeah, right there the third house down, the one with the pretty rosebushes."

"Family still there?"

"Just Payton's father. He like an old man now. He hardly ever gets out. All he does is drink all day. He never got over it. Neither did I, but I got another child to worry about."

I put my hand on her shoulder and thanked her for her time, and walked toward my car parked four houses down. I walked by the house with all the roses and, though I didn't want to, I walked up the empty drive to the porch and knocked. If it was for a story, I'd like to think I'd leave this brokenhearted drunk father alone.

But for my shooting, I had to try and ask a few questions. I knocked, but no one answered the door. As I walked back to the sidewalk, I stopped to admire this beautiful red-and-white rose in the yard. I took a sniff. Whoa. What a fragrance. It was like a perfume factory in one little flower.

CHAPTER 18

Down the street, on the other side of Central, Eddie Sims had been sitting on a maroon velvet couch in the Desmond family living room. In the two chairs opposite the couch were Terminal, clutching his own 15-shot SIG SAUER P226 Elite, and his mother, a red and white pillow on her lap. His father, Cleveland, was working late at the post office in Compton on Long Beach Boulevard. He'd be home soon. Bobby wanted to resolve this before his dad got home. He could manipulate Mom, Dad wasn't so easy.

Sims held paper towels to his temple to blot the blood.

"I am going to ask you again, why are you here?"

"Bobby, don't do anything rash. The man may have a perfectly fine explanation. I do not want violence in my home. Cleamon never got violent in the house and I don't want you to start. This is my church, my temple, you know that. Now put that gun down. Let the man speak. Put it down now, son."

I love this woman, Sims thought. He had managed to get his mind into first gear and come up with a story.

"Talk, motherfucker," said Terminal putting his SIG in one pocket, Sims's nine in the other.

"Bobby, watch your language."

"Why did you come to my house, mister?" she said.

Eddie lowered his head and blew out enough air to fill about two medium balloons. "Obviously, Mrs. Desmond, Bobby, I made a mistake in coming here. Especially at night. Especially bringing a gun. I should have left it in my car."

Fuck. Why did I mention a car? I'm an idiot.

"But," he sought to save himself, "I have heard so many stories about violence in Los Angeles. I live in Las Vegas."

"I don't want your bitch ass life story," Terminal snarled. "Why did you come here? Tell me now or we gonna do a one-on-one interview in the garage."

"I came here, well, I have been meaning to come here for a long time."

"Point, bitch. Point, bitch. Get to the fuckin' point, bitch. You startin' to really boil me. You don't want to see me boil. I din't get my name selling cotton candy, bitch."

"Bobby."

"Okay. I came here to thank you for your son, Cleamon. He saved my life once. Or at least saved me from a serious beating."

"Details, bitch. Details."

"What did I tell you, Bobby? I don't like that word."

"Okay. Details, motherfucker. That better, Ma?"

"Don't be wise, Bobby. Look how this man is shaking. Something about you looks familiar. Do I know you?"

"No, ma'am."

"Do you want a glass of water?"

"Yes, please. That sounds great, Mrs. Desmond." It bought him a little time, too. Mrs. Desmond walked into the kitchen.

"You might charm my mother with that 'Mrs. Desmond' shit, but it's not her you gonna have to convince if you want to live tonight."

Terminal's mother returned with a glass of tap water. Sims drank lustfully. "Okay. Go ahead, sir. What is your name, anyway?" she asked as she returned to the kitchen to get water for herself.

"Eddie Payton. Like the football running back," said Eddie Sims, immediately cursing himself for using a combo of his son's and his own first names. But, it was all he could think of. And you can't pause when someone asks your name.

Mrs. Desmond returned and sat.

"That was Walter, stupid," Terminal said. "Sweetness."

"Yeah, well, but the Payton part I meant."

"You gonna die here, motherfucker, but I guess it's gonna be of old age. Get on with it before I shoot you outta sheer boredom."

"Bobby."

"I was in the Los Angeles County jail. Over there in Men's Central."

"For what?"

"Like for a traffic thing. I had some warrants. This was years ago. Like in the nineties."

"When?"

"I really ain't sure. Like '99, maybe even 2000. Sumpin' like that." Sims was praying Big Evil had been there then and not in a state prison or out on the street.

"Go ahead. Go ahead. Go ahead."

"Well, I was up in there and—"

"Where?"

"I told you the county jail. CJ."

"Where in CJ, motherfucker?"

"Bobby."

"Up there in ninety-five hundred. Thousand guys in that one room." Sims had indeed once been to the County Jail back in the eighties for a battery charge that was eventually dropped and he had spent three days in ninety-five hundred, then the first stop for most inmates. Ninety-five hundred was a filthy, stifling football field-size room so overcrowded half of the inmates slept on the floor.

"So anyway, I was there, and I had a bunk. And this Kitchen Crip wanted it. He just got in and he didn't want to sleep on the floor. He had two other Kitchens with him."

"How you know about the Kitchens? I mean, you live in Vegas. I might could see you knowing Grape Street or the Sixties, but not the Bitchin' Crabs."

"You know, just heard of them because I used to live in the Nickersons years ago," said Sims, starting to feel a little confident.

"Oh, you an OG Bounty Hunter, Blood? That what you tryin'

to tell me? Buzz, I'll call Big Hank and Donnie check your ass out right now."

"No. I didn't bang."

"You lived in the Nickersons and din't hook with the Hunners? Man, you are a pussy. So anyway, go on, punk."

"Anyway, I didn't want to give it up. The bunk. I was feeling bad enough, and I sure didn't want to sleep on no goddamn floor. So I told him to find another bunk, and just like that he tomahawked me in the throat and pulled me off the bunk and his boys started stomping me. I was covering up, and I heard one of them say, 'Oh, shit.' I looked up and saw Big Evil, I mean Cleamon, right above me just kickin' ass. He knocked out two of them, and the other guy ran away. I thanked him a lot. And got to talking with him, and I said I wanted to pay my respects to him and his family, and he told me where he lived and all that. And he said it was no big deal because he enjoyed beating up Crips. I mean Crabs."

"So you waited all this time to come by and thank him? You know where he's at now, right?"

"Yes. I meant to come by, but I moved away to Vegas and I just kept putting it off. Then I saw that article in the *Times* the other week where that reporter who wrote about Cleamon got shot and it reminded me I needed to thank him or his family. That's all."

"Okay, shaky boy. You thanked us. Now you can go."

"Thank you, and if you talk to Cleamon tell him I said thank you, if he even remembers me."

"I will," said Mrs. Desmond. "But you should be more careful. You can get hurt around here."

His heartbeat coming back inside of ribs and chest plate, Sims was led out the front door. Bobby turned back to his mother. "Mom, I gonna let him out, but I just wanna have a word in private with the man."

"Be nice, Bobby. I believe he really wanted to thank our family. He seems so meek."

Outside, Bobby put an arm around Sims's shoulder. "I'm gonna have to keep your gun for a while. Let's me and you have one more little talk in the garage." The Desmond family single-car garage was behind the backyard, the entrance off the alley. The same alley where Sims had parked his Cutlass.

"I am done talking. I need to get on. I said my thanks, and I have to be on."

"No, you're not." He took Sims's own gun and stuck it in his ribs. "Open the garage door. It's not locked. Never is." Terminal noticed, but paid little attention, to a Cutlass parked about a hundred feet down the narrow, trash-strewn alley.

There was no room for a car in the Desmond garage. It was more a storage room/gym. There was a bench press set with 315 pounds, a worn-out heavy bag, a chair fit for the curb, and a cluttered work-bench with tools, extension cords, boxes of car parts, and a TV in the corner sitting on a stool. Terminal closed the door and turned on a light.

"I don't want my moms to see what's going to happen to you."

"Hey, hey. What are you talking about? I just came by to thank your family."

"Who the fuck are you? And why did you come to my mother's house with a gun? I'm tired of asking that question."

"And I told you already. Cleamon saved me from a beating at county."

"Evil wasn't in the county jail those years you said. He was at the SHU in Corcoran fucking up Mexicans in those gladiator fights the guards set up. Here, I wanna show you something," Terminal said. He grabbed a remote control and pushed a button and a fight came on the TV. It was like one of those grainy, poorly filmed fistfights posted on YouTube. Terminal watched engrossed and smiling for thirty seconds or so.

Eddie Sims was mesmerized as he watched the wicked brawl be-tween two black men.

"You see who that is, punk? That's my brother fighting at the county jail. Men's Central. The sheriffs up in there had heard about the SHU fights in Corcoran, so they copycatted. The guards up there used to have fun betting on who would win. Tell you the truth, I don't even blame them guards. I'd be doing the same thing I were them. Boring being a guard. Shit, I'd rather be an inmate. Anyways, these here fights, usually be a brother against a Mexican. But for my brother, for Big Evil, they ran outta Mexicans to give him a good fight. Image that. Running out of Mexicans."

Terminal lit up a joint and took a deep hit. "Yep. They ran out of Mexicans. Mexicans is tough, real tough, but usually they small. Thing Mexicans is good for, other than making tacos, is they do bring up that good cartel shit. Florencia and 38th Street and them. You gotta give them points for that."

He got back to admiring the video. "That's how bad my bro was. Is. So this sick sheriff there, he knows Big Evil is going away to prison, to Ironwood, so for his last fight at county he sets up a gladiator fade with a tough black inmate. That there who he's kicking ass on. You know him? That's King Funeral of the Hoovers. 'Bout to get his ass straight out for real kicked. See?"

Sims just watched, trying not to shake, but failing badly.

"Now, bitch, this is an old-school tape. So old they used to have the date on the screen. You see? Now read that date."

Sims saw the date on right corner of the screen, but said nothing.

"June 17, 1994. So how the fuck he gonna be at county in 1999 or 2000 when he was at Ironwood? Last time he was in county was in 2004 when they got him for that bogus car wash thing."

"Maybe I got the years wrong. It was a long time ago. Maybe he came down for a court hearing or appeal or something. He saved me."

"My brother wasn't there, you lying motherfucker. Me and my bro are close. If he was there, don't you think I would have visited him? Callin' me a lousy brother?"

Terminal slapped him hard on the face.

"Take off your clothes. All of them. Shoes and your panties too, bitch."

"What? You're kidding, right? I'll . . . I'll . . . I'll just go on my way. Sorry to bother you."

Terminal took the gun and jabbed it in Sims's chest. Sims was shaking like the leaves of an old maple. "Now, bitch. I heard once you get the best interviews when the liar is in the nude. Some CIA interrogation shit." Terminal went to the workbench, took off his leather jacket, and put on some gloves.

A minute later, Sims was totally naked. His penis had receded into him. Only a nub protruded. Terminal laughed. Terminal made him sit on a chair, then tied two rounds of duct tape around Sims, who tried to object, but the 9mm at his temple put an end to resistance.

"Oh, a little dick boy," laughed Terminal. "A tiny bit boy. Wait a minute. Is that a dick or just a fat pearl tongue? I'm sorry. I thought you were a man, not a woman." He laughed louder, truly amusing himself. He took a gloved hand and grabbed the diminutive member and yanked it. "Maybe we can pull it out. I bet you don't have a girl-friend. I bet your wife left you for a man. Right, cunt girl? This is too funny. Maybe I'll put a leash on you and parade you around the neighborhood and let everyone laugh at you. Like a circus freak. You might like that, right, faggot? Faggots like that humiliation, ain't that right?"

He slapped Sims again. At this point, Sims was hoping he just would get shot in the head and end his miserable life. How stupid I was to think I could take these people on? He began to weep.

Terminal's laugh started small, then rose like a tsunami until its thunderous shrieking crescendo overwhelmed every sound in its wake. He had learned the laugh from his big brother.

"You know how you can tell if a guy's a faggot? We used to do this in Folsom all the time to the new fish. You be surprised how many faggots there are. But, you prob'ly already know you a dick sucker, right? But, we are gonna make sure. Okay, little buddy? It's a surefire way. Foolproof. And so simple. You make a guy suck your dick and if his dick start to grow and maybe even get hard, then you know he's a cocksucker. A faggot. I'm gonna give you that faggot test right now."

A horn sounded outside the garage. Terminal ignored it and pulled down his pants unleashing a thick cock hanging down his thigh. "You like what you see, don't you? You starting to get hard? Let me see, cunt."

Then the horn wailed, nonstop for twenty seconds. It was right outside the garage now.

"What the fuck? Hold on, bitch fag. Don't worry, honey, I'll be right back."

Terminal pulled up his pants, went out to the alley through a side door. A young Eighty-Nine Family member, an up-and-coming player named Showboat, was idling in his red Expedition. "Yo, Term, whose fucking car is that? Man, we supposed to keep this alley clear. That's Family policy, man. You know that."

"Hold on, Show."

He went back into the garage through the side door. "That your Cutlass?" The numb Sims said nothing. Terminal slapped him sharp in the face. "That your Cutlass?"

Slapped again. He went to Sims's discarded pants and rifled through them, pulling out some keys. He gouged one of the keys into Sims's cheek. "One final time. Now, is that your Cutlass?"

"Yes."

"Get up." He ripped the duct tape off. Sims yelped. "Let's go. I am tired of you." He grabbed him by the shoulder and led him toward the side door. He ejected the fight tape and took it with him.

"What about my clothes? Please."

"Where you going, you don't need no clothes."

When Showboat saw the naked Sims, he started laughing uncontrollably. "Term, I'm sorry. I din't know you had no date. Them Corcoran habits hard to break."

Terminal came to the passenger side of the Lincoln and smashed the window with the handgun. "Whud you say?"

"Come on, Term, I just jokin'. Why you have to go and bust my window?"

"Buzz I can. That's why. I'm teaching this bitch a lesson. Hey, did you ever see my brother's fight video?" Terminal held up the tape and tossed it onto the passenger seat of Eddie's Cutlass. "I'm a show this to you later." Terminal popped the trunk on the Cutlass and forced in the naked, shell-shocked Eddie Sims.

Terminal drove Sims to an industrial area alley in Watts, where he parked, a few blocks from the edge of the Jordan Downs housing project. It was a desolate place at night, next to Alan Engle Scrap Metal, a sprawling compound just west of Alameda Street. Term has killed people here before. One time he killed a fellow Eighty-Nine Family member and tried to toss him over the fence in with a huge pile of brass destined for a Shanghai warehouse. But he couldn't quite get him over the barbed wire, and the victim ended up being lodged onto the barbed wire like some sick modern art installation.

His mind was flashing back to that fond memory as he opened the trunk of the car. When the trunk was barely one foot open, a tire iron lashed out and struck him in the hip. With one hand Sims pushed the trunk open all the way and with the other struck Terminal's right wrist with the iron. The gun, Term's own SIG 9mm, fell to the graveled alley. The crazed naked man vaulted out of the trunk and began to savagely whale on Terminal's face and head. In a frantic rush, he grabbed the gun and fired two shots into Big Evil's brother's chest.

He dropped the gun, pulled out the keys that were still in the trunk lock, jumped in the Cutlass, and headed out the alley.

He was almost to the mouth of the alley at 94th Street when he realized he didn't have any clothes on. Sims jerked the Olds into reverse and headed back to Terminal's body. Sims was never good at backing up and he began swerving all over the alley, twice scraping the Cutlass against a building. Heart thumping wildly, he slammed on the brakes around where he'd left Terminal and stepped out.

He looked from outside the driver's door, but saw no body. Where could he have gone? Suddenly, a hand reached out from underneath the car and grabbed him by the ankle. Sims had parked right over Terminal. Terminal was bleeding out, but managed to grab the SIG SAUER near him and awkwardly fired across his body toward Sims's ankles and feet. He missed. Sims jumped back into the driver's seat. He drove forward ten feet and then reversed and crushed Terminal. He did that back and forth two more times, the Cutlass like riding a bucking bronco. He backed up some more and saw his dead enemy, jumped out of the car, pulled off Terminal's red Fresno State sweatshirt and put it on. It was too much trouble to get any pants. Thinking in a rush about fingerprints, he grabbed the SIG, too, got in the Cutlass, and drove off as wildly as his heart was beating.

The sweatshirt was sticky. It had two holes in the front and was covered with blood. He was glad one of Fresno State's colors was blood red. If a cop saw him, at least he would just see his shoulders, not his chest. At night, he might not be able to tell. Just don't get stopped. All the way home, that is all he mumbled to himself. Don't get stopped. Don't get stopped. Don't get stopped. He didn't.

He pulled into his driveway, scrambled out, hysterically opening the gate that separated the front yard from the driveway leading to the garage and backyard. Inside his house, he stripped off the sweatshirt and threw it in a tall kitchen trash bag.

He slugged Hennessy, showered, slugged even more Hennessy, and dressed. He took the trash bag to the car and drove away. As he crossed Central and passed the Desmond household, he said out loud, "Sorry, Mrs. Desmond. You want Bobby's shirt? It's holy." He laughed.

He drove a mile until he saw a Dumpster in an alley off Avalon, dropped the trash bag, covered it with other trash, and went home. He looked around the car to see if there was anything else he needed to get rid of. On the passenger seat floor mat, he saw the fight video. At first he was going to trash it, but then he got another idea that made him smile.

Some more Hennessy and he started to unwind. Started to feel proud. Started to feel real good. Like a real man. He packed some things and got in his car. Before his long journey, he had one stop to make. On Hoover Street. Sims laughed. They'd like fight films over there. And this movie was to die for.

He got on the Harbor Freeway north. Took it to the Hollywood Freeway. It was just past one a.m. when he passed Magic Mountain on Highway 5. Pelican Bay, California's most forlorn address, was less than seven hundred miles away.

CHAPTER 19

"How are you feeling, Michael?" Duke Collinsworth asked. I was the first one to the editor's office and was waiting rather uncomfortably for Harriet Tinder and Ted Doot to show up. I felt an avocado pit drop hard in my stomach when the paper's publisher, Jon Friant, walked in and took a seat after a quick handshake. I had never really met him. All I had heard about Friant was that his only concern was the bottom line. I had some minor trouble getting over the spelling of his first name. In almost all cases, Johns were cooler than Jons, who, in my limited experience, tended to be pompous assholes. What a difference an *h* makes. Friant asked how I was. I responded, as I always did when asked that, quoting Sky Masterson from *Guys and Dolls*: "Healthy at the moment." Like Friant could give a fuck how I felt.

The others soon joined in around the oval mahogany table.

"Well, I'll be honest with you, Michael, this is not good. Not good for you. Not good for the paper," said Collinsworth. "Not good for anyone."

"Except Miller and the LAPD," said Tinder.

"Yes, Miller is loving this," said pumpkin head Doot.

"Any ideas how to get out of this mess?" Friant asked. "First off, let me just say I am here almost as much out of curiosity as I am as the paper's publisher. I will not make any decision, but to be honest, I am curious about the whole thing. I don't understand it."

"What don't you understand?" I asked, my concern mounting when I heard the word "decision."

"I don't understand why the hell you or anyone would say what you did. I don't get it."

Tinder piled on. "Yes. It's hard for us, hard for our readership to relate to someone who wants, or at least says he wants, to get shot. Explain that for us. Please."

"I understand it does sound strange to someone who doesn't speak that, um, that language. Like a foreign language, it would seem strange."

"What language are we speaking of?" asked Doot. "Oh, let me guess. Street language? Street talk?"

"Well, for lack of a better term, yes."

"What's a better term then?" said Tinder.

"Bullshitting."

"Were you drinking during this interview? Drinking alcohol?" said Doot.

"The guy I was with was a big shot in one of the biggest gangs in town, and he offered me a drink of his prized cognac. To refuse would have gotten this interview off badly. He would have been insulted, and trust would have been in jeopardy. So, to answer your question, yes, I did have a bit of his cognac. A couple small sips. I was not in any way drunk or remotely close to being so."

"Too bad," said Tinder. "That might explain your bizarre behavior."

"Michael," Collinsworth said, "I understand your beat is a difficult one. It was your idea to cover gangs, and I agreed that they needed to be covered. And I do not claim to know the intricacies of that world. How language is used. Still, I would think, given what happened to you, you must understand the seriousness of this."

"Duke, there is no way in hell I wanted to get shot. That is simply ridiculous."

"So, it's safe to say that you were simply joking with this guy, right, Mike?"

"That's all it was, Duke. Joking. I love life. I love my job. Why would I risk it? It doesn't make any sense at all. I can't believe anyone would have himself shot. Especially me. I have a lovely girlfriend. I'm healthy. I have a great job. My dream job."

"But," Collinsworth countered, "you just said this is one of the biggest or baddest, as you say, gangs in the city. Killers, I would assume. Don't you find it bizarre to be talking to one of them about the benefits of getting shot? I mean, to these guys, if I'm understanding you correctly, shooting someone is about as grave an act as anyone of us here getting a cup of coffee."

"I don't know how else to say it. I didn't want to get shot. We were joking."

"Okay, Michael, we just wanted to clarify a few things and we needed to hear your side," said Collinsworth. "Mike, I know you've had a rough few weeks, plus this has got to be frustrating, so why don't you just go home now, get some rest. We're just gonna go over a few things, get our strategy together. You know, we've been inundated with interview requests, not only for you, but for us, too."

"Duke, I am really sorry all this happened," I said, intentionally not addressing Tinder, Doot, or Friant. "I'm really sorry to put you through this, to put the paper I love through this. I'll know better not to joke with anybody anymore."

"Just take care of yourself, and we'll see you when you're ready to come back to work," said Collinsworth. "Don't even think about work for a while. Get your health back. Work is not as important as health. Go home, Mike. Rest up. Feel better."

I walked over to Greg's desk, a slight smile on my face, a weight lifted off my shoulders. Atlas relieved of duty. Greg was on the phone, but I gave him a rare double thumbs-up and a big smile and indicated I'd call him later.

At home, I grabbed a novel, *The Last Good Kiss* by the late James Crumley, and laid on the couch and began to read. I was almost done with its famous opening line when the phone rang. I finished the line, ". . . drinking the heart right out of a fine spring afternoon," then picked up.

"Hello, Michael?"

"Yeah."

"Hi, Mike, it's Duke Collinsworth. How are you?"

"I'm good. I've just been relaxing, reading a good book."

"Sorry to bother you. I talked to your cousin a little while ago, and he told me how strong you were."

"Oh, yeah?" I replied, my curiosity redlining. Why didn't he ask what "good book" I was reading, I thought. This must be serious.

"We really have thought long and hard about this. You've had some good times here and some hard times. I know you had a couple of warnings about drinking. But, though I haven't been here long and don't know you really well, I've heard from many people you're a good guy. And I believe that. You're old school, and so am I. You know you have a lot of friends here at the paper. Still, I have to think of the paper first. This has been a difficult situation for all of us, but I'm going to have to ask you to resign."

Revenge. The word had a raw, wicked urgency. But, I never liked that word. Someone had messed with you and now you had to get back at them. That was revenge and who wanted that in their life. Still, in addition to finding the guy who shot me, all I could think about after I was forced to resign was revenge on King Funeral. At least I had a mission or two in life. Not the missions I wanted, just the missions I got.

Many years ago, I had bought a Special Air Service British Commando knife, a Fairbairn Sykes MK 3. I had always admired the SAS, though I'm not really sure why I got it. I guess just to have it. Display it. It's a beautiful knife. The knife is illegal because it has two sharp sides, but it was legal to sell it as a display item. I was going to display it all right. Right up Funeral's ass.

What I most wanted to do, what I fantasized about, was to step to

him on Hoover Street in front of all his boys and kick the motherfuck-
ing shit out of him right there. I was strong. Before I was shot, I could
bench press 225 pounds seven times. I was fearless. I once took on six
guys a block from the Forum in Inglewood just before a Lakers playoff
game back in 1999. I ended up with a broken jaw, a busted nose, two
black eyes and thirty-five stitches on my forehead from a well-swung
red Craftsman pipe wrench. And *I* had started the fight, coming to
the aid of a female friend named Omega. Just a friend, at the time.

I was a good street fighter. I once beat up a Samoan when I was
seventeen. Truth be told, the Samoan boy—my friend and neighbor
and Blinky's little cousin—was only fifteen, but, still, *he was a
Samoan.*

Yeah, I was strong and fearless and a good street fighter for a journalist.

That was the key. *For a journalist.* For a street gang leader, I
wasn't any of that. Well, maybe fearless. Or close to it.

So that scenario of kicking Funeral's fat ass was just a lead pipe
dream, a brutal fantasy. Besides, he'd be surrounded by a swarm of
young Hoovers eager to make a rep. Still, I had to get back at Funeral
for ratting me out. Maybe I'd do it the Hoover way. I'd bring my gun.
Just for protection. I didn't even know if he'd be there, at the shithole
apartments where he grew up and still kept a unit, the place where
I interviewed him. But I had to go check it out.

I drove along the eastern fringes of Hollywood Boulevard, two
starstruck miles from where the Academy Awards are held. This was
Little Armenia. I motored past the Armenian-owned flower shop,
the Armenian-owned butcher and market, the Armenian-owned
photo studio, and the Armenian-owned pastry shop famous locally
for their baklava, to the bail bonds office run by Sharky Klian, my
Redwood Saloon drinking buddy. It was in front of Sharky's small
office next to the Redwood that I had been shot, but this office was
his moneymaker. The Armenian Power gang members of the neighborhood kept him busy.

"Sharky, I need a favor."

"You need a job, from what I heard," Sharky said with a laugh.

"I need a gun cleaned. Cleaned and ready to use."

"What? No, Michael. No, don't do anything stupid. It's not worth it. Knowing you, you'll get shot again. How about a shot instead?" He reached for a bottle of Johnnie Walker Black.

"It's not like that, Shark. I've had this three-eighty Beretta, model eight-four, thirteen shots—"

"Mike, I know how many shots it has."

"Sorry, Anyway I've had it for ages and never cleaned it and just want to have it cleaned, that's it."

Sharky was reluctant, but he took the gun.

The next day, I picked it up. On my way out, I stopped at Hank's Saloon on Grand Avenue downtown, had two quick drinks, left, got back in the car, popped a stick of Big Red, and took 8th Street to the Harbor Freeway south. I drove very calmly. The radio was off. The only sound was the quiet hum of the 4.0 V-8 Lexus. My car was in need of some cosmetic work, but I kept the engine in fine tune.

I exited the Harbor Freeway at Slauson Avenue. Not the fastest way to get to 74th and Hoover, that would be Florence, but I took Slauson to let the street atmosphere soak me, to get immersion. I drove past Figueroa and then made the left, turning south onto Hoover.

It would be a quick hit or miss. Funeral had long ago reached the status that he didn't always hang out in the streets, certainly not on a corner leaning against a street sign, foot propped against the pole, another firmly planted on cement, a hand on a forty-ounce bottle of Olde English.

As the street numbers got higher along Hoover—61, 62, 63—I began seeing an occasional gang member. They were not as obvious as they had been in years past. Nowadays, even nongang members often dressed like gang members, with baggy pants and white t-shirts to fit a hippo. I had a good eye and could usually tell a thug from a dresser. As I drew closer to Funeral's apartment on 74th and Hoover, gang members became a little more obvious. One there, three here, a couple more in a driveway. It wasn't like the old days along Colden between Fig and Hoover where there'd be couple hundred homies hanging out, but the gangsters were still around. Those who weren't locked up or buried.

I drove past 74th Street and Hoover to recon the area. There were at least two Hoover Criminals in front of the forest-green and Band-Aid colored two-story apartment building where King Funeral grew up. The color scheme alone could make someone angry. There were several no parking signs on the side wall of the building, each with a car parked in front of it. On the other corners of the intersection were Susy's Market, and two churches, the Greater Harvest Baptist Church and the Faith Church of God in Christ. I drove all the way to 84th Street before making a U-turn. Between 84th Street and 74th Street there were eleven churches. People prayed a lot on Hoover Street.

I turned right on 73rd Street, a block past Funeral's, made another U and parked facing Hoover Street. If I needed to make a quick escape, all I'd have to do was turn right on Hoover, quick right on Florence, and half mile to the freeway. I had considered calling Funeral and tell him I was coming over, but then realized how stupid that would be. I hadn't yet realized how stupid the whole plan was.

I wondered if I was out of my mind, but then I squashed that thought. Don't even answer the door when doubt knocks.

This was Funeral, a street legend, accustomed to prison attacks by men far tougher than me. I knew I couldn't go in scared.

But, if you don't fight back at the big things, then you start not fighting back at all. Sometimes in life, you can allow people to step over you, I figured. But, not this time. Everybody needs to have their own Stalingrad. You can only be pushed so far back against the Volga. This time I would have to make a stand and fight back.

I got out and popped the trunk and reached for the Beretta inside my gym bag. Clunk! The trunk bashed down against the back of my head. For a terrifying second, I thought Funeral had snuck up on me and slammed the trunk down on me, but then I realized that was not the case. I cussed myself. I had purchased a set of trunk shocks on eBay about four months ago because mine were shot and the trunk lid would not stay up. Damn, I'd had those trunk shocks for months and still hadn't installed them.

I tucked the gun under my black long-sleeve t-shirt into the waistband of my black pants. My SAS knife was taped upside down to my outer left leg just above my ankle.

Walking up Hoover Street, I was startled by that sound of "When the Saints Come Marching In" coming from my pocket. Francesca was calling. It was around ten p.m. I didn't answer.

I walked another half block, then leaned against the wall of a long-ago closed café called Soul Murray's. An older black man, about sixty, sixty-five, pushing a shopping cart filled with a bucket, brushes, shoe polishes, soaps, and rags with a cardboard sign that read "Noble's Rollin Carwash and Shoeshine" rolled by. He stopped. "You lost, young man?"

"No, sir," I replied, trying to think of the last time I called anybody "sir."

"You police?"

"Nah."

"Then you *must* be lost."

"Depends how you mean *lost*."

The man nodded, gave up a small smile, started to say something, then changed his mind, and headed on his way.

"Say, mister," I said. The black man stopped. "You ever think about adding a 'g' to that sign a yours? To that 'Rollin'?"

"No. I like the sound of it. Noble's Rollin Carwash and Shoeshine. Got a nice ring. I'm Noble."

"Figured."

"Why you ask, anyways?"

"Well, and I know it's stupid and sorta sad really, and you prob'ly know this anyway, but that's just the way the Rollin Sixites spell 'rolling' and they're much hated around here. By the Hoovers. Hate for you to get hurt just 'cause of that missing *g*."

"You sure you ain't a cop? But, yeah, I know that. But, see, I likes the sound of it this way and I just don't want to have to live my life like that. Fearing over the spelling of my own business. And I, myself, might just be that 'missing *g*' anyway. You feel me, young man? I wasted lotta years long time ago, lots of years, over some of that stupid gang shit 'round here, but I'm still here pushing."

"Keep pushin' till it's understood, right?" I said. "All right, man. I can appreciate that. Didn't mean to be nosey. You take care yourself, Noble. That's a good name."

"It's noble," said the man and he pushed on up Hoover. Then he laughed and said, "It's kinda funny. You worried about *me* getting shot. You look out now."

I stood there for another two minutes. Thinking about what I was gonna do. Thinking about the gun. Thinking about Noble and the years he lost for, I guess, doing some violence. Then I walked back to my car and stashed the Beretta deep in the trunk underneath the spare tire in a bag with the tire iron. I sat in the car for a minute then drove to 74th Street.

There were two orange-clad Hoover Street Criminals in the yard of the two-story apartment where Funeral had grown up, where I had interviewed him and been secretly taped. These Hoovers were real, not wannabes. When I walked up to the building, one of them went to an oleander bush and grabbed something. "Funeral around?" I asked.

"No, Officer," said one young Hoover, about sixteen. "You should go, Officer punk."

I wasn't in any goddamn son of a bitchin' mood to take orders from a sixteen-year-old though I know in my travels sixteen-year-old gang members are some of the worst ones and will shoot you within beats of your heart. But tonight I just didn't want to walk away. I headed toward the staircase of the dump.

"I said he wasn't here," said Sixteen. "I say you be better be going."

"And I say shut the fuck up. I came to see King Funeral, not your juvenile delinquent ass."

I think that caught him off guard. Lot of these guys are used to getting away with anything and when you call them on it, well, it's a gamble, but a lot of times they back off. Because so many of them are really just punks. 'Course a lot of times they don't back off. I guess I gambled good with him.

The other Hoover, who went into the oleander bush to retrieve something, was about twenty-one, give or take. Kinda hard to tell at that age. He came to his partner's side. "Don't be talking to my homie like that, motherfucker. Don't your fool ass know you in Hoover 'hood?"

"Fuck you, idiot, I been to Beirut 'hood. This ain't shit to me." I don't know what it was that made me feel so strong, so determined, so crazed, so I don't give a fuck. For a second or three, I wished I had indeed brought that Beretta with me. "Now I'm going to knock on Funeral's door, and we'll see if he's man enough to answer the door."

Just then Twenty-One, who was less then four feet from me, said, "Oh, no you're not," and reached into the waistband of his orange-and-black Nike basketball shorts. I may have never moved so quick, taking one step and hitting him with maybe the best left hook I'd ever launched. I put everything into it—my thigh, my torso, my shoulder, my forearm, my fist, and my fury—and it landed flush on his jaw. Rocky Marciano on Jersey Joe. He went down and out on the Southside of Los Angeles. As out as some fool trying to stretch a double into a triple off the right arm of Roberto Clemente. As he hit the weedy lawn, a .357 Magnum jerked loose from the hand in his waistband. I grabbed the gun. The sixteen-year-old froze. Didn't run, didn't charge me. Just froze, like he was in shock.

"I'm not here to hurt you. But, you ain't gonna go gather up your homies, you feel me? Walk the stairs with me, or you gonna be hurtin' immensely. You know what immensely means?"

"Not really."

"Well, you don't wanna find out. Now get up these stairs."

Fortunately, he believed me. He could've run off, and I wouldn't have done a thing. What could I have done, anyway? Chase him through Hoover Criminal 'hood? I'm not sure who was more nervous, him or me. But it was a strong nervous. My blood was surging. I never felt so alert, so focused.

We took the stairs. I really didn't want to knock on Funeral's door with a gun in my hand — might send the wrong impression — so I opened the chamber and jiggled out all the shells, put them in my pocket, and laid the gun on one of the steps. I went to apartment number 7, where I'd been taped, and pounded on the door like a madman. I pounded on that door for twenty seconds, I bet. Felt like two minutes. I guess he really wasn't there. I didn't think Funeral would hide from me. Part of me was glad he didn't answer the door. I went downstairs, picked up the gun. The sixteen-year-old came down with me. The twenty-one-year-old was still where I left him, groggy, but awake.

"You ever come by here again and you're a dead white motherfuckin' bitch."

"Here's your gun," I said. I grabbed it by the barrel and swung it like a hammer, the butt hitting him in the nose. Not super hard, but hard enough to drop him again. I figured he could get another gun very easily enough, so I tossed the gun from where it came, the oleander bush. I kept the bullets.

I turned to Sixteen and said, "I know it's easy for me to say, but you ought to get out of the gang life before it's too late. It's just not worth it." And then I said as loud as I could without screaming, "Tell Funeral Michael Lyons came by looking for him." Then I left.

I stepped to my car parked down the street about a football field away. I felt Hoover Criminal sights on my back, imagined a laser target on my nape. It tingled. Still, I walked, though I wanted to run, wanted to sprint like Jerry Rice in his beautiful prime, racing down the sidelines.

Just then, an LAPD patrol glided down Hoover. The white cops inside noticed the white man outside, a rare sight in these parts. Hoover Street wasn't even a drugstore for the white man. Those who did brave South Central for their crack preferred the quick and easy freeway on- and off-ramps near Figueroa Street, a half mile east.

The cops continued a block down, then made a quick U.

I had driven up Hoover heading for Florence, where I made a quick right on the red, but without coming to a totally complete stop. What they call a California Stop. I thought, as I made that right on red, that California had Girls, Cuisine, Dreamin', Redwoods, Condors, Rolls, and even Stops. Bet no other state has all that.

Then, as I approached Figueroa, just a half block from the freeway, almost home free, I noticed the cherry top lights flashing in my rearview.

"Shit." Maybe it's not for me. I pulled into the Standard Station at the corner of Flower Street and Figueroa. The cops pulled in behind.

"License and registration, sir."

"What I do?" Damned if I'd call these guys 'sir.'

"License and registration, sir. I would prefer not to ask again."

I nodded and slowly reached into my pocket for my wallet, removing the California driver's license. "Reg is in the glove box. Okay?"

"Get it slow."

I handed it to the officer. The second cop, short and stocky, was at the passenger-side window looking in. The first cop went back to his car. The other motioned for me to roll down the passenger window. I did and asked sarcastically, "Okay if I get some gas while I'm here?"

"Stay in the car," the stocky cop ordered. "Can I ask what you were doing on Hoover Street?"

"Is that illegal?"

"I'm just curious," said stocky.

"I understand. I'm just curious, too. Curious as to why, in the

LAPD division with the most killings, robberies, and rapes, at least tied with 108th Street, why you're wasting your time on me?"

The first cop came back. "You been drinking?"

"No"

"Then why do you have a Big Red wrapper on the floor?"

"Big Red's illegal. Being on Hoover Street is illegal. I guess, though, in the Seventy-Seventh, drive-bys and robberies are okay. That it?"

"Looks like we got us a smart-ass here," stocky said. "Why don't you get out of the vehicle?"

"Is that a question?" I asked, living up to his expectations. Just then, I realized I still had that damn SAS knife down my leg. Dumb ass. How stupid can one man be? Even in the cool night air, sweat seeped out onto my forehead.

"Get out." I did, as carefully as I could to make sure my pants didn't rise above my ankles.

By then, a small group of blacks at the mini-mart were watching. One of them couldn't resist. "Get your video phone, homie. This is history. LAPD stopping a white man." Several people laughed. Some gave and got loud side fives.

Another in the crowd yelled out, "Arrest that gang member, officer. Protect and serve us. Yeah, he a Blood. Denver Lane. Take him away before he robs and shoots us po' black folk," said another black man, laughing his ass off.

The two cops looked at each other. Now they regretted pulling me over. They decided they needed to at least make a show of it. "Look, man," the first cop said to me. "Here's the deal. We pulled you over because you made a California stop."

"Please. You gotta be kidding. You were profiling me. DWW. Driving while white in the neighborhood. That's some bullshit."

There were more taunts from the crowd of ten, twelve people.

"Well, that's not the point now with your fan club over there all riled up. I gotta make a show of it and get you on your way. So spread 'em. I gotta frisk you," said the first cop.

"Ah, Officer, can't I just get on my way? I was coming to Hoover to see an old friend. That's it. He wasn't home. Plus I got friends at the Seventy-Seventh. You know Detective Mo Batts? He's a friend of mine." Mo wasn't really a friend, but I was getting desperate. "Sal LaBarbera in Southeast is my main."

"No worries, but, for that mob's sake, I have to frisk you and then you can go. What's the problem? Now spread 'em. Assume the position."

Yes, worries. Oh, shit, I put my hands on the hood of his car, spread my legs. The officer patted me down. Then he came to the bottom of my left pants leg.

The crowd was cheering as I was cuffed. A muscular, forty-something man with a Southwest College sweatshirt, working at the gas station, came out of his bulletproof glass-enclosed workspace.

"You gonna have to move that car. It's blocking my business."

"I'm cuffed, man. Can you guys move it?"

The cops said no. Said I was lucky they didn't impound it, but since I knew Mo, they gave me a break.

"Then I'm gonna have it towed," the attendant said.

"Shit. Hey, my keys are in my front pocket. Can I give it to him?"

"It's your car. Do what you want. You want to fill out a stolen car report now or later?" The cops and even the gas station man started to laugh. At that point, I wasn't even concerned about the car. I was just glad the police hadn't looked in the trunk and found the gun.

I managed to get my keys out and hand them to the worker. "When I come back, I want to see a full tank. What's your name?"

"Rasheed. But, man," said the worker, "you're going to Seventy-Seventh Street. You better hope you *do* come back."

The holding cell at the LAPD's Seventy-Seventh Street Division had nine Latinos from God knows where, five African Americans, and one Armenian man. But, I knew here in jail, I was simply a white boy.

The Latinos used to be called Mexicans, but now with all the Salvadorans, Guatemalans, Hondurans, and whatnot, they all got lumped into being Latinos when it came to jail.

In the county jail system of Los Angeles—Men's Central, Twin Towers, Wayside—it wasn't about Crips and Bloods, or Criminals vs. Crips or even various Crips against other Crips. When it all came down, it was about Latinos versus blacks. I hoped my complexion, light for an Armenian, didn't possess the unifying power to bring the blacks and Latinos together to stomp me into red pilaf.

I considered trying to start a conversation with the black guys, but, lately, the jailed population had become such a bizarre, intertwined group of shifting alliances that it was far too risky to say your friends with guys from one set or another. The latest was that the Hoover Criminals had teamed up, incredibly, with their once deadly enemy, the Eight Trey Gangster Crips. Shit, but who knows? By next week, that could all change.

Rather than try to forge a relationship with either the blacks or the Latinos, I considered turning to a combination of Jesus, Muhammad, Abraham, Buddha, Gandhi, Mother Teresa, hell, even Reverend Ike, and whoever else was rumored to have any sway at all regarding these matters. Hell, I shouldn't even mention the word "sway." That's the very derogatory term for the Swans, one of the oldest Blood gangs.

I wished Blinky, the Samoan from my old neighborhood, would walk in. Instead, I got the next best thing.

"Lyons, get your ass over here." I looked up to see Detective Mo Batts towering over the stocky uniformed cop outside the cell. Batts had overheard the two cops talking about a white guy they had arrested for carrying a concealed weapon. Batts had overheard my name mentioned and stopped the paperwork.

"Sal, you not gonna believe who we got—well, who we *had* in the holding tank here," Batts said into phone at his desk, while his thumb and forefinger very gingerly glided up the double-edged SAS killing knife. I, without cuffs, was sitting across the desk. "Your boy

Lyons himself. No bullshit. Concealed weapon. No, a knife. Nice one. And not the kind you'd use to cut a T-bone."

"For self-defense, Detective Batts," I said.

"Shuddup." Batts talked for a while, then hung up. "For some unknown reason, I guess Detective LaBarbera thinks you're on the up-and-up. Says he owes you one. So, we gonna cut you loose. I'll keep your pretty blade, though. You do know taxicabs won't come here. It's not worth the gamble.

"And Lyons, I know you're crazy, but it's on tonight 'round here. We've had seven drive-bys already this shift. Three dead. That's why I'm still here. So, don't be walking. You best make your phone call for a pickup. Sal may think you're all right, but I'm not convinced. You get that one call, so make it good."

"Tell me this is a bad joke," Francesca said. I was lucky she had picked up the phone.

"I wish. Can you come get me?" I pleaded. Mo Batts had his gigantic fist in front of his mouth, trying unsuccessfully to stifle his laughter.

"Oh, Michael. I can't right now. We are too busy. I'm in the weeds." I heard in the background some orders come into her. "I gotta go."

"Wait. Wait. Can't you have one of workers, one of the cooks or bussers come get me? It's only like fifteen minutes away."

"I don't want my cooks knowing the man I live with is in jail for God knows what. Is this gonna be on the news? In the papers?"

"No, no. It's nothing. When can you get here? An hour? All right."

"Wait, Michael. Damnit. You know I'm gonna need some real good directions to get to your damn Southside."

Two hours later, I walked out with a pissed-off Francesca. "Where's your car?" I asked.

"My car? You think I'm going to drive a hundred and sixty thousand dollar Porsche down here at night? I wouldn't even bring it in the day. Christmas morning I wouldn't drive it here."

"Okay, okay."

"I got Luis's car. I don't even know what it is." Luis, the barback at Pizzeria Zola, had lent her his Ford Escort without questions.

Driving up Broadway to Florence, just a few blocks north, Francesca said, "Hospitals, gunshot wounds, breaking news, jails. Where are you gonna pop up next? The UN? Okay, let's hear it."

I told her quite a bit of my night. She said not a word but shook her head like a bobblehead Kirk Gibson speeding down Stadium Way. We pulled into the brightly lit Standard gas station. I got out and started filling Luis's car with the good stuff. The ninety-one octane.

"Big shot with the expensive gas. Probably doesn't even have a car now. Where is it?"

The Lexus wasn't in sight. I went inside the mini-mart. There was Rasheed. "Where's my car?"

Three police cars, lights twirling, sirens blaring, barreled west on Florence. A minute later, another one sped by. Then another two. "Someone must've straight-out ran a red light," I said. "Where's my car?"

"You the reporter that had hisself shot, right?"

"No. Where's my car?"

"You sure got out quick. White boy's rights, huh? And I know you're that reporter. Why did you do that? Word 'round here is that was Funeral from the Hoovers on the tape. That was stupid."

"Ah, man. I didn't do that. But, you know, if you want to believe that, there ain't nothing I can do about it. I did trust you with my keys. Now *that* was stupid."

Francesca marched into the mini-mart, her patience usually long as the wind, was gone with it now. "How long are you going to be here?"

"Not long."

"What exactly does 'not long' mean. A minute? A day? Should we set up camp? Maybe make a tent. I mean pitch a damn tent.

Build a goddamn campfire. Roast some marshmallows. Raise some fucking chickens. I just want a rough idea. A month? A year? What? I need to tell my son I moved into a gas station in Watts."

"Vermont Knolls," both Rasheed and I said. Rasheed was enjoying this immensely.

Rasheed laughed heartily. "You two. I could listen to you two all night. Serious. What's your comeback line, reporter, man. I wanna hear it."

"Knolls?" said Francesca, looking left, then right.

I stared at Rasheed who was busting up. Finally, he tossed me my keys. "It's in my driveway, three houses down on Flower. Thanks for the show. I get bored later, I'm gonna watch it on reruns," he said, nodding up to the security camera mounted high on a facing wall.

Rasheed, still grinning, walked from behind his enclosed area, over to the chiller. He pulled out a forty ounce of Olde English "800" and handed it to me. "You might need this tonight. Looks like you got yourself a special occasion."

CHAPTER 20

Just after ten a.m., before it got too crowded, I went to The Grove, the promenade attached to the old Farmer's Market at 3rd and Fairfax. At Barnes & Noble I stocked up on books and magazines that would help my born-again freelance career: *2014 Writer's Market*, *Starting Your Career as a Freelance Writer*, and *100 Best Magazine Markets*.

I walked back to the Farmer's Market—the one where there are no farmers—went to Short Order and had an Ida's Old School Burger and a Charlie Brown, a milkshake with 114-proof Old Grand Dad bourbon. With a red pen in hand, I began searching and marking the Writer's Market for magazines to query.

I flashed back twenty-one years, when I was a nineteen-year-old aspiring writer with no clips, scanning the same book in search of a forum to showcase my first story, which would become that magical clipping that would unlock doors of editors throughout the country. How I longed for that first byline. It would finally come in *Cycle News*, a report on a motocross race in Santa Maria. It felt so good. Countless times did I proudly gaze at my name— "By Michael Lyons." It did not fling open a new world for me, but still, it was the start.

I was doing the same thing again, but now I had scads of clips. Excellent ones. Prize-winning clips. So many grand clips I felt it was beneath me, the best street reporter in the city, to even have to talk about them or include them in a goddamn query letter. Still, it was kind of exciting. Like starting over. Like being young again.

On my way out, I walked over to Littlejohn's to get a pound of English toffee for Francesca. She loved that stuff, one of her few indulgences, one of my many. Then to Bob's Donuts to get glazed crumb and chocolate for Francesca's son, Oliver, and his buddies.

The sweets reception was disappointingly lackluster from Oliver and Francesca, both busy, he on his Mac, she on her Samsung. I headed to my cottage on Landa Street.

Not ten minutes after I got home, my front door was rattled with one powerful knock. I knew that knock.

"My two favorite detectives. Come on in," I said, hoping LaBarbera and Hart were not here regarding my attempted visit last night to King Funeral. They were, but not for the reason I thought.

I tried to be nonchalant. "What brings you here? You find the guy who shot me?"

"No. We have a few questions," Hart said, looking around my neat one-bedroom pad.

"Okay. You guys want some coffee? Water?"

"We're good," Hart said.

"How about some Olde English?"

Hart ignored that and asked pointedly, "Where were you last night between midnight and midnight twenty?"

"Why?"

"Just answer, Lyons."

"What happened?"

"Where were you?"

"I'm a suspect in something?"

"Answer the fuckin' question, Lyons," said an annoyed Hart. LaBarbera just studied me.

"You know where I was. And Sal, thanks, man, for last night. I know it was stupid. Thank you."

"You've helped me. Now we're even. Just answer Johnny's questions."

"You know where I was. At the Seventy-Seventh."

"Records show you got out of the holding cell at 10:07."

"Yeah, about, I guess. But, then I was with Mo Batts for like two hours. That's always a real pleasure."

"Yeah, Mo said you got your ride right about midnight. So where did you go when you left Seventy-Seventh?"

"What happened?"

"Answer, damnit."

"My girlfriend picked me up. Francesca. One of the barbacks at her restaurant lent her his car. She didn't want to take her car down there."

"Why? What kinda car does she have?" asked Hart.

"Porsche. Turbo Cabriolet. Silver."

"Damn. What the fuck does she see in you?" asked Hart.

"Fuck you, Johnny."

"What I wanna know," LaBarbera said, "is how do a famous chef and a crime reporter get together?"

"I'll tell you the story one of these days. Now why are you guys here? What happened? Tell me."

"After you left with her in the bartender's car—"

"Barback."

"Whatever."

"We left, went to the Standard station where my car was and then we went home."

"Lyons, a good D.A. would pick that story apart," Hart said. "A good deputy district attorney. Like that fine-ass Sandra Core."

I was shaking my head. Exasperated, I went to my kitchen, opened the refrigerator, pulled out the forty-ounce Olde English bottle, cracked it open, and took a swig. I held it out for the detectives.

"Damn, you *are* ghetto," said Hart. "You actually drink that piss?"

"Only on special occasions. Now, you ever gonna tell me what happened last night?"

"Shortly after you left the Seventy-Seventh, Funeral got shotgunned."

I was truly stunned. "Holy smokes."

"Holy smokes? I didn't know anybody still said that," said LaBarbera. "Olde English, holy smokes. You really are old school."

"He's dead, right?"

"Like that nail right there in your door," said Hart. "Funeral ain't muscular anymore. Lost a whole lotta weight. He's not getting an open casket, either. Shotgun will do that to a human. One of the uniforms told me they found parts of his face *across the street.*"

"Damn."

"Look, Lyons," Hart said, "He gets shot around midnight. You get released around midnight. Your lady takes you to get your car, but you have two cars. So you have to drive back separately."

"She followed me home. She doesn't know her way around the Southside."

"You were literally one minute from Funeral's place," said Hart. "Plenty of time. You tell to her hold on one minute, kill Funeral, come back, and drive home."

"This is ridiculous. You're kidding, right? Come on, Sal, Johnny. You don't believe this."

"Mike," Sal said. "You know damn well, it would be derelict in our duty if we didn't consider you. If only to check you off the list. You know that. Let's face it. You're there. You hate Funeral. You have access and motive."

"This is bullshit, and I think you two know it. You cut me loose last night, and now you're questioning me on a murder?"

"Gets worse," said Sal. "Three guys at the apartment said a man fitting your description came by around ten looking for Funeral. One of them said you told him to tell Funeral you would be back."

"Of course they gonna say that. They're criminals. That's the name of their gang. Criminals. Hoover Criminals. They killed their own guy and are going to blame me," I said.

"Look," said Hart, "He made you lose your job. That made you crazy. Right now, you are the only one with motive who was seen at his apartment."

"Are you nuts? Funeral had a hundred enemies. Funeral has enemies going back twenty years. Enemies up and down that very block. Plus, you know better than me the Hoovers have as many in-house killings as the Sixties or Grape Street. Come to find out, they are their own worstest enemy."

"Worstest? You might wanna go back to college and take a grammar class," said LaBarbera. "You've been on the street too long."

"Yeah," Hart added, "Did you get fired for that tape or for your sentence structure?"

"Nothing's worse than getting accused of murder by two wannabe English professors. Look, I admit I was pissed after I lost my job because of that tape. But, maybe it was one of those blessings in disguise. The *Times* editors didn't give a shit about my beat, your beat. And yeah, I was disgraced, still am, but, mark my words, I'll be back stronger than ever. Sal, you've known me for a long time. Did you ever believe I set up my own shooting?"

"I already told you that. Jesus, how many times you want me to say it?"

"I guess I just need to hear it again."

"Keep asking me, I'm gonna start having doubts. Look, we even told the chief that we didn't buy that shit for a minute."

"Really?"

"Yes. We don't bullshit."

"Thank you. That means a lot. So Funeral is dead, huh? Well, he was a killer and a rapist anyway. 'Member, when he raped that kid at Corcoran?"

Many years ago, while he was in Corcoran, the guards mistakenly—or so they later claimed—put a hundred-thirty-pound eighteen-year-old white meth hound from Merced in a cell with King Funeral. Funeral sodomized him for three days before the guards transferred the shell-shocked kid to his proper cell where he bashed his head against a wall and hung himself with a bedsheet.

"I could give a fuck Funeral is dead."

Hart checked out my pad. He sauntered into the bedroom like he was a potential buyer, walked into my bite-size kitchen.

"I'm serious, Lyons," said LaBarbera. "If there's anything you need to tell me, do it now."

I took a long, slow breath. "Look, Sal, Johnny, come on. I didn't shoot that pig, but, I'm not gonna lie, I kinda wanted to. And yeah, I *was* there last night, but I never saw him. I was there way before midnight. Before I got arrested."

"Arrested for having a knife," said Hart. "So, you are admitting to two homicide detectives that you were where a man was killed, on the night he was killed, you had a motive to kill him, *and* you had a knife. And Batts said some *commando* knife, I may add."

"You just said Funeral was shot and, anyway, Mo kept the knife."

"For your information, Lyons," said Hart seriously, "Funeral got shot between midnight and twelve fifteen according to the neighbors. And you can't prove to us that you didn't sneak away from chef girl and kill this guy."

"This is absurd. To think I walked up with all his boys around and shotgunned Funeral while my woman was patiently waiting at a gas station at Flower and Florence. Clearly, you don't know my girlfriend."

"I repeat, I don't think you can prove that you didn't," said Hart, still in the kitchen. The detective opened the refrigerator, took out the Olde English, twisted the cap off, took a sniff, and made an unpleasant face.

As he did, a slow smile came to my face. "Wait, wait. I *can* prove I wasn't there at Funeral's place during that time. Let's take a ride."

Two hours later, I was dropped back home, cleared of the killing of King Funeral, thanks to Rasheed and his security camera at the Standard gas station.

"One more question, Mike," LaBarbera said. "Why'd you go by last night to see Funeral, anyway?"

"Sal, I'm really not sure. I . . . I don't know. Part of me wanted to hurt him, part of me was, uh, was scared of him, tell the truth. I still wanted to humiliate him, but, I realized he wasn't worth it. He just wasn't. In the end, I guess I just wanted to let him know I was still standing."

"Well," said LaBarbera, "he's not."

"I gotta say, in a way, I was flattered you guys thought, or even considered I killed Funeral. But guys, I'm a writer, not a fighter."

"Please, Lyons," Hart said. "We pulled your sheet. Barroom brawls. Shooting near Compton, in Dominguez. The Rustic Inn mean anything to you?"

"Man, I was like a teenager. Coming to the aid of a friend. Self-defense."

"Take your pick, huh?" said Hart. "Shit, when you got busted at the Rustic, you were, what, twenty-seven? That's an old-ass teenager."

"Every time in my life I got into trouble, it was for coming to help out a friend or cousin who was in a serious jam."

"What I wanna know is how'd you ever get hired at the *Times* with a record? Especially, as a crime reporter."

"Johnny, don't you think the science reporter should have some experience in science? Or the medical reporter know something about medicine? So why shouldn't the crime reporter have a little experience in crime?"

Sal laughed. "You got a point there. Just try and stay outta trouble."

"Sonny Barger told me that once. Hey, you ever gonna find the guy that shot me? Or is he dead?"

"Where have you been?" asked Francesca. She was sipping a glass of red wine, sitting on a small green leather couch in the cool, dark den, her favorite room for relaxation. But she wasn't relaxed.

"Trying to solve a murder, baby. Murder is my business." I knew the fake tough-guy routine never worked on her, but I enjoyed it. Sometimes in life you just have to entertain yourself if no one else will. "Seriously, guess who got killed last night while we were at that gas station getting my car?"

"What do you mean 'guess'? That's a stupid request. Is this some twisted, morbid game show?"

"King Funeral."

No reaction. None.

"The guy that taped me and played it for the cops. That guy that basically got me fired. He got killed last night. Near where we were. They actually were thinking maybe I did it because I was down there last night."

"Michael, you live in a strange world. It's like another planet from what I know." Francesca could be warm, sexy, and cuddly. She was extremely generous and giving to friends in need. And she could be distant and cold. "Look, maybe this isn't going to work out. I know we've been together for a while and had some great times, but I've been thinking, we are just so different. So, so different. When people ask us how do a chef and a crime reporter get together, it's a good question. We are from two completely different worlds. That scene last night at the jail. At the gas station. You with a knife. That's just not me. And we argue about little things. I don't like to argue, even over little things. Like the other night when I told you I'd never heard of that singer they showed on that commercial for those soul singer CDs."

"Jackie Wilson."

"Yes. Hey, I'm sorry I never heard of Jackie Wilson, but you had to make fun of me."

"Come on. I was just playing with you. I don't care if you never heard of Jackie Wilson. I just thought it was kinda funny since you love Van Morrison so much."

"What does Van Morrison have to do with it?"

"Forget it. The main thing is I love you."

"No, you don't. You don't love me."

"Don't say that. Don't tell me who I love. I love you. We have a great time together. When you aren't working."

"Well, someone has to work."

I took the blow with a smile the way Roberto Duran would do when Sugar Ray Leonard stung him. But it stung, all right.

"No, I think sometimes you take advantage of me, Michael. You use me. We go to Italy. We go to the French Laundry. You are the big shot at Zola. I know you like that. Walk in and everyone treats you like you're the boss. They all like you, but it doesn't hurt that they think I am your girlfriend."

"Of course, I like that. But, that is not the reason I love you. And what do you mean they 'think' you're my girlfriend? You *are* my girl-friend."

"I think maybe we shouldn't see each other for a while."

"What? What do you mean a while? A day?"

"I mean maybe a few weeks. I mean maybe a lifetime."

"A lifetime?"

"Let's see how it goes. We are just too different. Maybe you should find yourself a wild girl who knows who Jackie Wilson is."

"Fuck Jackie Wilson."

"Why don't you go home now? Don't call me."

"Just like that?"

"That's how it happens. Just like that."

I knew when not to argue. I headed for the door. On my way, I tried to kiss her on the lips, but she leaned way back. It reminded me of the way Ali used to lean back when Ernie Tyrell threw a jab at him.

As I drove home, I put on an oldies station hoping for a long shot that Van Morrison would come on singing "Jackie Wilson Said." He didn't.

That night and the next morning, I was as low as I had been for ages. Lower than when I lay in the hospital bed with bullet wounds. Lower than when I was fired. I could feel the sadness and weakness deep in my bones. I had a great gal and my stupid actions were going to take her away.

I longed to call her, but knew well enough never to call from a point of weakness. Our routine was that I would leave her house in the morning and she would call after her morning walk. That next morning I ached for that phone to ring. She usually called my home number because my cell phone was so erratic in my hilly neighbor-hood. I was too old for this. Acting a damn fool. I waited for the call from her. It didn't come.

• • •

I had to keep moving. I wanted to stay home and drink and drink and listen to Sinatra and pass out on the couch. But, thank Zeus, I didn't.

Instead, I went to the county jail looking for Deputy Sarkis Sarkisian. He was there and gave me some time in a small office near the visitor's room. I asked if he had heard anything about my shooting, any rumor, any buzz, anything at all about King Funeral, a smidgen that I would find of interest. He told me a story that fascinated me. Not only did the story itself fascinate, but the mere fact that I had never heard it before was perplexing.

In the mid-1990s, Sarkisian told me, there was a period where both Big Evil and King Funeral were trustees at the jail. Because of their reputations, the sheriffs used them to help keep the relative peace inside. Big Evil ran the entire Bloods module and King Funeral ran the large module containing the Hoovers, who were then Crips, as well as several other Crip sets. There were other trustees as well, Wild Cat from the Rollin Sixties, and guys for the Mexican gangs, usually shot callers for Geraghty Loma, White Fence Florencia, 38th Street and 18th Street. In return for trying to keep their modules quiet—they were not always successful—these trustees were granted extra access to the jail, more time outside their cells, better food, and use of a phone when they wanted it, which was often.

"One day," said Sarkisian, "Funeral and Evil, they got along all right, anyway they were relaxing in a small, empty barracks-like room when a sadistic old white deputy sheriff named Dean Boylston came in with a new sheriff he was training. Boylston was about like fifty or so. Been at the jail his whole career."

"Yeah, and?"

"Well, this was around the time they were having those gladiator fights in the SHU up in Corcoran. So Boylston orders, more or less, Evil and Funeral to get it on. Whoever wins the fight gets even more privileges."

"So what happened?"

"Long story, long, bloody story short, Evil kicked his ass."

"I'd have had my money on Evil."

"No, you don't understand. He kicked his ass."

"What's not to get?"

"No, I mean literally. He got him down, started to choke him out. Then Boylston made him stop. Kept screaming, "No killing! No killing!" So Evil straight out pulls Funeral's jailhouse pants down and his underwear and literally kicks him in the ass. Then with his other foot, kicks him again and says, 'I kicked your ass twice.'"

"Whoa. Humiliation."

"That's not the worst of it. This Deputy Boylston, he got one of them big old video cameras and he taped the whole thing. With that tape, you know, that old tape. What do they call it?"

"Not eight millimeter?"

"No, no. Used to be all popular, till DVD came around."

"Oh, ugh, VHS."

"Yeah, that's it. VHS. He tapes it, even does some commentary like he's Howard Cosell, ya know, like 'in this corner from Seventy-Fourth and Hoover, da da da' and down goes Funeral and so on. He tapes it and keeps the tape. He goes to Evil and told him something like 'if you brag about this fight, or if I hear about it from anyone not in this room, then your privilege is gone.' And to Funeral, he tells him 'if you don't keep the Hoovers in line, I'm gonna release this tape and everyone gonna see how big bad King Funeral got his ass kicked. Twice.'"

"So no one ever saw the tape?"

"As far as I know, no gangbangers did, but who knows for sure? Some deputies saw it. I never did, but that's how I heard about it. Boylston died a few years back. But, his partner, the rookie, he's still around. I think you might have heard of him. He joined LAPD years ago. He's a detective now."

"What's his name?"

"Johnny Hart."

• • •

I drove to Southeast Division, aka 108th Street. I didn't even call. I figured if Johnny wasn't there, I could go to the projects or visit my sister in G-Town.

But, Hart was there.

"Why didn't you tell me about the tape?"

"What tape?"

"The one where Big Evil kicks King Funeral's ass at Men's Central."

"First of all, I was told to keep that secret. And what does it have to do with you?"

"You kidding me? Big Evil and King Funeral have a lot to do with me. I was accused by you of killing one. I made the other one famous. This tape might have something to do with my shooter."

"How? Mike, believe me I thought about it and if there was a connection, the slightest hint of a connection, I would be on it and you would know about it. But, I can't see any connection at all to what's been going on with you."

"It's too much of a coincidence. And I don't get why Evil never told me this story."

"It's a big deal to you, but to Evil it probably wasn't that big of a thing. How'd you find out about it anyway?"

"That's what I do, try and find out about things. Like who shot me, since you haven't found out. But, there's got to be a connection. Does Sal know about the fight, the tape?"

"Of course. What do you think? You think I keep things from LaBarbera?

"We talked about it and couldn't come up with any tie-in to you. We are on this case, but like I told you time and again. It doesn't look gang related. Not yet, at least."

"Were there copies made of that tape? Do you think the Hoovers got a hold of it and that's why Funeral got splattered?"

"I don't know. The deputy who filmed it, who started the fight—"

"Boylston."

"Yeah. What an asshole. But, he was my trainer when I first was working jails. Anyway, I don't know if he made copies or not. I know he used to threaten to release it to fuck with Funeral. Funeral would've lost all his power if that tape got out. This was before the Internet was super huge like it is now with all this YouTube shit and all that, but even then it woulda made the rounds."

"I bet it got out."

"No, I think Funeral was killed because someone, maybe Mayhem or even his nephew, what's his name, Tiny Trouble, might've bragged about how his uncle helped him get out jail by dealing with the police."

"This is maddening."

"Hey Mike, we're still on your case, but, and I think Sal might've told you, we're not on it exclusively. We're getting fresh homicides, two, three a week. They need us on other stuff. We're not giving up at all. We'll get the guy. I just don't think it's related to that tape."

"You still have the tape?"

"I never had it. I saw the fight, when it happened. But, I never saw that tape. I think Boylston took it to his grave. Maybe now he can still taunt Funeral with it in hell."

I wanted a drink in a friendly place. I went to the Redwood Saloon. I hadn't been there since that jacked-up news conference. I had a double Jack on the rocks.

"Hey, Jack," Danny said, "You see the paper today? The mayor and the chief's gang list?"

"No. What're you talking about?"

"They made a list of the eleven worst gangs in the city. Said they were gonna target them. Put them out of business."

"Never happen. Who made the list? Where's the paper?"

"Where it always is. You haven't been here for so long you forgot?"

I walked over near the juke, went through the paper, found the story, and walked outside.

On the sidewalk where I was shot, I read the story of the eleven worst gangs in the city as selected by the chief and the mayor. It was bullshit. The list contained five of the toughest gangs in Los Angeles, but had another six that were insignificant. They'd left out at least five gangs that were not only among the worst in the city, but among the worst in the nation. The Bounty Hunters, Florencia, Eight Trey Gangster Crips, East Coast Crips. The mayor and the chief of police were so clueless as to what was going on in the streets that they didn't even put the Hoover Criminals on the list. Their leader had been killed, they play a major role in the jail system, they have turf that stretches for miles, and they weren't even mentioned among the eleven worst gangs. The powers that be know so little about what's going on in their own streets that they probably hadn't even heard about Funeral's killing.

Ten minutes later, I called Laurie Escobar, a friend of Francesca and the editor of the *Los Angeles Weekly*. I told her the story I wanted to do: blast the mayor and the chief for their errant gang list and come up with the real eleven, or in my story, the twelve worst gangs in the city. The Dirty Dozen. Corny, I know, but Escobar liked the idea, but was uneasy about me doing it.

"I have to tell you, Michael, I'm a little uncomfortable about having you write for us at this moment."

"Because of that tape, right?"

"Yes, because of that tape."

"Laurie, you know Francesca pretty good. Do you actually think I would risk losing her to get shot? It's absurd to even think that. Yeah, that was me on the tape. Everyone knows that. I never denied it, but I wasn't fired for that tape. It was an excuse to get rid of me because Doot and Tinder and I didn't get along. Plus those editorials that Collinsworth wrote and the tape embarrassed them. Laurie, this is a good story. We can beat the *Times*, and beat the mayor and the chief. I know I can get LAPD gang and homicide detectives who will agree with my list. The mayor and chief have one gang from Torrance and one from Canoga Park on their list, but they don't have the Hoovers, the Bounty Hunters, Eight Trey Gangsters, Florencia. Their list is a joke. There's no reporter who knows the streets like me, you know that. Gimme a shot."

She agreed to give me the story. I think her friendship with Francesca helped me. The pay would be fifty cents a word, twelve hundred words. I could sure use six hundred dollars.

She gave me the number and e-mail of Doris De Soto, the hard-charging news editor at the *Weekly*. De Soto loved the idea. Anytime she could criticize the mayor and the chief in one story, she was all aboard.

It was Friday afternoon. The *Weekly* came out on Thursdays, so Doris told me to get it to her Monday evening or Tuesday morning at the latest, and they'd run it next week. Cool. Or, as Big Evil would say, "bool."

The *Weekly* was a free paper loaded with advertising for tit enlargement, butt reductions, butt additions, even anus tightening. Nevertheless, the paper was well regarded. They often beat the *Times* on political and street stories and their television, movie, and restaurant critics were respected.

For the next four days, I felt a live wire coursing through my veins for the first time since Francesca told me to go home. I was hitting the streets with the vigor of the Michael of old. I had a routine. I would spot my potential interviewees, drive a bit past them, get out the car, notebook in hand, a minimum of two ink pens handy, and, as nonchalantly as possible, step to them. Could be one guy, could be seven. "Excuse me, fellas, my name is Michael Lyons. I'm a reporter. I'm working on a story about that stupid list the LAPD came out with about the worst street gangs in the city. You guys see that list?" I quickly wanted to establish that I was against the LAPD's list.

It is uncommon to get a hit on your first foray into the streets. Usually, you strike out several times before you get something worth writing down or even get someone to talk. I spotted a possible gang member on foot turning from 53rd Street onto Hoover. At first, as is so often the case, I figured it wouldn't be worth it and I'd drive on. But, like a good reporter, I decided what the hell, don't be lazy, so what if I strike out. I've struck out a lot. So did Babe Ruth.

I drove past. Parked along Hoover near 54th Street. I confronted the kid, and this time I hit a home run. He was a for-real Hoover Criminal. The Hoover, nicknamed Set Trip, gave me a good interview, some good quotes. "Why weren't the Hoovers on the list? We the most hated gang in L.A. We even hate each other."

"Is that what happened to King Funeral?

"I don't know nothin' 'bout that," Set Trip said, glancing around as he spoke. Chances are the young thug knew who had killed King Funeral—most likely another Hoover. Like all the super gangs in L.A., they had plenty of in-house killings. Maybe it had been Funeral's cooperation with the police over the tape of me that did him in. The detectives wouldn't find out until someone was arrested for a felony and, utterly fearful of prison time, gave up the shooter of Funeral as a deal to get cut loose. That guy would have to leave town.

I knew it was a long shot, but I played it anyway. "Say, you heard about that reporter who was shot downtown, right?"

"Yeah, I heard. We ain't as stupid as everyone thinks. I read the paper. I even heard about a couple wars we was into. They should just send the Hoovers over there to Iraq and Afghanistan, Syria too. We clean that shit up in a week."

"Yeah. But the reporter. You hear anything on the street about who shot him?"

"All I know is who didn't shoot him," Set Trip said.

"Who didn't shoot him?"

"Hoovers didn't shoot him. He'd be dead if we shot him. Same with Grape Street. I don't know but if I had to guess, I'd say it was a loner."

"A loner? What's a loner?"

"A loner, you know, a loner, some guy not in a gang, not in a set. Just some guy that reporter pissed off."

I don't know why, but I couldn't resist. "Say, Set Trip, that reporter who got shot, that was me."

"No shit? Well, I be goddamn. I be getting interviewed by somebody famous and shit. Good for you. Welcome to the club." He lifted his shirt and showed off a serious stomach scar. Then he wound up and gave me a hard side five.

I was really just joking with King Funeral when I said getting shot has its benefits, but, truth be told, in certain neighborhoods getting shot does get you some quick respect. Ask Set Trip.

Back at home, I was strong enough to get back to exercising vigorously. I was doing a set of push-ups, sit-ups, and the all-important pull-ups when the phone rang.

"We lost Term." I recognized Detective Sal LaBarbera's voice.

"Term? Terminal?" I asked incredulously. "Big Evil's brother?"

"Lyons, how many Terminals are there?"

"What happened, Sal?"

"Someone called in a body by that Alan Engle, what is it, that ugh, recycling center. Not recycling, but—"

"Scrap metal place. The big one near Jordan Downs, right?"

"Right. So patrol goes over there. It's a homicide. They call over here and Waxman goes over and it's Bobby Desmond. They barely recognized him, but he didn't have a shirt on and they saw all the tats. Waxman said he got two in the chest, but a major-ass beating, too. Face smashed in like with a baseball bat or pipe, plus tire treads on his body. Broken leg. Was run over. This was very personal. Term's not getting an open casket."

"Holy smokes. Must be the trend. Like King Funeral. Jack 'em up so bad the family can't even say good-bye at the funeral. You tell his parents yet?"

"I went over there, but no one was home. They're working folks. We're trying to keep it quiet until they know. I'm telling you, but I am counting on you to be quiet, too. Oh, wait a minute. You can't do a daily for the *Times*, can you? Sorry, I forgot you got your ass got fired."

"Screw you, Sal. What about Big Evil? He know?"

"He probably knows by now. I wanted to tell him myself, but he was in the hole. He'd jacked somebody."

"Typical Evil."

"Anyway, he's getting or got out today. Apparently there's a guard up there, some white guy, who is on good terms with him, and he said he'd tell him."

"Anyway, Sal, what do you think? In-house?"

"Most likely. Terminal had a lot of enemies. Eighty-Nines and the Swans. Not to mention all the Crip sets around them. It was definitely not a random thing. The level of violence was, like I said, very personal. Whoever killed Terminal had someone they loved killed by him."

"Or his brother. Well, that narrows it down to what, thirty, forty people. Look, this could be a great story. An Evil follow-up. Can I tag along? Be the fly on the wall?"

"The other day we questioned you in a gang murder, and now you want to tag along with us? What makes you think you aren't still a suspect in the Funeral killing?"

"There you go flattering me again. Come on with the tagalong. I'll make you famous again."

"Last thing I need is for you to make me famous. I'll pass. But maybe I'll run that by the bigwigs. Who are you working for?"

"I could freelance Terminal's death to a lotta places. Maybe the *Weekly*. Maybe a magazine piece. I got that worst gang piece coming out Thursday in the *Weekly*. I'm back on it."

"Call me tonight, Mike, but, you for sure can't go to the Desmond household tonight when we notify."

"Why not?"

"You know why. First of all, it's not right. Second, she still hates your guts. From that magazine story on Evil. I saw Mrs. Desmond a few weeks ago when we were doing a 'cide on Eighty-Seventh Street and Wadsworth. She drove by and stopped when she saw me. Said it was too bad you didn't die when you got shot."

"Lovely woman. She raises the two biggest killers in the city, and I'm the bad guy. You know what, Sal? That's okay. I know she tried to raise them, worked hard and all that. Sal, to change the subject, my shooting, anything new?"

"Still working it, but nothing yet. We'll get the guy."

"What about King Funeral? Who killed him?"

"It's looking in-house. There haven't been any paybacks on the Sixties or Eight Treys or Main Street or anybody else. Of course, no witnesses have stepped up. Probably have to wait till some Hoover gets busted, starts to panic about being locked up, and gives up some Funeral info as his get outta jail card. Same ol', same ol'. Word might have leaked that Funeral gave us the tape, and, you know, any cooperation with the police, even if it was to bring you down, even to get someone out of a jam, is a serious violation of the gang code."

"Say, wait a minute, Sal. What about me?"

"What about you?"

"Funeral gets killed. Terminal gets killed. I get shot. Don't you see a pattern?"

"No. Not unless you're a shot caller."

"It just seems like a coincidence, and I don't believe in coincidence."

"Michael, that's my line."

"Yeah, well, I'm gonna find out before whoever shot me comes back."

"I'd tell you to be careful and don't do anything crazy, but I'd be wasting my time."

CHAPTER 21

The day before the Desmonds were to receive that hard visit from detectives, their son Cleamon got an intriguing visit from a stranger. To visit an inmate in California prison, the inmate must send you a visiting form, which is completed and returned to the California Department of Corrections, the CDC, in Sacramento.

But, there is a way around the visiting form. If the prison is more than two hundred miles away from the address on the potential visitor's California driver's license, they can visit an inmate unannounced as long as the inmate approves the last-minute in-house request. Abnormal is the case when an inmate, lonely for contact with the outside world, will deny a visit even if he has no idea who the person is.

Eddie Sims presented the top-of-the-line fake ID he had purchased near McArthur Park a week ago for eighty-five dollars. He used the name Barry Sanders, the great Detroit Lions running back, another favorite of his son, Payton.

Cleamon "Big Evil" Desmond was brought into the visiting area by four guards, one of whom held a shotgun. Desmond was denied his "super trustee" privileges after he knocked out a guard during a basketball game. Now he was cuffed, his hands locked to a chain around his waist, his feet shackled. Six foot three, about two-thirty. Graceful in chains. No unneeded fat. Fast as a jaguar. His muscles bulging, but not muscle-bound, his skin shiny, his eyes bright.

A guard released his right hand so he could use the phone to talk through the thick wire-meshed glass. Cleamon was curious who was here to visit. Sure wasn't the real Barry Sanders. A minute later,

Sims came in, sat down, and picked up the phone. It took thirty seconds to come on.

"Who are you?" Evil asked as the phone went on.

"A friend of Bobby's."

"Bullshit, motherfucker. If you a friend of my brother's you wouldn't be calling him Bobby."

"A friend of Terminal. I didn't want to be rude."

"Rude? To me? That's impossible."

"I doubt that. I mean, don't you think if someone did something wrong to you, or bumped into you without saying excuse me, wouldn't that be rude?"

"That would be stupid. There's a difference. Now, who the fuck are you?"

"I'm a friend of your family," said Sims, starting to feel the security of the thick glass between him and the man who had killed his son. "In fact, I met your mother the other day. Nice lady. Lovely lady. Nice-looking older woman."

"Now you starting to get stupid."

"No, I meant that as a compliment. I'm sorry, I meant no disrespect. But, Bobby, I mean Terminal, your mother kept calling him Bobby, I guess that's why I keep calling him that. Anyway, I used to work on Terminal's car. He was a good rapper. Could get down. He used to freestyle at the shop where I worked."

"Where was that?"

"Frank's over on Central and Ninety-Second."

"Yeah, know that place. So why you here?"

"Well, I was in the area, visiting a cousin in Eureka and figured I would come by and pass on my respects and condolences to you about Terminal. Like I said, he was a friend. He even showed me the video of you kicking Funeral's ass."

"Shit, I forgot about that. I wonder how he got it."

"I don't know. But, anyway, I been locked up myself and I know it's nice to get any visit, even from a stranger. Break up the day, you know?"

"I know."

"It must've been hard to hear the news about Terminal while you up in here. Were you two close?"

Big Evil thought back to another lifetime when he and his little brother used to play on the streets and sidewalks of 89th Street and 88th Place. That's as far as they were allowed to roam. Their parents made life for the brothers in their volatile neighborhood as good as they could. Cleamon and Bobby rode new Schwinns when the other kids on the block had rusted hand-me-down Huffys. The Desmond parents opened a new world for their sons with trips to Yosemite and Mount Shasta and Pismo Beach while the other kids on the block never ventured west of the Harbor Freeway, the Westside. Cleamon smiled when he thought about those trips. He laughed when he thought about how he taught his little brother how to fight, especially the time he broke Bobby's nose and told the crying eight-year-old that one day he would thank him for that punch.

When he'd heard the news of Terminal's violent death, he'd felt only rage. But now, thinking back on those days, he got a rare visit from sadness, felt the unfamiliarity of moisture in his eyes.

"Man, whoever you are, he was my little brother. Things didn't work out how my parents planned it. But, he was my little brother. I loved him like only a brother can. I wish I could have been with him that night. I wish."

"That's sad, man," Eddie said, as serious as can be. Then he went for the kill shot. "You know, Big Evil, I had a wish just this morning, too."

"Oh, yeah? What that be?"

"I just wish you could've been there and seen little Bobby's face when I shot him and drove my car over and over his punk ass."

Evil boiled, his rage about to explode. Sims didn't let up. "Gonna be casket closed for Bobby. Face looked like a watermelon dropped from the Empire State Building."

With peerless fury, Big Evil slammed his forehead into the wire-stuffed glass separating him from Sims. An unholy wail, like that of a Cape buffalo-gored lion, erupted from Evil's crazed mouth. The guards rushed to him, yelling for backup. With his one free hand he struck the glass three furious times before the guards tried to tackle him. One guard went for the shackled, but bucking legs. Not a smart move. The other went Barry Bonds on Evil's shoulders with his nightstick. Two more guards entered the room. One with a taser that had little effect. Five men were on the shackled Evil while he screamed, "That guy killed my brother! He killed my brother! Get him! Get him!"

The guards were too busy to pay attention to the words. They were struggling to get the upper hand. They didn't have it. Two more guards showed up, both with shotguns that were useless in the cramped quarters.

By the time they finally got control, Eddie Sims was halfway to Eureka. At first, he considered just dumping the Cutlass at the airport and getting a flight to Los Angeles, if they had those flights, or to Sacramento. He didn't want to chance driving seven hundred miles. They probably got some video in the lot, in the prison itself. It would be sad to leave the Cutlass. He knew he would never see it again.

But, then he gambled. Who is going to believe Big Evil? And after the fight he most likely put up—Sims had seen the opening salvos—he must certainly be in the hole by now with no communication with the outside or inside world.

So he drove home. However, just to play it cautious, he took the long way, heading down from Eureka, then heading east at Fortuna along meandering Highway 36, past sycamores and pines, past fields of wild fennel, to the two-horse towns of Platina and Red Bluff. There, he checked into a sixty-one dollar room at the Red Bluff Travelodge on Antelope Boulevard.

He put on the local news channel based in Sacramento and saw nothing about himself or Big Evil or Pelican Bay. Checked the papers in the morning. Nothing. Why worry? No one would believe a killer like Evil.

He filled the gas tank and zipped down Highway 5. Just past bankrupt Stockton, he chicaned over to Highway 99, which went through the heart of the San Joaquin Valley, past Modesto, Merced, Fresno, Visalia, Corcoran, and Bakersfield before it met up again with Interstate 5.

Seeing Big Evil try to attack him, even through bulletproof glass, was terrifying. He loved it. If he died right now, it would be worth it for that moment. But he moved on to more pleasant thoughts—his next victim.

CHAPTER 22

Detective Ralph Waxman was the primary investigating the wicked killing of Terminal, but it was Sal LaBarbera and Johnny Hart who went to the Desmond household to give the parents the grim news. Sal had known the family over twenty years, having first come in contact with them while investigating an assault when he was a patrolman. A black man had been badly beaten, pulverized into a temporary coma in the alley by the garage. Young Cleamon was questioned but not arrested.

Throughout the following nearly two decades, after the brothers, Cleamon and Bobby, had grown into Big Evil and Terminal, LaBarbera would visit the home on a nearly monthly basis, looking for one or the other of them, sometimes both. Mrs. Desmond would be pleasant sometimes, curt others. "I am sick and tired of you coming around here every time someone gets shot. Are Cleamon and Bobby the only suspects in this city? Get out of here. Tired of your damn knock, too."

So, when they heard that powerful single knock on the door, the Desmonds knew who it was.

"Hello, Detective Sal. Johnny. So who did Bobby supposedly shoot now?"

"Can we come in?"

"Here we go again. I'm too tired to argue. I had a strange day." She unlocked the security door. They walked in.

Hart couldn't resist. "What was so strange about it?"

"What do you want?"

"Is Cleveland home?" At that, Cleveland Desmond entered the front room.

"Sit down, ma'am, Mr. Desmond," Sal said in a quiet tone.

"Oh, my God. No!" Mrs. Desmond said in a trembling, terrified murmur. She began moaning, slowly, like a forty-five hit single on thirty-three rpm. Her husband rushed to her side and put his arm around her. "Please, Jesus. Please. Don't let it be. Please, Jesus."

Sal shook his head. "I'm sorry. Bobby is gone. They found him in an alley in Watts this morning. I'm really sorry to tell you this."

Betty slumped, her husband guided her down on the couch. He sat next to her, gently running his hand over her hair. There were just a few tears slowly leaking from her heartbroken eyes. It was the news they had been avoiding, but at the same time expecting, for more than fifteen years. Now the news landed home with death's abrupt splat, like a big city Sunday newspaper landing on a rainy driveway. The couple sat there in silence. Finally, Mr. Desmond said, "Let's pray, dear." He handed her a framed photograph of their slain son and she held it to her chest.

Sal and Johnny got up. "We'll be outside. Please come get us when you are done. We need to talk. Our thoughts are with you."

Johnny chimed in, "Sorry for your loss."

They stepped off the porch and walked toward the chain-link fence near the sidewalk. Johnny said, "You know, Sal, in a way I really am sorry for their loss. Not that I'm sorry about Term getting killed. He can rot in hell for all I care. Things would be better 'round here if he got killed fifteen years ago. But, how can such a nice couple as those people inside raise two kids who killed over, what, thirty-five, forty people?"

On cue, maybe two, three blocks away, five-rapid fire gunshots were heard.

"That's how," said Sal. Neither bothered to call in or investigate the shots. Mere gunshots around here didn't merit investigation. Someone needed to get hit. "I mean, if Cleamon had been raised in a nice neighborhood, with these parents, he could've grown up to have been a CEO or something. He was, he is a leader. He's probably running the black rows up at the Bay right now. Bobby, I don't know about him. He was more the joker."

"Yeah, he was a funny guy. 'Cept when he killed someone."

Five minutes later, they were back inside. Mr. Desmond was cracking the seal on a bottle of Rémy Martin XO.

"Bobby brought me this Rémy three, four years ago. I never opened it. Would you like some?"

"No, thank you, Mr. Desmond."

"Honey, have a sip with me. For Bobby." He poured a smidgen in a glass for his wife. He poured himself three fingers into a snifter. They tapped and looked heavenward.

"I know it's rough, but the sooner we get on this, the better," Sal said. "I tried to get ahold of you earlier, but I didn't have a work address or cell. We want to catch the person who killed your son."

She gasped at that. Cleveland kissed her cheek. "Honey, Bobby's in a better place now."

Sal and Johnny looked at each other. "Anyway," said Sal, "when did you last see Bobby?"

"Last night around seven, I think. It was dark."

"Earlier, you said its been a 'strange' day," said Hart. "What did you mean?"

"Well, I meant, well, the day wasn't so strange. Just a normal day at work, but last night was weird. Now I wonder if it had something to do with what happened to Bobby. I can't believe he is gone. Does his girlfriend know? His boys? Does Tamara know?"

"You are the first family we've told," said Sal. "We kept it from the media."

Johnny and Sal both thought *not that the media would give a damn about a killing down here now that Lyons was not at the* Times. Sal continued. "I tried to get ahold of Cleamon up north, but he was unavailable. There is apparently a guard there who is on friendly terms with him and he was going to tell him. So he knows. Please go on about last night."

She told them about the visit from the man who came to the door and had a gun and claimed he wanted to thank Cleamon for saving him from the Crips in jail.

Johnny took notes.

"When did he say that happened? Cleamon hasn't been in county for a long time as far as I know," Sal said.

"I forgot what he said. But it was a long time ago. In the late nineties maybe."

"And he was just now getting around to thanking you?"

"Said he had been out of town, Las Vegas, I think. Yes, it was Las Vegas. And he read or heard about Mike Lyons getting shot and it mentioned that Lyons jerk had wrote a big story about Cleamon, that phony story full of lies. So I guess it made this guy think he never did thank Cleamon or his family. He was really nervous. Bobby had his gun and was using curse words a lot. I told him to calm down."

"Mrs. Desmond, could you describe him with as much detail as possible? His height, weight, tattoos, earrings, any marks, scars. Anything."

"That's the thing. There was really nothing distinctive about him. He was average height and weight. I didn't see or notice any tattoos or scars or earrings. Medium complexion."

LaBarbera glanced over at Hart who was busy taking notes.

"What was this guy's name? Did he introduce himself?"

"Oh, Jesus, what was his name? He said it, too, because we asked him, but then I went to get some water. He was so nervous. Bobby would know. Oh, God!"

Mr. Desmond held his wife again. "Honey, he's in a better place."

"Mrs. Desmond, try and think of his name."

She racked her mind. "It had something to do with a football player. I wasn't really paying that much attention because he had got me thinking about Cleamon and I was just thinking back to when Cleamon was a little boy. So I was here, but I wasn't. I remember, though, it was something about a football player and Bobby saying something back like he had the wrong name. That make any sense? That help?"

"Well, not really. At least, not yet."

The phone rang. "Good piece in the *Weekly*," LaBarbera said. "Still got it."

"Thanks. You catch any flack from the brass?" I asked. Sal had been quoted as saying the mayor and chief's list was "odd."

"Not a word. Anyway, Johnny and I just finished and we're gonna go out for some pizza. Can you get us into your girl's hot restaurant? You wanna meet us?"

"Sure." I hadn't seen Francesca for nearly a week. This would be an excuse. "What time?"

Though always booked, the Pizzeria as well as the Osteria next door, would keep one table in reserve for Francesca. I called and asked for that table. They were happy to give it to me. They wondered where I'd been. I was waiting at the front desk, talking to Lance, the maître d', when the detectives arrived. We were quickly seated and offered menus.

"So how'd it go tonight?" I asked. "The notification. What was their reaction when you told them their son was dead?"

A bottle of red wine came.

"Before we even told her, she knew," said LaBarbera.

"Mom's intuition," Hart added.

"Compliments of the kitchen, Michael," Pilar, the beautiful server, said. She placed down three appetizers. The detectives dug in. I sipped the wine.

"So when did the parents last see him?" I asked.

They laid out the story for me. The armed stranger who came to thank Cleamon and the family for saving him in county jail. Terminal terrifying the nervous visitor. The name she couldn't remember. The football player thing.

"You mean the stranger's name was the same as a football player?" I asked.

"The guy said his name, and then said, 'like the football player.' And then Term tells the guy something like you mean so and so and he corrected the name to match a football player."

"You mean," I said, "like he said his name was 'Joe Wyoming, like the football player's' and Term corrected him? Something like that?"

"I guess."

The pizzas came. We ate in silence for a few minutes. Pilar brought another bottle. We ate and drank. The pizza was superb.

"So," Sal said between savoring bites, "Johnny and I were thinking the killing of Term and your shooting might be connected."

"Fuck, Sal, I told you that already. You asked me if I was a shot caller."

"Well, it clicked for us when Mrs. Desmond said there was 'nothing really distinctive' about the guy who came to visit. Those are the exact words you used. And what's the connection?"

Hart's mouth was full of the meat lover's pizza yet he mumbled a response that was impossible to understand. But I knew what he meant. "Big Evil."

"Exactly," said LaBarbera. "Now it may just be a coincidence, but I don't believe in coincidences. Mike, I want you to come with us over to Mrs. Desmond's house, the sooner the better, so you two can go over what this guy looked like."

"Just for the hell of it, let's say the shooter is the same guy. What does that tell us? He got something against Evil?"

"Yeah. Evil killed someone he loved, and he can't get to him at Pelican Bay, so he gets to Evil's little brother. That story you did made Evil a legend. He was a legend in the 'hood, but people all over the city never heard of him until you wrote that magazine story.

And that courtroom piece you wrote about his trial. That could piss someone off. How Evil was smiling, how the evidence was thin."

"He was, it was."

"So, Mike, Johnny and I figured, the shooter figures you're the easiest one to get to, a journalist, and it was you who made Evil famous. His loved one is gone, Evil is living the big-shot life, so take it out on you."

"Well, just saying that's true. You think he's done? Like, who's next?"

I got a major chill. If it was the same guy who shot me that killed Terminal, he must be a total bad-ass. But even that didn't add up because the guy that shot me, he just didn't seem like a badass killer. Even then, I thought about keeping my Beretta close.

Leaning on his unmarked Charger parked under a no stopping sign, LaBarbera said, "We can't get dragged down chasing a ghost here on the football name thing, but we'll take a look. This was a personal attack on Term. He or Evil killed someone's loved one, and that someone took it out on Terminal. Let's go through the files and get a list of all their victims. See if one of them has a name that stands out."

"That's kinda ridiculous, man," I said. "I mean half the guys in the NFL have last names to match homicide victims. Williams, Brown, Jones, Jackson, Johnson."

"I know, but something might pop out. We look into everything."

"Maybe," Hart said, "this guy was going to the Desmond home to kill the mother. Get back at Evil that way, and he just ran into Terminal."

"Are you two thinking that the guy that Mrs. Desmond said came to the house, and—and what's her first name anyway? Why we gotta call her Mrs. Desmond all the time? Like a show of respect because she raised two of the biggest killers in the city?"

"It's Betty, but, we just got into the Mrs. Desmond thing. She's a nice lady and I think she tried, her husband tried, they just couldn't compete with the neighborhood. It was a tug-of-war, and the gang beat the parents for Cleamon and Bobby."

"Anyway," I said and then frowned, "what was I saying? Damn, I forgot already. Mrs. Desmond, why we gotta call her, oh, yeah. The guy that came to the house that she was talking about, you thinking he killed Terminal? Based on what she was saying about how nervous he was when he had a gun pointed at him, how the hell is someone like that gonna take out Term?"

"Mike, we are not concluding that that guy did anything, but a guy coming to her house with a gun is something we look into. It would be poor police work not to. You know that."

I went back to Osteria where Francesca was very busy, but she leaned over the countertop, kissed me on the cheek, and quietly said, "I've missed you."

That's all I wanted to hear.

CHAPTER 23

The next morning Homicide Detective Johnny Hart was playing a long shot. Hart was hoping one of the names of the victims of Big Evil and Terminal would lead to the mysterious man who came to the Desmond household the night before Terminal's ravaged body was found. He had a list of 127 names of victims, victim's families, and victim's known friends and associates. The brothers Desmond had amassed a frighteningly extensive roster of sufferers, dead and alive.

LaBarbera, taking a short break from a meeting with superiors on the progress of several homicide and shooting investigations, including those of Bobby Desmond and Michael Lyons, approached Hart's desk. "Anything pop?"

"Sal, this is ridiculous," said a frustrated Hart, his third cup of weak in-house coffee in hand. "First of all, the guy that came to see them, if Mrs. Desmond is accurate, seemed like he was about to soil himself, not to brutalize one of the baddest Bloods in this whole jacked-up city. And secondly, yes, I've got enough football-related names on this list to make a decent NFL team. Got a Joe Green—"

"Mean Joe Greene. But, with the third 'e'"?

"No, Sal. No. But, if Mystery Man said Joe Greene, I don't think Term would ask that third 'e' question. You see what I mean? This is a waste of time for a superior detective. Me."

"Where is he from?"

"This says, hold on, um, Maywood."

"Who else you got?"

"Got a Steve Smith. Victim."

"Steve Smith?"

"Carolina Panther receiver."

"Oh, yeah. He still a Panther? But, no. Too common. Don't you have anything that sticks out? No Unitas? Jurgenson? No Tarkington?"

"Damn, Sal, how old are you? Those are some triple OGs."

"Yeah, yeah. I knew this was a shot in the dark. Figured, though every now and then, you get an upset. Ask Man o' War."

"How about Payton Sims?"

"Payton Sims? I know that name. Payton Sims. Oh, yeah. Of course. He got Uzied walking to the car wash on Central. The one the task force finally got Evil for. Evil and Poison Rat."

"Yeah, Payton Sims and Marcus Washington."

"Yeah, but, I don't see any football name connection."

"Payton Sims. Walter Payton and Billy Sims."

"A stretch, but yeah, okay. Or Phil Simms," said LaBarbera. "Won a Super Bowl."

"Yeah, but Phil Simms has two 'm's."

"How're the Desmonds supposed to know that?"

"Sal, you're the nit-picking detective asking if Joe Green had the "e" at the end."

LaBarbera nodded in admission. "Okay, okay. Where'd Payton Sims live? I remember it was close, because he walked to that car wash. And you remember we could never figure out why anyone would walk to a car wash? Think about it."

"Maybe," Hart said, "the shower at his house was broke and he went to wash himself."

"You're stupid. Anyway, where'd he live?"

"Let's see. Nine twenty-seven East Eighty-Ninth Street. That's right across Central from the Desmonds."

"Interesting. His family still there?"

"This is old, but says survivors were his parents who lived there. Edward and Jennette. Should I check it out?"

"Yes. Let's cover all the bases. Tell Waxman to check it out. It's his case. I gotta go back to this bullshit meeting."

• • •

On his trek from Orange County, Detective Ralph Waxman chugged along in his son's 1991 Honda Accord, heading toward Edward and Jennette Simses' home in the Kitchen, a neighborhood where he had investigated several homicides. He didn't want to take his own car, a maroon Cadillac STS, so he traded with his nineteen-year-old son who was so thrilled with the swap he didn't even ask his dad why.

Waxman stuck to the slower lanes of the 91, 605, and 105 freeways as his son's Honda was misfiring badly. Kids these days, Waxman thought. He was planning on dropping the car off for a tune-up later, not that his son would even notice the difference.

As he exited the 105 and lumbered up Central Avenue, past the infamous Nickerson Gardens housing project and the all-boys Verbum Dei High School, past the Watts Community Action Labor Committee and Ted Watkins Park, past boarded-up two-story apartment buildings and store front churches, past enough liquor stores to get Moscow drunk, Waxman thought Johnny Hart's request to check out Ed Sims was a waste of time.

Waxman had called Sims from the road, saying he wanted to go over some details of his son's case. Purely routine, he said.

Sims was waiting for him on the porch. He hadn't bought Waxman's "purely routine" bullshit. What did they have on him? A witness? DNA in the alley? Had he cleaned his car's bloodied underbelly thoroughly enough? He came close to panic. He sipped some Hennessy. He considered running. Pack up the Cutlass and hit the road. He drank more Hennessy. And more. The French brandy started to work its dangerous charm. He relaxed. Fuck it. I'm dead already. It doesn't matter.

He had checked the load on his 9mm. It was full. Sims had decided he was not going to prison. Not even jail. He switched off the safety and stashed the gun under the pillow of his son's bed.

Sims heard the coughing Honda Accord before he saw it. When he did, it made him sad.

"Hi, I'm Detective Ralph Waxman, LAPD." They shook hands. Waxman smelled the booze.

"You need a tune-up. Heard you belchin' a block away."

"Tell me about it. My son's car."

"Let's have a look. I'm a mechanic."

"That's okay. I'll take care of it later."

"Take a minute. C'mon. Pop the hood and start her up."

Five minutes later, Sims came out of Frank's Auto Supply, his old place of employment on Central Avenue, with a Phillips screwdriver, a feeler gauge, and a package of contact points. He took out the old points and showed them to Waxman, who knew as much about car engines as he did about nuclear physics. "See these points right here, all pitted. That's your problem. My son, Payton, had a Honda just like this. His first car. Hell, his only car. I changed the points probably five times."

He put in the new points, had Waxman blip the ignition to get them in the right position so he could measure and set them. Cinched them up and they were on their way. Night and day.

"Damn. What a difference. What do I owe you?"

"Just a ride home."

Waxman took out forty dollars. Sims refused, but Waxman insisted, and he took it. He already had that money spent. His Hennessy was running a bit low, and he could use some more bullets. Hopefully, he thought.

Back at the house, Waxman took a look around. Roses in the front yard, older Cutlass way up the driveway, bars on the windows. Inside, Sims didn't hide the booze. He poured a glass, didn't bother to offer any, and took a gulp. "Ever since I lost my son and wife, this has been my best friend."

"Your wife was killed, too? I didn't know that."

"She left me. After Payton did."

"Sorry."

"At least I did something this morning. I love to fix cars." He took a gulp. "I know this lady, Dorothy, she's 'bout seventy-five. Runs the Watts Rose Garden. All by herself. Over a hundred bushes. She told me once, when she be working on those roses, she's in her own world. Her rose world, she calls it. This beautiful world of sweet smells and all them colors. She don't even see them thorns, even though they scratchin' her crinkly, ol' black skin. That rose garden? It's two blocks from Jordan Downs, Grape Street Crips, one of the worst places in the city. Hell, you know that." He took another belt. "But, anyway she's right there and she's in paradise. I saw you checkin' out my roses by the driveway. Dorothy planted them. That one there, the red one all creamy in the middle? It's called Double Delight. It's my favorite. They call it that because it's beautiful and smells sweet too. Just like a fine woman. What I'm getting at is, I guess I'm rambling now, but that's how I feel when I work on cars. It's like the car is sick, and I'm the doctor in my car world."

"Well, Doctor, thanks again."

"Anyways, I know you didn't come to my beautiful neighborhood to get a tune-up. What's happening?"

"Mr. Sims, did you know a Bobby Desmond? Better known as Terminal."

Sims took a shaky sip. "His brother killed my son."

"You heard anything about him lately?"

"Heard he got hisself kilt. Gotta say I din't burst into no tears when I heard the news. In fact, I think I had a drink to celebrate." Sims took another drink. Laughed.

"Mr. Sims, where were you last Tuesday night?"

"Is that when he got it? Now you're flattering me."

"Sir, tell me your whereabouts Tuesday from six p.m. until eight a.m. the next day."

"I love it when you guys call people 'sir.' I knows what 'sir' means. Means 'asshole.' Anyways, sir, I don't think I can prove it by anyone, but I was right here. Probably passed out on this here couch. Sometimes I don't even make it to the bed, sir."

Waxman tried to ignore the "sir" comments. It wasn't easy. "I'm sure it has been tough, sir, but what's it been? Eight, nine years?"

"Seems like last week to me," said Sims taking another sip. Then another.

Waxman asked why Payton would walk to a car wash.

"I wondered that, too," said Sims. "But, I think I might know why. The other day, I don't know, a week ago, a month ago, I was outside and a neighbor walked over and told me he was going downtown and wanted to trade me a five dollar bill for a bunch of quarters. You know, for parking. I told him I'd go in inside and check, but he said it was all right, he'd just go to the car wash. You know, those change machines them places have to get quarters to start the wash. Maybe that's why he went. Man, that made me weak all over when the neighbor said that. Quarters. Get killed for wanting some change."

Waxman just nodded.

"Sometimes I sleep in Payton's room. I'll show you." He led the way to Payton's room. It's very neat, preserved, just the way it was when Payton slept there, except for the used 9mm under the pillow. Sims glanced at the pillow. He hoped he wouldn't have to go for it. He wasn't going to prison, he'd rather die. Detective Waxman was not part of the Revenge. He had nothing to do with Big Evil living the good life in prison. Still, if he had to use it, he would. As Sims looked at the pillow, Waxman looked at the three Pop Warner football trophies on a dresser. On the wall was a framed poster of number thirty-four of the Chicago Bears.

"I loved that guy," said the detective. "I was a Chargers fan, but I loved Walter Payton."

"Everybody loved Sweetness," said Sims getting emotional. "I named my boy after him."

•   •   •

Later, at South Bureau, Waxman saw LaBarbera. "I went and saw that Edward Sims, the father of Payton Sims, one of Evil's victims."

"Ralph, I know who he is. And?"

"He's a beaten-down drunk. No way in hell he coulda got the drop on Terminal. No way. You were right about the Walter Payton thing, though. Even had a poster of Sweetness in the kid's room."

LaBarbera nodded and walked away.

"Say, Sal, let me know if you ever need a good mechanic around here."

Back on 89th Street, Sims packed a large suitcase, a case he had bought with exhilaration years ago in anticipation of where it would take him. He remembered so vividly walking into the house with the suitcase, putting Sammy Davis Jr. on the turntable and moving the needle to the fourth track—"Faraway Places"—taking hold of his wife and dancing around the room as Sammy sang of going to Bombay and Rio, Beirut, Barcelona. The years chewed away at that joy until the day Payton died and it was vanquished. He'd never used that suitcase until that bitter day. He threw it angrily into the trunk of the Cutlass, took a last look at his home, and backed out of the driveway. He was to the curb when he looked at his roses, his glorious rosebushes. He pulled back up and ran over Double Delight.

At the Bank of America on Central and 104th Street in Watts, he withdrew all his savings, just over $1,400. He rented a room at the Dare-U-Inn, a 32-unit, U-shaped motel on Main Street in an industrial area between Gardena and Compton. The Dare-U-Inn offered a nice degree of privacy as it catered to the illicit affair crowd or couples who stayed with other family members and couldn't really let it all hang out. He paid the Korean owner for a week in advance, $280 in cash. The clean, large room had a TV with cable. He wanted to watch the news tomorrow morning.

CHAPTER 24

That night a hard rain fell.

Leslie Harrington cherished the rain. Loved the sound of it beating on the window, the sight of it splashing on the panes. The coolness it brought. The excuse to light a fire in her Rustic Canyon home in Santa Monica. When it came down hard, she loved to curl up on her couch, wrapped all cozy in her favorite red comforter, Central Coast Chardonnay within easy reach, and watch *Casablanca* or *Waterloo Bridge* or *Here Comes Mr. Jordan*.

She was content, even if she was alone, which she usually was lately. She loved to walk down to the deserted beach at night, no umbrella, just her hooded parka, and watch the silent rain meet the roaring surf of the sea. If there was thunder and lightning, all the better. But she would gladly settle for just the rain. She knew how to settle.

She settled a lot in court. She knew if you could settle for something just a little less than what you wanted, more often than not, you'd win the case. She was a Los Angeles County Deputy District Attorney. A rising star. Her star had begun to shine years ago when she sent one Cleamon Desmond away for the rest of his life for ordering the murder of two men on Central Avenue just north of Watts in Green Meadows.

It was in that trial that she'd really learned to settle. Of course, she wanted the death penalty for this murderous thug known as Big Evil, said to be responsible for more killings than anyone else in the history of Los Angeles's world-famous gang warfare. He'd beat many cases before. She knew this case was weak, hinging mainly on the testimony of another gang member, Freddie Gelson, who agreed to testify if he was granted a new life far away from 89th and Central. She laughed when one of the detectives, John Hart, told her "No problem. We can put Gelson up at the Rio Palace. Not the one in Brazil, though. The one on 105th and Broadway."

She also knew that in the wake of a then-recent Illinois decision to ban the death penalty, unless you had a without-a-doubt case, it was much harder to get a conviction on a capital case than a LWOP, life without the possibility of parole. Also in this crime, Desmond had not been the triggerman. That meant, as dim-witted as it was, even though he had ordered the hits, some jurors would rationalize "well, he didn't actually pull the trigger that killed these people." That was the breed of jurors she encountered.

So she went for LWOP and won the trial. She gained the admiration of her peers. She had put away the most feared gang member in the city. Big Evil didn't even seem to mind. She had, however, gained the intense hatred, the pure loathing of the father of one of Big Evil's victims.

On that rainy night in Rustic Canyon, that father, one Edward Sims, was parked on her street, watching her watch the rain and a movie. Watching her drink some white wine. He put down his binoculars and cracked a new 750 ml of Hennessy, courtesy of an unwitting LAPD detective. He took a sip and smiled as he wondered if that detective could be considered an accomplice for what was going to happen in Rustic Canyon tonight.

Eddie Sims leaned over onto the passenger seat, out of sight, whenever he heard or saw a car coming down the street. There were not many cars, but Sims figured anyone who saw a black man here might get suspicious, just as anyone seeing a white man on his block would. The difference was that on his block the white man, unless he was police, might get his ass kicked and robbed. Over here in Rustic Canyon, they'd just call the police. Roll the damn SWAT team just because a brother parked on the street. And with binoculars? Prob'ly get five years. What the charges, man? BMPWB of the Rustic Canyon Criminal Code. Black man parked with binoculars.

He had made up his mind even before he'd shot the reporter that he would never go to prison. He had two options—to get away with it or to die resisting. At this point, he was so far gone, he didn't even care. At the same time, he felt very much at peace. He was hoping to get away with this, but knew in the long run, he would not. In a way, he felt Eddie Sims was already dead. It was very freeing to live when you are already dead.

And that was sad to him. Eddie Sims, he thought, had been a good man for many years. A decent man. A man who always tried to do the right thing, even if he made some wrong decisions. Like when he asked Jennette to marry him only two minutes after she told him she was pregnant. He knew she wasn't the woman he wanted to spend a lifetime with, knew she was more interested in diamonds than in sharing a life together in a modest home. Eddie knew that with just his high school education and limited mechanical skills he wasn't going far. He just wanted to work, get a good job, pay for the baby's education. That's what he wanted most, to make his baby's life better than his had been.

Eddie's life as a youth was rough. He had lived in the largest and, probably, worst housing project in the United States, the doomed Robert Taylor Homes on the South Side of Chicago. But, his family—mother and two brothers—got out when he was seven. His father had been locked up in Joliet for armed robbery and manslaughter. Received twenty years, but only did six months because he got shanked to death in the yard by the cousin of the man he killed during the botched liquor store robbery on 66th Place and Blackstone Avenue.

The family moved to his mother's mother's two-bedroom home in South Central on the corner of 76th and Wadsworth, just a mile north from the home he'd rented for the last ten years. In South Central in 1971, his two older brothers had joined the original Crips gang, founded by the legendary Raymond Washington who lived just two doors down.

Back in those days, there was just one gang called the "Crips"—not like now where there are a one hundred different Crip gangs—and they fought with their fists. But, soon the guns came with bloody, reckless vengeance. The older Sims brothers were both killed fighting against the Swans, part of the newly formed alliance of black gangs—Bounty Hunters, Piru, Brims, Denver Lanes, Bishops, Van Ness Gangsters—that went under the umbrella of the Bloods.

Eddie never joined the Crips. Never took retaliation against the Bloods, either. His mother would curse him for this. "Your brothers, my two sons, get killed by Swans and pussy bitch Eddie just wants to stay home and work on his shitty old Oldsmobile. I'm glad your father is dead. He'd be 'shamed of you. Little bitch."

But Eddie didn't have it in him to kill. It didn't seem to him it was courageous—or took—courage to kill. It wasn't toughness. He guessed it was hatred and despair and a never-ending tormented feeling that it was better to kill and get killed than to just go on living. That was the way Sims felt now.

Eddie kept working on that Oldsmobile, a '67 442 with its 360-horsepower force air engine, that was his pride and joy. To his sadness, he sold it when times demanded. He would eventually get another Olds, an '84 Cutlass, from his earnings as a mechanic at a ramshackle auto supply/repair joint. He made enough money to get by and salt away some for his son's college fund. It wasn't much money he stashed—sometimes only five bucks a week, but it was enough to be a source of pride for Eddie Sims. That's what kept him going, his beautiful, sweet son, Payton.

Payton was named for Eddie's favorite football player, Walter Payton aka "Sweetness." Jennette didn't want the name, but let Eddie have his way after he bribed her by offering up his entire next paycheck if she named the boy after the great Chicago Bear running back. "What's in a fuckin' name?" Jennette had said. "For your paycheck, as pathetic as it is, you can name him Gale Sayers for all I care."

Eddie always remembered that because he was stunned his wife even knew who Gale Sayers was. Musta seen that TV movie of the week about Brian Piccolo getting cancer. Everybody in the whole country saw that tearjerkin' motherfucker. Even Dick Butkus probably cried.

CHAPTER 25

Leslie Harrington was crying. She knew this was going to turn out bad. When Vivian Leigh says to Robert Taylor: *"I loved you, I've never loved anyone else. I never shall, that's the truth, Roy, I never shall."* That's when Harrington always lost it. She had seen *Waterloo Bridge* four times and always hoped for a happy ending.

Outside, Sims had picked up the binocs and watched Harrington bawling like a jilted fourteen-year-old girl. What the fuck was she watching? Maybe I should just knock on the door while she's vulnerable and gut her with this KA-BAR.

Sims knew a gunshot would shock and awe this block, and the police would swarm in a minute. So he was planning on sticking her with the Marine Corps knife his slain son had owned. Payton Sims had told his father when he was eighteen that he wanted to have a gun for protection in the gang neighborhood they lived. The elder Sims said no, though he felt good that his son had come to him to ask for permission. Eddie told his kid that a gun could only get him in trouble. "If you have to use a gun, only two things happen—you lose and get shot, you win and go to prison." When Payton asked, "What about a knife?" the father reluctantly agreed. Payton researched knives, considered the British SAS commando knife, but went for the Marine KA-BAR. Eddie never forgave himself for not letting his kid get the gun. It tormented him.

Eddie switched to a pleasanter thought. The split-second look of horror on Terminal's face when he realized he was about to get shot. How he wished he could have videotaped that and shown it to Evil. He looked over through the window that Harrington left uncurtained because she so loved to see the rain splash. The room had changed its hue. The movie or whatever she was crying about, must've ended, and she'd turned off the tube.

I guess I got away with both of them, Sims thought. Not a word about shooting the reporter. That was, what, weeks ago? Losing track of time. Terminal was a couple days ago, but if they had something I would have heard. That visit from Detective Waxman went well. That fool had no idea.

Sims knew this would be different. He had no feelings about it. He was going to kill Harrington for her decision not to seek the death penalty. Sure, he knew the California death penalty was a joke. You get it and live another fifteen years minimum, but at least it was death. Not life. Evil was living the life of a star up in Pelican Bay.

The problem was going to be that killing a deputy D.A., a white woman, in Santa Monica, would be a national story, would bring in twenty-five detectives, if they had that many. Sims knew a world-class manhunt would be launched to find Leslie Harrington's killer. This wouldn't be like the search for Terminal's killer. No one cared about Terminal other than his family and the overworked detectives assigned to the case. But Leslie Harrington was going to become famous.

As he sat there, Sims decided he was not going to kill Harrington that night. Just getting the lay of the land, getting a feel for the block so when he came back he would be comfortable in the kill zone, would be enough for that night. But, when the front door suddenly opened and Harrington came out in a hooded sweatshirt and walked to the sidewalk, her arms spread, relishing the raindrops falling all about her, Sims flung open his door.

Harrington heard the door and looked quizzically at the black man moving oddly quick around his car. Not running, but speed walking. In a spark, her mind thought of those speed walkers in the Olympics. Then, in another flash, she thought, *what is this man doing here? Why is he moving fast?* She was wine-buzzed and still in movie mode, and this was like a movie. It took a second, maybe two, to realize this was not a movie. The guy coming her way was not Robert Taylor or Humphrey Bogart.

Then she felt paralyzing fear. She couldn't scream, she couldn't move. He sprinted to her now. She felt nothing but sadness, for Vivian Leigh and for herself. Sims was on her now. She said not a word. She was like a guilty, standing mannequin, ready for execution. He pulled her head back savagely and, with the glistening, razor-sharp KA-BAR Marine blade, cut her pretty throat. It severed the jugular vein and carotid artery. Her head shook involuntarily side to side as if saying "no." The blood sprayed out like water from sprinklers on the Dodger Stadium infield before a hot summer day game. Then she collapsed.

Her gushers of blood mingled with her beloved pools of raindrops. It reminded Sims of strawberry Kool-Aid. He never liked strawberry. He was a grape guy.

Molly Brink had her routine. Every morning at six-thirty she'd be out the door with her Rottweiler mix named Scruffy McDoo, a slobbering, loveable 100-pound rescue mutt. Molly lived in the Santa Monica flatlands, but enjoyed the cool morning air and slight uphill grade of Rustic Canyon. It was McDoo who first detected something amiss as they turned off West Channel Road onto Rustic Canyon. The rain had stopped hours earlier, but the sidewalks and streets were still wet. The scent of death was in the damp air.

Molly sensed McDoo's bizarre behavior and she got an extra chill, the goose bumps roiling up her spine all the way to her neck and jawbone. Then she saw a form in the low ivy around an old oak tree. She slowed and almost tiptoed up to it. A body. A woman. She inched closer and then she saw the throat. Or what was left of it. Molly started retching.

In fifteen minutes, the street was a beehive of police activity. A dozen Santa Monica PD cruisers lined the normally tranquil street. Detectives, crime-scene people, the coroner's van. Officers were going door-to-door, waking neighbors with the horrible news. Trying to see if anyone had seen anything, anything at all even remotely unusual. They got next to nothing. One woman did notice an unfamiliar car on the block a house away from Harrington's, but did not know the type of car other than to say "I just noticed it because it wasn't new and all the cars around here are new." They got her to say it was a dark car with two doors.

When the crime scene was in full chaotic bloom on Rustic Canyon, the killer of Leslie Harrington was in a deep sleep at the Dare-U-Inn. Eddie Sims had driven fretfully from the killing zone, but once he got onto the Santa Monica Freeway, he mellowed and began to get a peaceful high. It was not like the adrenaline-fueled energy he had after Terminal's demise. This was a calm, tranquil feeling, his reward for killing the woman he blamed for not sending Big Evil to San Quentin and death row.

When Sims awoke at seven, although Leslie Harrington had not been identified publically by name, the story was breaking news.

There was a time when Eddie Sims would have been disgusted by such a heinous attack. An innocent young woman killed because she didn't go for death. Killed because she went for life. Feeling sad? Feeling bad? Fuck no. That was the old Eddie. The weak and meek Eddie who had let his wife get away with cheating on him and bragging about fucking two men at once. The weak and meek Eddie who couldn't protect his only son. Fuck that pussy Eddie. That Eddie was dead. The new Eddie was taking no prisoners. New Eddie was without heart. It was already time to focus on his next victim. After that, Eddie would get the blood-sucking reporter, kill him this time, then go for his grand finale. As for the reporter, he fantasized about just walking right up to him in daylight and shooting him in the head. Just like Denzel did in Harlem in *American Gangster*, then calmly walk away with everyone looking on. But, that was Hollywood. This was Los Angeles.

● ● ●

Sal, Johnny, and I met at the Desmond household. They had agreed to the meeting, but Mr. Desmond asked them to come early, by seven, so he would not have to be late for work.

Sal rapped his trademark powerful one knock on the Desmonds' security door.

"When'd you start doing that knock?" I asked.

"On patrol. In the Seventy-Seventh. Everyone was doing the five rap hard knock. Bang, bang, bang, bang, bang. Gangsters heard that, knew it was police. So I went with my one-punch knockout knock. It confused them. I think they were expecting follow-up knocks, but just got the one. So they would come to the door to check it out. Like, what the fuck was that? A knock on the door or a single gunshot."

I wasn't sure if LaBarbera was messing with me or not, but I went along. "So like before you got married, did you do that knock when you went to pick up a date?"

"No," said Sal. "I'd give them the nice, soft triple knock. Then when I took them back home, that's when I'd give them the hard one."

"Damn, Sal, I didn't know better, I'd say that was Johnny talking." Hart shot me a look.

Mrs. Desmond opened the door. "How many years have I been hearing that dreadful knock of yours? I hope this is the last time."

Mr. Desmond appeared behind his wife, his bloodshot eyes peering over her shoulder and straight into my face.

"You two know Michael Lyons."

There was a moment of uncomfortable silence. Then I spoke. "Mr. and Mrs. Desmond, I was very sorry to hear about what happened to Bobby. I'm sorry for your loss."

Mrs. Desmond said nothing. Her husband nodded and opened the security door. They all settled on a couch and three chairs. The fifty-inch Panasonic plasma HDTV Terminal had bought for his parents was tuned to the *Today* show, but the sound was off. The house was hospital-operating-room clean. It would have taken an elite team of Salvadoran housekeepers an hour to find something in need of wiping.

Hart opened up. "We are trying to see if there is any connection at all between Bobby's death and the shooting of Lyons here."

"What could possibly be the connection?" asked Mr. Desmond.

"Cleamon," said Hart.

"I don't understand," said Mrs. Desmond.

"We," Sal said, "are working on a few theories. Now, of course, it would be productive if someone in the neighborhood stepped forward with some information, but so far nobody has. No surprise there, but, with all due respect, your son had more than his share of enemies."

Silence from the parents.

"One of the theories we are exploring, and I have to emphasize this is only a theory, is that the shooter is trying to get back at Big, uh, at Cleamon, by hurting people close to him."

"This here so-called reporter here wasn't close to my son," said Mrs. Desmond, the sound of indignation clear. "He wrote those lies that my son was a mass murderer." LaBarbera, Hart, and I all resisted the urge to say, "He was."

Sal went on. "This theory is that the shooter hated Cleamon. Maybe Cleamon hurt a loved one of his or hers and that person is fixated on getting back at him by killing anyone associated with him, like his younger brother Bobby and Lyons here, who wrote an article that kind of made him famous."

"Infamous," said Mr. Desmond.

"Okay," said Hart. "So let's talk about the man that came to see you. We just want to eliminate him. First, Mike, describe the man who shot you."

"I've told you this before."

"Tell Mrs. Desmond."

"He was black."

"Of course, he was," said Mrs. Desmond with a sneer. "White people do not shoot."

Hart couldn't resist. "That's true. But, you can't rule out those crazy Mexicans."

Even Mr. Desmond laughed briefly.

I continued, "He wasn't noticeably tall or short. Wasn't really dark or light-skinned. I do remember thinking he was kinda old for a banger. Not that I don't know some older gang members. Wild Cat from the Rollin Sixties, for example."

"Listen to him. Knows Wild Cat," Mrs. Desmond mocked. "From the Sixties. Very impressive. Good for you, street."

Though annoyed, I went on. "He was maybe forty-five, fifty. No tats or facial scars that I noticed. He had a purple scarf covering most of his head and forehead. That's Grape Street Crips, Betty."

"Oh, really?" asked Mrs. Desmond sarcastically. "He knows what purple stands for. Very street. Let me ask you something. Are you one of those white guys who wishes they was black so they can join a tough street gang? Or are you the white guy that got his ass kicked by African Americans in school and now is trying to get even? I bet you're one of those white boys use the word 'nigga' all the time."

"Settle down, dear," Mr. Desmond urged.

"Yes, let's move on," Sal said. Hart said nothing. He was enjoying the exchange.

Mrs. Desmond continued, "Actually, I think you are just some little white guy making a living being a parasite on the misfortunes of black folks in the neighborhood. I bet there are no black folk in his lily neighborhood."

"Look, I know you didn't like the story I did on Big Evil—"

"Cleamon is his name," she interrupted firmly.

"To you. To me, he's Big Evil," I said getting tired of her pompousness. "Always was, always will be."

"He is Cleamon Desmond here, you understand?" said Mrs. Desmond.

"Tell that to the families of all the people he killed," I said, unable to keep my calm.

"Get out of my home. Now!"

"Honey, relax," said Cleveland Desmond. "We need to do this. Get it over with."

"Okay, okay, everybody calm down," said LaBarbera. "Let's get back on point. What else?"

"That's really about it, Sal. I know that's not much. I only saw him for two seconds, and he was coming at me with a gun. Black guy, forty to fifty, purple scarf, medium height."

"Very descriptive," said Mrs. Desmond. "Narrows it down to only about a hundred thousand people. You call yourself a reporter? I thought reporters were supposed to be good at describing people."

"Not when they are shooting at me."

Johnny turned to Mrs. Desmond. "Does that go with the man who came here when Terminal showed up?" He instantly regretted that.

"Detective Hart, I did not christen my son with that name. In this household, his name is Bobby. I know this person here does not respect our house, but I would appreciate it in this home that you refer to him by his Christian name. Not some name the LAPD probably gave him."

Mrs. Desmond continued, "The person that came here fits that vague description. I would add that he was extraordinarily nervous. Even when Bobby did not threaten him. But, it didn't seem like that meek man would or could shoot anybody."

"He did have a gun," said Hart.

"Yes, until Bobby took it off him. I think maybe he did want to thank us for Cleamon helping him out. Yes, it took five or ten years, whatever. But how many times do we want to thank someone and put it off or forget it all together?

"Just two weeks ago, I was thinking about a dear family friend and thought to myself, I'm going to write her a letter. An actual letter. How much would she enjoy that? But, I put it off, and last week she had a stroke and died. We put things off we shouldn't."

"That's true," said Sal. "Okay, you mentioned the football comments between the guy and Bobby. Do you remember hearing the name Walter Payton, the football player?"

"I don't remember."

"How about Sweetness?" I asked.

Mrs. Desmond said with a nod, "Sweetness. Yes, yes, sweetness. That was it. I remember because in the middle of all this commotion, I thought it odd for someone to mention the word sweetness. What does that mean, sweetness?"

"That was Walter Payton's nickname," said Sal.

"So," she asked, "is that of any significance here?"

"I don't know yet, but I kind of doubt it," said Detective Hart.

At that moment, Hart switched his attention to what was being aired. The *Today* show's Al Roker had been replaced by a pretty blonde with an umbrella and large breasts with a "Breaking News" banner across the upper part of the screen. On the bottom of the screen was "Rustic Canyon Santa Monica."

"Can you turn the volume up?"

News of the killing traveled fast though law enforcement. The lead homicide detective in Santa Monica had called a friend at LAPD's Robbery-Homicide division, Detective Rosemary Sanchez, who was stunned and deeply disturbed by the news. She had worked with Harrington on the Big Evil Task Force. Sanchez made some calls. The first one was to Sal LaBarbera, Sally LaBoo, as she affectionately called him.

LaBarbera, Hart, and I had left the meeting with the Desmonds and were on the cracked, graffiti-splattered, weedy, uneven 89th Street sidewalk when Sal's cell rang.

"Sal, it's Rosemary Sanchez."

"Rosemary. Oh, no. You didn't call me Sally LaBoo, this can't be good news. Is this about Rustic Canyon?"

CHAPTER 26

An hour later, the detectives were meeting with their superiors, including Chief Miller, Commander Kuwahara and Captain Tatreau. "First of all, we do not need, want, or even have a new serial killer in town," said the chief. "There've only been two killings that can possibly be tied together, so, by definition, that doesn't make it up to serial killer. At best, it is just a double murderer."

"Well, sir," injected Hart, "there would be three if you count the attempted murder of the reporter Lyons. Not that we even mentioned the term serial killer."

"I am not counting Lyons. Who knows who shot him? He, apparently, had lots of enemies, too. And I am still not convinced that that gang-member loving asshole didn't have himself shot."

Kuwahara spoke up. "Could any of this be related to the killing of King Funeral?"

"No," said Hart. "That's looking in-house. The common thread between Terminal, Leslie, and Lyons is Big Evil."

"Are you familiar with Big Evil, Chief?" Sal asked.

"He was around before I got here, but I am familiar with his legacy. Where is he? San Quentin. Death Row, right?"

"No, he didn't get death. He got LWOP. Pelican Bay."

"Go see him."

"Chief, how about we arrange to get him on the phone? We're kinda busy."

"Go now. I'll have the visit set up, the flights. You'll be back here by four. You need to see this guy in person."

• • •

Eighty-five minutes later the detectives were on a plane heading to Eureka, where a rental car was reserved for the seventy-mile drive to the prison.

That morning, Don Ball, the one guard at Pelican Bay who had a good rapport with Big Evil, went down to the hole. Ball, a large, pumped-up, red-haired white man, went into the cell alone, a major violation of prison rules and a rather stupid thing to do, though he had warned three guards to stand by.

Ball laughed out loud when he thought of the scene in *Young Frankenstein* when Gene Wilder is about to go into a locked room where the monster is and orders his cohorts not to open the door no matter how much he screams. Three seconds later, Wilder is yelling "Mommy!" Ball was still laughing as he went into Evil's cell.

"What's so funny, Big Red? Let a brother in on the joke. What up?" Evil was only slightly puffed up and bruised, but still sprouted a huge smile when he saw Ball.

"I'll tell you later, Cleamon. How you feeling?"

"Little sore is all. Red, I'm glad you came down. I 'preciate. What brings you down to paradise?"

"You're getting a visit from LAPD. Ever heard of, let's see," he took out a sheet of paper. "Sal LaBarbera?"

Evil revved up his laugh. "Sally LaBoo! Coming to the big house."

When he saw LaBarbera and Hart he flashed his bright smile. You couldn't help but like that smile, even if you knew it was the last thing many people ever saw. "Sally and Johnny up in the bay," he rumbled.

"Hello, Cleamon. Long time," said Sal. "Looks like you been fighting again."

"Six guards."

"Fair fight," said Hart. "Sorry to hear about your brother."

"Me too," said Sal. "Sorry 'bout Term."

"Yeah, it's hard. 'Specially not being able to do a fuckin' thing about it. But, fuck all that. Sal man, I've been trying to get hold of you. That's why I fought the guards. Why I was in the hole. This guy came here to visit me and said he was a friend of Term's and all and then he says he was the one that killed Terminal."

"What?" both stunned detectives said.

"Said like too bad I wasn't there when he killed him. And shot him. Ran over him."

"Holy fuck. Sal, we never released anything about the tire marks."

"What did he look like?" Sal asked.

"Man, he kinda nervous guy. Black. About I don't know, maybe fifty, maybe less. Look kinda plain, you know what I'm saying?"

"I'm thinking I do. But what else? How tall? Any marks? Scars? Weight? You know the drill."

"Well, he was sittin' down so don't know how tall he was, but he wasn't big, that's for sure. I could tell that. Thing I remember about him was that he was nervous, and I could tell he was lying."

"What do you mean? Lying about what? That he was the one that killed Term?"

"I don't know about that, but he was lyin' before he said that. Lyin' about how he was a friend of Term and that he was just up this way and knew I was here and wanted to say, you know, condolences. Plus, he called him Bobby. None of his homies called him that."

LaBarbera looked around the room and at the guards behind him. He was looking for a video camera in the visiting room. There was none visible. "Say, fellas, are there video cameras here to record the visitors or inmates?"

The detectives were in the same room with Evil and the six guards, not on the outside looking in as Eddie Sims had been. "None in here, sir," said a guard with sergeant stripes. "There are some video cameras outside this wall that film the visitors that come in here."

"Do you know how long they keep the tapes or film or whatever it is? Is it digital and logged to a computer?"

"I'll check, sir. But I kind of doubt it. We are very low tech here, sir."

"I'm Detective LaBarbera. This is Detective Hart. LAPD. All this 'sir' stuff, you're making me feel like I'm an asshole under arrest."

Polite laughter from the guards.

"You think this guy was for real?" Evil asked.

"I don't know, but he fits a very vague description that both Michael Lyons, the reporter, and your mother gave about a man who came to her house."

"That mothercuntin' fucker."

"Okay, anything else you can remember about him?"

"Only that he's a dead man."

"Cleamon, just help us find him. Had you seen or talked to Bobby lately?"

"I ain't seen him since my trial."

"He never came to visit you up here?"

"No. Kinda bothered me at first, but it's a long drive. Plus, I guess he was trying to get out the 'hood and all. It's almost funny, man. I get sent to Pelican Bay, get life without, and it saves my life. He stays out and gets the real death sentence."

"Yeah, life's a funny thing," said LaBarbera.

"You have any idea at all who would want to kill Bobby?" asked Hart.

"What's with the Bobby shit? My moms called him that, but he was always Terminal or Term to me. I gave him that name. But, yeah, the boy had his enemies. Shit, even beefed with some Bloods, guys in Swans, Blood Stone Villains, Pueblos. But, Sal, you know that already. That ain't no news."

"You want some news?" Sal asked.

"Talk."

"Remember Leslie Harrington?"

"Of course I remember that fox."

"She's dead."

"Murdered dead?"

"Yeah, found her body yesterday morning."

"Shot?"

"Stabbed."

"Damn, that's too bad."

"For some reason I wouldn't think you would be disappointed she was dead. She did send you up here."

"Her and you and about twenty other motherfuckers sent me up here, but, you all just doin' your job. I don't hold it against you guys or her. That's all part the game. Still, she was kinda special to me, even up here."

"How so?" asked Hart. "She visit? She write?"

"No. But lotta times I close my eyes and imagine it be Leslie suckin' my dick. Now, how I gonna imagine a dead girl sucking my dick? It ain't gonna be the same. I mean I can do imagination as good as anybody, you feel me, but even I don't want a dead girl suckin' on me."

"You always did have your principles, Evil," Hart said. "Anyway, with Terminal and Leslie both killed, and Michael Lyons shot—you knew about that, right?"

"Yeah, I heard about that nut Lyons. You know, I was pissed at his ass after that magazine story he did on me, 'member that? I told him so on the phone. My moms didn't like that story, about I killed so many people and admitted it, so I lighted him up. But, he came to me like a man. We straight. He even writes a letter every now and then, sometimes even throws in a twenty. He bool. I think the boy got a past his own self. They wouldn't let him visit me here 'cause he got some felony. I think he even got two felonies."

"He does. You have any ideas about him? Who shot Michael Lyons?"

"Nah. Like I said, I had a green light on him, but I cancelled it about, what, shit, I don't even know. Maybe five years ago. This time wasn't from me."

"See, the only connection between the three shootings that we can come up with is you. Lyons wrote about you. Made you famous. Leslie prosecuted you. Put you in here for life."

"Pending appeals, Detective," said Evil.

"Pending appeals."

"But, Sal, man, maybe they ain't even connected. Lyons, I know that crazy fool had a lot of enemies. Plus he be goin' out at night to the Nickersons, to Jordan Downs like he askin' to get shot. And my brother sure did have some enemies. He was fuckin' half the girls in town. And maybe Leslie, maybe it was just random or maybe an old boyfriend. What you people call a crime of passion. Was her pussy jacked-up? Mutilated and shit."

"Autopsy today," said Hart.

"Well, you get a jacked-up pussy or butter hole, then you'll know. Like Term sounds from what the homies tell me, he was all jacked-up. Oh yeah, that guy that came here? He even said something about they gonna have a closed casket. That's personal."

"But, still the three all had ties to you," said LaBarbera. "And now this guy that loosely fits the description that Lyons gave comes here. I don't believe in coincidences," said Sal. He left his card. "Call me collect any time. Cleamon, if I owned a gang, I'd draft you number one. But, Evil, I need you to get word to your boys to somehow cooperate with this.

"Cooperate? That's one of the ugliest words in the world."

"Somebody musta seen something," Sal said with deliberate drama. "Your mother and father could be next."

"Send that kite, Big," Hart urged.

Just then, the guard came back in. "Sir, I mean, Detective, sorry, but the videotapes get replaced. We're so outdated here we don't have computers that we can download onto. There are cameras in the parking lot, too, and in the lobby, but they get replaced also. But, I do have something for you that may help," he said, handing LaBarbera a printout.

"What's this?"

"It's a list of all the people that have come to visit Cleamon Desmond in the last twelve months."

Sal looked at the short list of names. He came to the last name on the list. "Check it out, Johnny. Same damn day Terminal was found, Big Evil got a visit from one Barry Sanders."

"Damn. It was him."

LaBarbera and Hart got up to leave.

"Wait, wait, wait," said Evil. "Shit, I almost forgot. Johnny, remember way back when that old guard had me fight King Funeral? And he videotaped it? 'Member? You were there. I kicked his ass."

"Twice. Yeah, of course. Lyons brought that up to me few days ago. What about it?"

"This guy that came to scc me, he said Term showed him that tape."

"This is too strange," said Hart.

On the picturesque drive from Pelican Bay to the Eureka, California, airport, studded with mighty redwoods and glimpses of the sea, they talked about the man Evil had described. "That's the third person that gave the same very general description of the guy," said Hart. "And I do not believe in coincidence."

"That's my line."

"What about that guy Ralph went to see? The Payton guy. Payton Sims's father. What did he look like?"

"I don't know. He just said he was a broken-down drunk. Drinking from a bottle. But, call Ralph. With a name like that, this guy is lookin' suspect. Plus using Barry Sanders's name now, the guy's got a thing for great running backs. Tell Ralph to get over to Funeral's place and look for that film of that Evil Funeral fight. What was it? What kind of film?"

"A VHS tape," said Hart as he got out his cell.

As LaBarbera drove fifteen to twenty mph above every posted speed limit, which varied on this windy road from fifteen to fifty-five, Hart called Waxman. It rang once and then the signal was lost near the overcast, north coast town of Trinidad. He tried again with the same result.

"Damn," said Hart as they drove past a sign welcoming motorists to Trinidad, population 314 people. "Shit, they got three hundred fourteen people here. Doesn't anyone have use for a cell phone?"

"Maybe they're the lucky ones."

Fifteen minutes later, outside of Arcata, Hart tried and got through, but just to Waxman's voice mail. Hart impatiently waited for the long-winded automated woman's voice to finish. Hart growled into the phone.

"I hate that part. 'When you are finished you can hang up.' No kidding, idiot."

The killing of Leslie Harrington was a giant SIWA. By itself, Leslie's death was huge news, the lead on all local television stations and on all the network news programs. It just about had it all. An attractive, white, deputy district attorney in a safe, wealthy, secluded neighborhood with her throat savagely slashed, nearly decapitated. Other than the involvement of a celebrity, a news director couldn't ask for anything more.

As for the part of me being a journalist, I craved the story. I wanted to break the story of a serial killer loose in Los Angeles. It could be my salvation, erase the doubters who still thought I had myself shot, deliver me from evil, thanks, in a sordid way, to Evil.

No one at the *Times* had discovered the common thread of the attacks on Harrington, Terminal, and myself. It would have been on their website by now and it wasn't.

It was Wednesday afternoon. The *L.A. Weekly* came out on Thursday, and they usually liked stories filed and edited by Monday. They might go with a hot story filed late on Tuesday. In extremely rare cases, blistering news could be filed Wednesday. I e-mailed and called Doris De Soto, the news editor at the *Weekly*. De Soto lived to beat the *Times*.

"Doris, Michael Lyons. I gotta great scoop for you, beat the

Times, but we have to have to get it in this week's paper."

"Lyons, it's Wednesday. What's the story?"

"There's a serial killer in Los Angeles. A great story."

"Details and don't make it long-winded. Speak."

"You heard about Leslie Harrington in Santa Monica this morning? The deputy district attorney."

"Stupid question. Go."

"Okay. She was killed by a guy who also killed Bobby Desmond. You know him?" I asked, instantly regretting it. No way she knew Terminal.

"No. Just tell the damn story."

"Bobby Desmond, street name Terminal from Eighty-Nine Family Bloods."

"Not another gang story."

"No. Lemme finish. Terminal was Big Evil's brother. Leslie Harrington was the D.A. who put Evil away for life. I was shot and I was the one who made him famous outside of the Southside. There is some guy going around killing or shooting people associated with Big Evil. Me included. This is a great story. We need to get it in this week before the *Times* figures it out. We can burn the *Times* with this," I said, playing to her weakness.

"What have you got? Just your hunch? It could just be a coincidence. What do the police say? On the record."

"Doris, I need you to give me a go ahead and I'll get all that. I don't know if can get the police to go on the record that there is a serial killer, but off the record I know some detectives who may be leaning in that direction."

"'May be leaning'? I need more than 'may be leaning.'"

"They are leaning. Way leaning. Leaning Tower of Pisa leaning."

"Listen. We can't just say there's a serial killer out there and panic the whole city. Santa Monica's in panic mode already. This guy, saying he is the guy, killed two people and shot you. Does that even qualify as a serial killer? He's no Gacy or Dahmer."

"Think about how many lives would've been saved if they'd

started reporting on Gacy and Dahmer after they killed their first two victims. This guy is a sick fuck, and he's getting sicker. First, he shoots me. Then, he gets Terminal. Shoots him, beats him with a crowbar or something, and runs over him. Then, with Harrington, he almost cuts her head off. He's escalating. It's classic serial killer. It's the reason he's living. And he'll do it again."

"What are you, Doctor Phil? Clarice from *Silence in the Lambs?*"

"*Of* the Lambs."

"What the shit ever. Look, we need some facts here. That's how journalism works. Here's the deal. I'll give you three hours. You got till 7. Not 7:01. We'll need something from the LAPD. We can throw in the brief stuff we already did. The thread being Big Evil, but the key is the LAPD. You need the chief. Can you get to him? Or Kuwahara?"

"Cool, I'm on it," I said.

"You don't get what I need, you don't get paid a nickel."

"I don't like nickels." I hung up. Actually, I did like those Indian head nickels.

I felt that glorious rush of deadline. I dialed the chief's cell. He picked up.

"Chief, it's Michael Lyons." Silence. "Chief?"

"Well, if it isn't the loser. I don't recall giving you my cell."

"Well, I got it. Chief, I am doing an article about Leslie Harrington. I knew her."

"I thought you got fired from the *Times.*"

"This is a freelance piece for the *Weekly.*"

"Oh, yes. How the mighty have fallen."

"Very original. About Harrington?"

"Hey, I saw your twelve worst, or, in your case, best, gangs story in the *Weekly*. Nice placement. Right between the tit enlargement ads and the sale on butt plugs."

I resisted the urge to say, "You might want take yours out once in a while," and just repeated, "About Harrington?"

"She was a wonderful, talented woman, and we are saddened at the LAPD. We are doing everything we can to assist the fine Santa Monica Police Department in solving this tragic case. Okay? I gotta go."

"Wait, wait, wait, Chief. One minute, please. Do you see any connection to her killing and that of Bobby Desmond aka Terminal and to my shooting?"

"I thought you were shot in the torso, not the brain. That is just plain stupid. First of all, I'm still not totally convinced you didn't plan your own shooting."

"Okay, leave me out of it. Is there a connection between Harrington and Terminal?"

"We are working to solve both cases, but we see no connection."

"What about the Big Evil connection? His younger brother. And it was Harrington who put him away."

"That makes no sense. I guess the shooting left you with a lack of oxygen to the brain. That happens."

"Is there a serial killer in Los Angeles?"

"Jesus, Lyons," the exasperated chief said, "Listen carefully. There is absolutely no evidence at all of a serial killer in Los Angeles. I've wasted enough time."

Next, I called South Bureau Commander Lester Kuwahara, who answered on the first ring. I identified myself.

"What do you want, Lyons? You shoot yourself lately? Maybe next time you can get an artery and bleed your ass out."

"Always a pleasure, Lester. Harrington and Terminal? A connection?"

"You talk to the chief?"

"Yes, but he's not up on the street like you are," I said, getting desperate with the flattery angle.

"First of all, you have lost it. Terminal had a hundred enemies. It was probably in-house. This is off the record, right?"

"If that's the only way. Anonymous sources?"

"Okay. You know the Eighty-Nines kill each other more than

they kill Crips. As for Leslie, she probably ran into one of those homeless sickos that live down there by that, that, that overlook thing. What do they call it in Santa Monica? You know that grassy part with a walkway just above the beach. They have a name for that place."

"The Promenade?"

"No, idiot. By Ocean Avenue. It doesn't matter. Anyway, she probably ran into one of those guys who followed her home."

"She drove a 2013 Maserati GT. You think some homeless guy chased her down? Maybe it was Usain Bolt."

"Who the hell is Hussein Bolt? What are you jabbering about?"

"The Olympic sprinter. And it's Usain. Forget it. Forget it. Anyway, do you think there is a serial killer active in Los Angeles?"

"Whoa. Now you've really lost it. Where do you get that? You used to be a good street reporter. Now you're a desperate reporter. Take my advice. Either get another line of work or try another city. Maybe Duluth. Better yet, Wasilla. You have no cred here."

I called De Soto back. "Doris, I'm on it. Talked to the chief and Kuwahara. They both deny any serial killer. They say Terminal and Harrington are totally unrelated."

"Wow. What a great quote. Maybe quote of the year, huh? Should I tell Escobar to stop the presses? Hire some paper boys to yell 'Extra, extra, read all about it.'"

"They have to be related. Me, too."

"Lyons, how can we justify a story about a serial killer? I told you we need something from the police. Not your hunch. I can see there might be a connection to Big Evil. He's a thread. But, Terminal, anybody with that name had to have lots of enemies. Coincidences do happen. That Terminal was killed is not even news. Harrington is the story."

"What about me getting shot? That's three connections to Big Evil. If I can get some detective, even off the record, can we do it?"

"We took a gamble having you write anything for us. You know better than anyone your cred took a beating, even though I'm sure you had nothing to do with your shooting. Still, it was a gamble for us, but you kicked ass. But, we need to be careful, and this is not a careful story. So, here's the deal. Get one of your detectives, even off the record, write it up, and send it to me by seven. No guarantees. I can clear a little space, eight hundred words, a thousand max if it works. Turn it in. I'll run it by the big shots if I think it has a chance in hell. Understand that this is not an assignment. You are writing on spec. Like I told you, we don't run it, you don't get paid jack shit."

"This ain't about money. Never was."

CHAPTER 27

After Kuwahara told Lyons he was crazy for thinking a serial killer was loose, the commander met with LaBarbera and Hart to discuss that very possibility. The detectives debriefed him about their visit to Pelican Bay. Waxman then described Edward Sims as about fifty, medium build, maybe 170, about five foot ten, similar to Evil's description of his visitor.

"Fourth person, same description, however vague it is," LaBarbera said. "Evil, Mrs. Desmond, Waxman, and Lyons."

"All right, boys, all right. Let's get down to it," said Kuwahara. "Waxman, get back over there. Now. We need a photo of this Sims guy. Show it to Mrs. Desmond, fax it to Pelican Bay. See if it's the same guy. And get it to Lyons."

"No problem, sir. I'm on my way," said Waxman. "I gotta say, though, if Sims is the guy that jacked up Terminal, then had the stones to confront Big Evil, even through the prison glass, well, then he is one Dr. Jekyll and Mr. Hyde motherfucker."

"Head down there. Be careful, this time. I'll have a patrol car meet you. I'll send two, make it three."

Waxman left and Kuwahara told the others he was giving them more resources—two more detectives and a liaison with Santa Monica "just in case there is a connection."

"Oh, there's a connection, boss," Hart said.

"So," Sal said, "working on the premise that this is the same guy, we came up with a possible list of potential victims. Check it out." He handed Kuwahara a paper with six names. Next to each name was from one and three stars. "The stars represent our guess at the likelihood of an attack."

The list included Mr. and Mrs. Desmond. Her name with three stars, his with two. Judge Reese, who presided over the Big Evil trial and urged Harrington to go for LWOP, had two stars. The next two, Helen Truman and Freddie Gelson, each had one star. Lyons's name was the last on the list, with one star.

"I don't know Truman or Gelson," said Kuwahara. "But, first things first. Does the judge know about this?"

"Yes, sir," said Hart. "The district attorney's office has assigned two of their people to be with him from the moment he leaves his house until walks into his chambers. And the same on the evening end. The judge was fine with that, but refused to have anyone spend the night. In his words, 'Anyone who comes into my house at night is getting a free ride in the coroner's van.' We hear he always carries his personal .38 snub-nosed."

"Great. What about the Desmonds?"

"They know," Waxman said. "We're doing extra patrols around their street. All shifts. They don't want a patrol car parked in front of their house or even on the block."

"Okay, the other two. Who are they?"

"Helen Truman is this white girl from Orange County who became a great love of Evil's," Hart said. "She was down on Crenshaw when they used to cruise, remember, and one night she ran outta gas or something happened to her car and was about to get jacked by some Sixties when Evil showed up and rescued her."

"We don't even know if this killer knows about her," added Hart. "But we are trying to track her and give her a warning."

"And this Freddie Gelson?" Kuwahara said. "That name rings a bell."

"Gelson was the guy whose testimony got Evil convicted," said Hart. "He got a deal with the D.A. to walk if he testified. That was the problem with getting Evil. No one would testify. But Gelson was in a car with Evil when they did a drive-by on some 97 East Coasts. Wounded two. Slightly. Gelson was the shooter, and he cut a deal and testified on that double that put Cleamon away."

"Why would the killer want to kill him?" Kuwahara asked. "Sounds like Evil would want Gelson dead."

"Not at all," said LaBarbera. "Gelson is the only possible way Evil can get out. If Evil's people get to Gelson's family, they might be able to force him to go on record saying he was lying or was coerced, and Evil might be granted another trial. With Gelson dead, Evil stays in the Bay forever."

"Okay, I'll call the chief and brief him," Kuwahara said.

Waxman called in. He had met patrol, and they cased the house. No sign of Sims. No car. "But, Sal, he must've left in a hurry."

"How can you tell?"

"He ran over his favorite rosebush."

I wrote the story. I got both Hart and Waxman to speak off the record, quoting the two anonymous police sources, that they were "definitely looking into the strong possibility that the shooting of Mike Lyons and the deaths of Leslie Harrington and Bobby Desmond are related." The relation? Cleamon "Big Evil" Desmond. I went into the backgrounds of both murder victims and their link to Evil, as well as my own connection via the magazine piece that some considered to be a glorification of the notorious gang leader. I included both the chief's and Kuwahara's fervent denials, as well as the denial of LaBarbera. "There has been no link detected. We do know that Bobby Desmond, who I am long familiar with, has beaten three murder raps and had a number of sworn enemies," LaBarbera said. "We are hoping someone from the neighborhood who may have seen Bobby in his final hours will step forward. They can call LAPD anonymously."

I sent it in an attached Word document to De Soto. She e-mailed back in two minutes. I was encouraged. All the message said was: "A good serial killer needs a name."

I e-mailed back immediately, not bothering to correct my typos: "I don't wanto give him a name. Maybe he will write n give me a name. Happened to Jimmy Breslin—son of Sam wrote, gave him a name. Remember?"

She replied quick. "Can't wait. TV will come up with a name. We need to. Good for the paper. You just hint at name. Let us read the story and everyone will go away with a nickname without you naming. Work on end. Send back five."

I rewrote the ending. De Soto loved it. My kicker was now: "Is there an Evil killer out there?"

"Great. Gotta run it by the brass," she e-mailed after she read. Fifteen anguished minutes later, she e-mailed back with the verdict. It was worth the wait. A serial killer was born.

The story came out first on their website, then on the racks. De Soto had many connections in the local television media and, wanting to build the buzz and humiliate the *Times* too, she e-mailed the story to the local stations early. Then she called her network contacts in hopes that they would mention the story in the five-minute teaser they aired at the bottom of the network morning programs. CBS and NBC went for it. Local channels 5, 11, and 13 aired it with gusto.

"Coming up, serial killer loose in Los Angeles."

"L.A. has a new serial killer. After the break."

By nine, the calls were coming into LAPD press relations from all over the country plus Mexico, El Salvador, Japan, South Korea, England, Armenia, Israel, and Russia asking about the Evil Killer.

The chief and Kuwahara were livid and privately vowed to fire the "police sources." The papers were snatched up quickly, serial killers being one of the favorite topics of Los Angelinos, in a league with the rain.

At Intelligentsia on Sunset in Silverlake, at Peet's on Larchmont, at Sqirl on Virgil, at Bob's Donuts in the Farmer's Market, at Stan's Donuts in Westwood Village, at Euro Pane on Colorado Boulevard in Pasadena, strangers were talking to each other about the new killer in town. Only a few things—riots and natural disasters—bring a community together like a good serial-killer story. And the fact that one of his victims, alleged victims, that is, was an attractive white woman, a deputy district attorney from an exclusive Santa Monica neighborhood, did wonders for the story. If it had been just Terminal, no one at the fancy coffeehouses and donut shops would even have heard about it. Southside homicide victims didn't matter to most cappuccino drinkers.

On the noon news broadcasts, the Evil Killer was the lead story. De Soto called me to say four local news stations had called, requesting interviews with me. In Los Angeles, a city with a stunted memory, I was no longer the disgraced reporter who had had himself shot, but rather the hotshot reporter who broke a serial-killer story. I refused all the offers. I'll admit it felt good to be asked, but it felt even better to tell them no. The chief called.

"I don't remember giving you my home number?"

"You were probably drunk, asshole. Look, Lyons, enjoy your fifteen minutes of fame. Or, in your case, fifteen seconds. You think you broke news with that story today? It will be old news tomorrow."

"How's that?"

"Well, the *Weekly* doesn't come out every day, right? I mean, that is why they call it the *L.A. Weekly*. It's not a daily."

"Brilliant. No wonder you're the chief."

"It just that the *Weekly* is going to come out looking weakly."

"Huh?"

"Get it? Weakly. W-E-A-K-L-Y. That is weakly because, gang lover, that news you supposedly broke today will itself be broken by tomorrow. The *Times* and everyone else will have a much bigger story tomorrow."

"What will they have?"

"We got a suspect already, loser."

As the chief gloated, his bodyguard, a sergeant from Metro Division, walked into his boss's office. He motioned for the chief to cover the phone, then whispered, "Judge Reese hasn't come back from lunch. He apparently slipped out the back way from his chambers. That was two hours ago."

The chief didn't bother telling Lyons he had to go. He just hung up.

CHAPTER 28

Detectives caught an unexpected break—cooperation from Eighty-Nine Family Bloods. Collect calls from Big Evil to members of the Eighty-Nine Family ordered anyone with info about Terminal's final hours to notify his mom. Evil didn't want to ask the boys to give the information straight to the police. He still had clout, but when one is serving an LWOP sentence, the general feeling from the homies, especially the young ones, is "What can he do to me? He's in for life without." Most knew Evil could still do a lot, but not like the old days. Once the Joint Task Force brought Evil down, Eighty-Nine Family was not the same. Though they were never a huge gang, like, say, Grape Street or Rollin Sixties who each had more than a thousand members. But, the seventy or so members the 89s did have were true hard-core gangsters. Real riders, ready to die for their cause, whatever that was. They didn't even know. Now their ranks were depleted, cut down by bullets and long prison terms. Yet, when Evil let those still on the streets know that his mother could be in danger, to a man, they said they would tell her whatever they learned.

One of them, Showboat, told Evil he would talk to her immediately. After he did, Betty Desmond called Sal, got his voice mail, called Hart, got him.

She told him someone had seen Terminal drive away that night, after he threw a naked man in the trunk of a blue Oldsmobile Cutlass Supreme that was blocking the alley. Showboat wasn't a Cutlass man, so he just said this particular model was from the 1980s. It was something to go on. Hart let the troops know.

"Shit," Waxman said when he heard from Hart. "Johnny, I think that Sims, I think he had a Cutlass. It was a either Cutlass or the Buick, ugh, Buick had a version. What was it? Regal. It was a Regal or a Cutlass."

"Okay, check out Sims with DMV. That's a common name, so have 'em cross the address. Get a driver's license picture, too."

"Jesus, Johnny, I'm a damn detective, too. You gonna wipe my ass for me?"

Hart hung up.

An hour later, Detective Waxman's phone rang. It was the DMV. Edward Sims had a blue 1984 Cutlass Supreme SL Coupe registered to him. Waxman got a chill. They agreed to e-mail Sims's California driver's license photo to the homicide table at Southeast Division, to South Bureau Homicide, to Press Relations downtown, and to Pelican Bay. Hart would notify the prison of the impending e-mail.

Don Ball, the Pelican Bay guard, went to the tier in the SHU where Big Evil was held. "What up, Big Red?" Evil said cheerfully. "When we gonna do a guards versus inmates game again?"

Big Red didn't say a word. He just held up the DMV photo of Eddie Sims. Evil grabbed the bars and tried to shake and break them à la King Kong.

Detectives went to the Desmond house with the photo. Betty Desmond, who had taken a leave of absence from her job, was home and confirmed that that was the man who came to her house. Hart e-mailed the photo to Lyons. "Is this the guy who shot you?" was in the subject box. Lyons studied it for a long time, trying hard to focus on those terrifying moments on 2nd Street. He couldn't say for certain it was the same man.

Meanwhile, the chief's aides were setting up a press conference to announce Edward Sims as a "Person of Interest."

"Stupid story is not even one day old and we got the suspect," the chief said to Lieutenant Lucy Sanchez of press relations. Then he remembered Judge Reese. Damn, he thought, it would be nice to have the big breaking news press conference at five, but, shit, this can't wait. "We have to protect the judge, Lucy. We can't wait. Notify the media immediately. They need to put this picture out now. And the car and license plate."

Those in the LAPD who were involved felt a surge. They were close to getting this guy. Only one detective was depressed over the recent development. Waxman. "Zeus all mighty," he muttered to himself when he was alone. "I had a serial killer, the Evil Killer, give my kid's car a tune-up." On top of it, the kid hadn't even noticed the car was running better. Waxman had to tell him, which brought an, "Oh, yeah, Dad, I thought something was different."

CHAPTER 29

For Eddie Sims, finding his prey was not particularly difficult because he had learned the virtue of patience. Sims had studied the whereabouts, the comings and goings of Harrington, Lyons, and Judge Reese for weeks. He had patience now, a quality quite underrated, especially by the impatient. He learned of Lyons's saloon habits. He found out where Harrington lived alone, simply by waiting near the courthouse parking lot and following her from a safe distance. When she rode out the Santa Monica Freeway to its end near the ocean, he followed a few more blocks, then pulled off. The next day he resumed where he had stopped. Her radiant red Maserati GT was not hard to catch sight of, though in this part of town Masers were no rarity. In just three days, he knew where she lived.

He did the same with Judge Reese. After several days on him, he discovered Reese had a fondness for slipping away around noon and wildly smacking balls at the driving range of the Wilshire Country Club near Rossmore Avenue and Beverly Boulevard. Although the club was private, Sims had gone to the pro shop and bought a Wilshire Country Club golf cap. As he entered an older, gray-haired man was leaving and telling the shop's only worker, "Thank you, Dial." Dial, Sims thought, what kind of sorry-ass name was that? Named after some soap. What's with white people and their kids' names?

Sims had given himself a minor makeover. He'd shaved his head, but not the three-days' facial growth. He'd brought boots that gave him an extra two inches. Wrapped two sweaters around his belly. He had wrapped three, until he realized the third one, with green-

and-gold diamonds, was Payton's, a birthday gift from Lisa, his one and only girlfriend. He took it off. He didn't want Payton along for the Revenge. His knife, okay, his sweater, no.

Sims's biggest worry now was his Cutlass. He considered leaving it at the long-term lot at LAX, which was the classic place to leave a criminal car. But, he needed a car and he couldn't rent one without using his real driver's license, since it matched his only debit card. So he chanced it with the Cutlass and drove five minutes to Western Avenue in Gardena, where he knew of two used car lots. He parked the Cutlass on an industrial stretch of Gramercy Place at 169th Place near the back end of the Gardena Villas Mobile Home Park. He walked the block to Fujishima Motors on Western Avenue next to a UPS facility, and, after a test drive that didn't even leave the lot, drove out ten minutes later in a once-silver eight-hundred-dollar 1991 Ford Taurus with 190,000 thousand miles.

He took Western to Redondo Beach Boulevard, hung a right past Normandie Avenue, past the Nahas Department Store, past the Memorial Hospital of Gardena, past Larry Flynt's Hustler Casino, past Vermont Avenue, and onto the northbound Harbor Freeway. He was going golfing. Or at least to the range, looking to get a hole in one judge.

Up the Harbor, he tuned the radio to KNX News Radio. Traffic was humming along nicely. As he neared the Manchester Avenue off-ramp, he gazed to his right, to the east, just two miles away where he once had a content life with a wife, an energetic son, some rose-bushes, and a never-ending rotation of cars in need of tune-ups. He stared east so long that when he returned his eyes to the freeway, he had to slam on his brakes to avoid rear-ending a tricked-out lime-green Nissan 350Z.

Off to the northwest, dark clouds were heading toward town. Traffic slowed considerably by the time he hit Vernon Avenue near the Coliseum. It usually did. Then he heard the radio report. "We now go live to Hal Hansen at the Police Administration Building for breaking news."

Howitzer Hal, as usual, laid it on thick. "This is Hal Hansen and we have cracking news on the case of the maniacal serial killer known as the Evil Killer. Just moments ago, the LAPD released a photo of a man, Edward Sims, aka Eddie Sims, aka Barry Sanders. He is said to be a 'person of interest' in the case. Go to our website, losangeles dot cbslocal dot com to see his picture. Sims is described as black, forty-nine years old, five foot nine, a hundred seventy pounds with no distinguishing marks such as tattoos or scars. He drives a 1984 Oldsmobile Cutlass Supreme SL, blue with California license plate zero-three-two ISN. Once again, LAPD has not said he is a suspect, but rather a 'person of interest.' That sounds interestingly suspect to me. Stay tuned to KNX for further updates."

The in-station radio broadcaster asked Hansen what citizens should do if they spotted the man. Sims was sweating now. He was thankful for the anonymity of the Ford Taurus, but wished he had parked the Cutlass farther away from Fujishima Motors. Oh, so they find the Cutter, he thought. What difference would it make now?

"Do not, I repeat, do not attempt to apprehend this man. He is considered very dangerous and possibly armed like a Navy SEAL, Force Recon Marine, or a Delta operator," said Hansen, lapsing back into his over-the-top military ways and convicting Sims already. "This man has nearly beheaded a deputy district attorney with, what sources tell me, may have been an unforgiving Special Forces knife. He is alleged to have brutally killed one of this city's most violent gang members, a gang member so dastardly he was known on the streets as 'Terminal.' Let the SWAT unit handle this bad guy. If you see him, notify LAPD at once. This is a nine-one-oner if there ever was one."

Even Sims, with all he had going on, had time to realize Hansen sounded like a buffoon. He lumbered up the Harbor Freeway at fifteen mph, then to a stop, then back to twenty mph past the Coliseum, the USC campus, the Shrine Auditorium, and Felix Chevrolet. He dared not look at the drivers surrounding him. Were they staring?

After passing the Adams Boulevard off-ramp, Sims moved to the right-hand lanes and transferred to the westbound Santa Monica Freeway, taking the swooping two-lane 270-degree right transition ramp so slowly he was nearly rear-ended by a UPS truck that had veered off to pass him on the outside. It gave Sims an idea.

At the Wilshire Country Club, Judge Reese was getting his unwind on. He was sick of the security detail put on him. Yes, it might be for his own good, but it was stifling. Besides, the judge had his reliable snub-nosed .38. A Colt Detective Special. Lately, he would never leave home without it.

Before he got his bucket of balls, Reese told club staff that if there were any phone calls for him, any at all, he was not there. He turned off his cell. His shoulders were knotted. He needed a massage. He had no idea about a possible break in the Evil Killer case. He was enjoying the cloudy day. It looked like rain tonight.

When the word came in that he was missing, desperate LAPD detectives tracked down his wife, Jackie, who was lunching with the ladies at the Water Grill. Jackie told detectives her husband loved to golf at the Wilshire, Los Angeles, and Bel Air country clubs. They dispatched units to all three courses, most to Wilshire since it was closest to the courthouse. Jackie called her husband's cell phone. It went straight to voice mail.

At that point, the judge had nine balls left in his bucket. A patrol car was coming Code Three, lights and siren, from Hollywood Division less than two miles away. Others were scrambling from wherever they were. Cars were heading in from Olympic and Wilshire divisions, too

Sims, in his Taurus, entered the parking lot of the Wilshire Country Club and was greeted by a sunglassed Asian parking valet seated in a director's chair who figured this guy was not a member. He put his hand up for Sims to stop. The judge was down to three balls.

"Help you, sir?"

"I just have a delivery for the pro shop," Sims said, patting a box in the small rear seat. "Golf shirts, I think."

"I can take them here."

"Thanks, but I had direct orders to hand them right to the pro shop. To Dial."

"I can do that."

The judge was done driving.

"Thanks, but I was told to hand them over to Dial personally."

"Well, I don't even think Dial is in today. I haven't seen him."

Sims spotted the judge, his Callaway FT-I driver over his shoulder like a baseball bat, heading toward his British Racing Green Jaguar XJR coupe.

"Okay, well, no problem. I'll just come back tomorrow," Sims said, blood now pounding against the walls of his veins at the sight of the kill. "I'll just turn around up in here."

He pulled the Taurus into the lot, turned it facing out back toward the entrance. He took a deep breath, got out of the car, walked toward the Jaguar, 9mm by his outer thigh.

"Judge Reese."

The judge looked up and sensed the danger. He panicked and went for the Jag door and urgently flung the Callaway driver at Sims while he fumbled for his .38 Detective Special. "C'mon, Snubby."

The parking valet watched in horror, unable to speak. Sims sighted his Beretta.

"You bastard," the judge said as he finally pulled out the snub-nosed .38. But, it was too late. "Bastard" was his last word. Three bullets missed him entirely, but two tore into the judge, one entering his mouth, the other just above his eyebrow. Like Terminal, there would be no open casket for the judge.

Sims dashed to his still-running car. The stunned valet sprinted away up Rossmore screaming, "Help!" Sims floored the Ford, didn't let up as he exited, and made the right-hander onto southbound Rossmore, tires squealing, car starting to slide into oncoming northbound traffic. The worn Bridgestones eventually took hold, and the Taurus ricocheted forward. A lady in a Maxima slammed on her brakes to avoid the reckless driver.

Sims kept the gas pedal down as he streaked south toward 3rd Street where he made a wild right, then a quick left onto Muirfield Road, the most prestigious street in Hancock Park. He abandoned the car and walked quickly back to Beverly, then back to Rossmore where he waited with Mexicans or Salvadorans or Guatemalans, all females, for a bus. Slow-ass bus, hurry up. No wonder everybody drove a car in this jacked-up city.

Back at the Wilshire Country Club, the first LAPD cruiser on the scene bounced into the parking lot where Judge Reese's body lay on its back, his face ruined. Lights still revolving, the sedan screeched to a halt, the doors flung open as the officers, guns drawn, huddled behind the car.

"He's gone. The guy who shot the judge. He's gone. He tore out going toward Beverly," said a timid country club employee from near the pro shop. By now, the parking attendant was back, and he told the officers the car was a Taurus, silver or light blue and the "driver was a black guy, forty or fifty, something like that."

Three minutes later, after Chief Miller, Commander Kuwahara, and the detectives got the news, all doubt was gone. An all-points bulletin to be on the lookout—a BOLO—for Edward Sims driving a Ford Taurus was issued. Minutes later, the car was found by passing cops, suspicious of a tired Taurus on a street of ten-million-dollar mansions.

Sims got off the bus at Alvarado Street and checked into a fifty-two-dollar room at the Royal Viking, paying for two nights up front. The motel, across the street from the Royal Thai Massage, Viva Bargain Center, and Tango Room cocktail lounge, had seen better times as evidenced by the razor wire atop its chain-link fence. Sims wondered if he had ever seen razor wire protecting a motel from the streets.

Then again, he thought, maybe it was to protect the neighborhood from the motel.

Upon entering room 41, he turned on the television. Before he had two sweaters off, "Breaking News" was showing helicopter views of the Wilshire Country Club with an inset of Sims's driver's license photo. He glanced at a mirror and back at the photo. The shaved head helped.

He could hear the faint sound of scattered, soft rain against the window. He thought of Leslie Harrington and her rain. He craved a cognac, but he stayed inside till darkness fell.

Sims left his room that cloudy, drizzly night at ten thirty, to get a loaf of Weber's white sandwich bread, a jar of Skippy's creamy peanut butter, a liter bottle and a 200-milliliter bottle—what many still called a half pint—of Hennessy, and a non-Major League Baseball-sanctioned L.A. Dodgers cap at Crest Jr. Liquors three blocks west on 3rd Street just past St. Vincent Medical Center. The Korean owner and Mexican American helper barely noticed him, paying rapt attention to the Lakers-Suns game at Staples that had gone into double overtime. Outside, he grabbed an *L.A. Weekly*.

By the time he made it back to his room at the Royal Viking, half the half pint was warming his guts. He watched television. More on the shooting of the judge, but no breaking news. He laughed at that. He knew the next time there was breaking news on his case it would be "live" on 89th Street, right in front of Mr. and Mrs. Desmond's house.

All night, he lay awake on a hard, queen-size bed, tossed and turned like a an old, out-of-balance washing machine in a North Compton coin laundry, and drank from the upended Hennessy liter as if it were mother's milk. It was L.A. cold outside and the heater inside didn't work. Still, Sims was sweating. He threw off the sheets and toxins oozed out of him. He thumbed though the *Weekly*. He read a feel-good piece about a woman who had been wounded in Hyde Park by a stray gang bullet, but had recovered enough to start her dream job of driving a bus. It didn't make him feel good. He missed a piece by Michael Lyons about a serial killer.

He laughed when he thought about King Funeral. On his way to Pelican Bay, he had dropped off the tape, which he had taken from Terminal, to the homies at 74th and Hoover with instructions to watch it. He knew where to drop it because on the video, the announcer—actually the deputy Boylston—introduced Funeral as "The King of 74th and Hoover." Sims relished having the power of death.

Sims actually looked forward to death after he completed the Revenge and it was a peaceful thought. Nothing but sleep lay ahead for him. That sounded nice. An eternity of peaceful, ultimate slumber. Lay me down next to Payton in the cold Inglewood Park dirt.

That next morning was a dazzling Los Angeles day, like the day Lyons had been shot on 2nd Street. The gray sky had turned cerulean blue strewn with three gigantic, billowy clouds, the kind you want to take a nap on. From Sims's second-floor room at the Royal Viking, even Alvarado Street looked clean.

That afternoon, Lyons went to a joint press conference the mayor and chief of police gave on the steps of City Hall, across the street from a former heroin mart now awash in bougainvillea. He stayed way back, away from TV reporters and their cameramen. Both the mayor and the chief admitted that a serial killer, dubbed the Evil Killer, was loose in the city. Lyons felt a tinge of not quite pride, but satisfaction when he heard that. They took turns answering questions. Lyons had no questions, he never did near a TV camera.

"Chief Miller has assured me everything possible is being done to track this deranged man down and bring him to justice," the mayor said. He rambled on for a few more minutes before the chief took over.

"Yes, there is a serial killer on a rampage. However—and I cannot stress this enough—" the chief said, "the people he is targeting, all of his victims, have a direct connection with an incarcerated gang leader named Cleamon Desmond, better known as Big Evil. The suspect's son was ordered killed by Cleamon Desmond years ago. The suspect, Edward Sims, is seeking revenge in his own sick way. At this point, we believe both Judge Harold Reese and Deputy District Attorney Leslie Harrington were killed because they did not go for the death penalty against Cleamon Desmond who is serving a sentence of life without the possibility of parole in Northern California. He will never get out of prison, but, apparently, that was not enough for Edward Sims. We now believe that reporter Michael Lyons may have been also a victim of this sick individual."

Lyons walked away content as Miller continued. "Mr. Sims, if you can hear me, please turn yourself in before you and other people are harmed. I know and you know your good son would not want this."

Sims could hear him loud and clear at the Royal Viking. "Okay, Chief. Whatever you say. I'll turn myself in tomorrow. Right after I kill Big Evil's mother."

Mr. and Mrs. Desmond had been alerted that the Evil Killer had struck again. Still, they refused an offer by the LAPD to be put up at a hotel near the airport. They were proud people and they were not going to run. LaBarbera and Hart had made a special appeal to Mrs. Desmond personally, but she was unfazed. "If the good Lord feels it is my time, then it is my time. Thank you, Sal, and thank you, Johnny, but this has been my home for forty-one years, and I am not being forced out of it by anyone except Jesus Christ himself."

In Orange County, sheriff's deputies had tracked down Evil's white girlfriend Helen Truman, who was delighted to be put up at a hotel room until the killer was caught. She had hit a stretch of bad road and was back living with her mother in Santa Ana. She hoped Sims wouldn't be caught anytime soon.

CHAPTER 30

Sims wanted to get as close as possible to the Desmond household. He knew there would be, if not a straight-out stakeout, at least a near constant patrol in the area. Maybe even a cop planted inside the house, though he doubted that, knowing the Desmonds.

That day, the subject of a massive manhunt ate peanut butter sandwiches washed down with Hennessy. He even watched old sit-coms: *Happy Days*, *Good Times*, *The Jeffersons*. He spent another sweaty night at the Royal Viking, and he finalized his plan.

The next day, wearing the Dodgers cap, sunglasses, and two sweaters over a brown shirt and pants, he boarded a southbound RTD bus on Alvarado. At Washington Boulevard he transferred to a westbound bus to Western Avenue where he caught a southbound bus heading for Gardena. No one had noticed him. Fellow passengers paid him no mind. They had their own problems.

An idea had come to him when a UPS truck passed him the other day on the big, sweeping transition from the Harbor Freeway to the Santa Monica Freeway. He knew there were always a lot of "Big Brown" trucks coming and going around Western and Artesia since they had a major facility two blocks away.

He headed that way and made his headquarters in what was becoming an urban dinosaur, a public pay phone booth, on the edge of an Arco station. He lifted the receiver and pretended to talk while he scanned for a UPS truck. There was a Del Taco right across the street and a Wendy's twenty feet from the phone booth.

After more than a hour, Sims saw what he was looking for. A UPS truck pulled into the parking lot behind Wendy's. The driver did not use the drive-through, either because the truck couldn't fit or maybe he just wanted to sit inside, enjoying that rare sit-down meal for a UPS driver who usually are on the run. Must've finished his route early.

Sims caught a break when he saw the driver was a woman, a small one at that. When she was done, she headed back to her UPS truck. About thirty seconds later, she was tied up in the back, her mouth wrapped in tape, being quietly assured she would not be hurt. "Just please don't try to jump out. I will not hurt you. Just sit still for twenty minutes, and this will all be over. Do you know who I am?"

She nodded.

"Okay, then. Then you know I am only dealing with people associated with Big Evil. So you can relax—unless you're a friend of Big Evil?"

She shook her head so violently she nearly pulled a neck muscle.

He took Artesia onto the 91 East and exited at Central. He headed north on Central, through and past West Compton, under the 105 Freeway, to the stretch of road Detective Waxman had taken to visit him. He passed the Nickerson Gardens, passed his bank, passed the park. At 94th and Central, Sims dialed 911 on the UPS driver's cell phone. "I just saw the Evil Killer get out of a car on 94th and Central and go into that market there. I am sure it is him."

"What is your name, sir?"

"Do I have to give it? I'm afraid. I am sure it is him." He hung up and tossed the phone out.

Though 911 had received more than three dozen such leads, this call was sent out on a special frequency set up yesterday solely for Evil Killer information. Patrol cars in the area, even those parked near the Desmond house, sped toward 94th Street. As Sims continued north on Central, he saw three cruisers zooming south. Sims turned left onto 89th Street.

A UPS truck was not a familiar sight in the Eighty-Nine Family 'hood, but it wasn't as if a spaceship had landed when Sims pulled the "Big Brown" P-600 UPS truck to a stop in front of Cleveland

and Betty Desmond's house. Dodgers cap pulled low over his forehead, sweaters off, he quickly got out and knocked hard three times
on the heavy metal security door.

Fifteen seconds later he heard a "Who is it?" He knew the voice.
He tried to disguise his. "UPS delivery for Cleveland Desmond."

"Just leave it," Betty Desmond said.

"That's fine." Sims left a box he had grabbed from the UPS truck
on the porch and began slowly walking back to the front gate. When
he heard the door open, he did not look back. When he heard the
security door open he did not look back. By the time Betty Desmond
had bent over to pick up the box, Sims was at the gate, but, suddenly,
he spun and dashed back to the front door. Before she could scream,
Sims had Big Evil's mother back in the house with a gun pointed at
her chest.

"Pleasure to see you again, Mrs. Desmond. So sorry about Terminal."

"Bobby."

"Let's compromise and just call him dead boy with the mashed-
in face. Just to let you know, in his last moments he suffered very
much, but not like I have." He walked her through the house. No
one else was there. He pushed her hard down onto a couch. "Sit
down. I have some calls to make. I will kill you in an instant if you
move or yell. I think you know I'm capable."

"What do you want? You're sick. What did I do to you?"

"Your son killed my son, and now he is paying the price." He
pulled out a piece of paper and began dialing. After five phone
calls—to police divisions at Southeast and 77th Street, the *Times* city
desk, Channel 7 Eyewitness News, and his estranged wife, a call that
didn't go though, Sims was ready for the Revenge's last act.

In fifteen minutes, the circus came to town. The SWAT team was
there. Hostage negotiators. At least thirty cruisers. The media throngs
had been pushed back more than a block. The square of Central,
Manchester, 92nd and Wadsworth was cordoned off. But LaBarbera

and Hart let me in. It was rare, but not unheard of, to let a reporter inside the crime tape. I had been inside several times, but never on such a dramatic scene. My friend and old pod mate, sexy Carly Engstrom, wearing knee-high white leather boots, was on scene, too, and yelling at Johnny Hart. Apparently, cop reporter Morty Goldstein, who never left the office, had told her to get down here, and the city editor agreed. Hart, eager to score points with Carly, walked over, took her by the hand, and led her under the crime tape to where Sal and I were with the others.

"Mikey, this is so exciting," she said and squeezed my hand.

"It is now that you're here," I said.

"You're right about that, Lyons," said Hart. "But, keep your pretty head low. You hear me. Do not, under any circumstances, act like Lyons."

Carly laughed.

The lead hostage negotiator decided he would have LaBarbera take first crack at Sims since he was so familiar with the case. LaBarbera was handed a small megaphone. "Mr. Sims, this is Detective LaBarbera. You want to get at Evil, but you are not getting at him from there. Give up and go to Pelican Bay."

"Shuddup. Don't lie to me. I'll go to San Quentin and you know that. Killing a judge and D.A. I'm not stupid. If you speak again, she's dead."

LaBarbera, not wanting to push a maniac, gave up the megaphone. Hart shook his head. "Great job, Sal. Whaddya get in hostage negotiating class? A D minus?" I had to muffle a laugh. To me, a D minus is the worst of all grades. It indicates that you tried and sucked.

I was huddled safely behind the stolen UPS truck with LaBarbera, Hart, Kuwahara, Engstrom, several SWAT unit members, and the lead hostage negotiator. I could tell Kuwahara was pissed at his detectives for allowing me to get in close, but was too busy to deal with that now—until I opened my mouth.

"Maybe I should tell him I'll trade places with her," I told the group.

"Shut the fuck up, Lyons, or so help me—" said Kuwahara. "No, no, just get out of here now. Go. Back away. Now!" Having no option, I obeyed, taking a couple of crouched steps away.

The SWAT unit snipers did not have a good shot. There was no good angle into the house. Back in the mid-1980s, the Desmonds, fearful of drive-bys into their kitchen, which faced the alley, had not only boarded up the kitchen windows, but had them cemented shut. This eliminated several angle shots.

CHAPTER 31

Sims was holding his pistol to the head of Betty Desmond, his forearm wrapped firmly around her throat, his mouth so close to her ear, she could hear the cognac sloshing. He yelled out that if they did anything, if he heard or saw anything like a "flash or bang or grenade, tear gas or any other tricks," he would immediately "kill the lady."

Outside, Hart said, "This guy is so far gone."

"Do we have a shot?" LaBarbera asked the SWAT unit commander.

"Not yet."

Inside, Sims said, "Say a prayer, Mrs. Desmond. One single woman created Evil and Terminal. You must be the mother of the year. I am the motherfucker of the year."

Betty Desmond looked around for something she could use to hit this deranged person.

Outside, I moved back closer to Sal and asked, "Who is the SIC?"

"What the fuck is the SIC?"

"Sniper in charge."

"Where do you come up with this shit?" Still, he pointed to a man on a porch across 89th Street and two houses down. "Don't do anything crazy now, Lyons."

"I'm not doing anything," I said as I scampered away to the house with the snipers, two on the roof, two on the porch. The taller of the porch shooters was in charge.

"Get outta here."

"I'm with Sal."

"I know who you are. You're a distraction, goddamnit. Get the hell out."

"One question. Just one. Do you know who Zaistev was?"

"The greatest sniper of all time. Not counting me. Now go!"

"That's what I wanted to hear."

CHAPTER 32

Inside the house, Sims spotted Mr. Desmond's prized cognac, the bottle of Rémy Martin XO that Terminal had bought for him years ago. "Look, the Desmond family has the fancy cognac. All my life, I wanted to try some of that XO."

"Help yourself," said Betty Desmond, praying for any distraction.

Sims dragged her to the cabinet where the Rémy glowed. "Open it and pour me a glass, a snifter. Let's do this right."

She reached for the curvy bottle, but then suddenly he tightened his grip on her neck and yanked her away.

"No, no. Not a good idea. You might try and hurt me with that bottle. Any woman that raised Big Evil must know how to go on the attack." He released his grip on her, but not his stare, not his aim. Without looking away from her, he thumb opened the Rémy Martin and lifted it. He considered pouring the amber into a snifter, but instead, eyes like a laser on Betty Desmond, brought the bottle to his lips and poured the cognac into his mouth. He put the bottle down, resumed his vise grip on her neck, and only then did he slowly swallow. He savored it as much as a man can with a SWAT unit waiting outside to kill him.

"Do you think it's a shame to drink this fine stuff from the bottle?"

"You're worried about shame now? Mister, you shamed yourself a long time ago. You shamed the memory of your son."

Sims ratcheted her neck even tighter.

• • •

Outside, I crouch-jogged back near Hart, who was now safely behind a patrol car with Carly Engstrom and two other cops, next to the UPS truck.

For some unknown reason, my mind clicked to a concert I recently saw at the Sports Arena before I was shot. It was Bruce Springsteen and the E Street Band.

In the midst of the chaos on 89th Street, I thought about that concert, and it gave me strength. The same strength I had when I saw Springsteen that night. When I heard him sing "Land of Hope and Dreams," a song about dreams not thwarted, and faith rewarded. It was so uplifting, so rousing, more than a church sermon, more than any speech. And I felt invincible. I was on my feet most of the concert. And now, here on the Southside, I stood up.

Without saying a word, I rose from behind shelter and walked to the gate of the chain-link fence and entered the yard.

"Lyons!" yelled Hart.

"Fuckin' Lyons, you're gonna get her killed," screamed Kuwahara.

I spoke loudly, as the irate LAPD command, foremost among them Kuwahara, now looked on and fumed in stunned silence.

"Mr. Sims," I said, "Payton would not want you to do this. You must know this. This lady is a good woman. Please, Eddie Sims, let her go."

Silence from inside.

"Look, you tried for me first, you can have a second chance right now. I'm the one that made Big Evil famous. I'll swap places. Let her go."

I was three feet inside the gate, right there on the front yard where Big Evil and Terminal were raised, and I didn't fear a thing. I thought what a wonderful life I have lived. Full of wonder and tears, full of love and imagination. And I felt strong then. Proud, too. And, I guess I was a little sad, too. I had a lot of thoughts going on. Still, I continued my fervent plea. "You know, Edward Sims, Walter

Payton was a great running back, a great man. He's up in heaven hoping and praying you'll let that woman go. So is your son, Payton. So is Gale Sayers."

CHAPTER 33

Hart looked over to LaBarbera who was still behind the neighboring UPS truck. "Lyons is an imbecile."

Commander Kuwahara scatted over to the Buick. "If that woman dies, Lyons is going down for accessory to murder. I am dead serious. Get him out or I'll have the SWAT unit shoot him."

"You're kidding, right, Lester?"

"Unfortunately, but not about the accessory part."

In the house, Sims was about to end this drama. "Say a prayer, Mrs. Desmond." She lowered her head, softly weeping. "Say a prayer for Payton."

Betty Desmond who had been shaking, suddenly calmed. She bowed her head and said, "Bobby, I'm coming to be with you. Payton Sims, I'm coming to meet you. Sweetness, you too."

Eddie Sims looked at her, raised his pistol, then opened the front door and fired.

CHAPTER 34

Nanoseconds after former Marine Corps sniper and current SWAT sniper commander Juan Jose Gallardo, Jr., son of a Vietnam War Marine Corps sniper, saw the door move, he fired, too. His projectile from the .50-caliber Barrett M82A1 tore through Sims's brain. Fortunately, Mrs. Desmond was five foot three and the lead whizzed above her, though she was showered with brains, bone fragments, and blood. She collapsed.

Sniper Gallardo yelled, "He's dead. All clear."

Laying twisted near the gate, his face and the right side of his head covered in blood, was the body of Michael Lyons. The cops rushed to the house, most of them going on into the house from front and back. LaBarbera, Hart, and a paramedic ran to the fallen, motionless reporter.

"Is he dead?" Hart asked the paramedic who was quickly at Lyons's side.

"He's got a pulse," the paramedic announced. His gloved hands, already streaked scarlet, were gentle on Lyons's face and head. "It might be a, no, it looks like a side head wound. Could even be a graze."

"Lyons. Lyons!" Sal bellowed.

"Wake your ass up, you motherfuckin' imbecile," hollered Hart.

I stirred a bit and then groggily opened my eyes and stared up at everyone for five dazed seconds until I could talk. "What, what happened? She okay? What happened? Somebody call me an imbecile?"

"I did," Hart said. "Gale Sayers isn't dead, you fool."

"Oh. Oh, yeah. What happened?"

"Sims is dead. She's not."

I closed my eyes, and I guess I went to sleep right there on the lavish 89th Street sidewalk.

I spent just one night at St. Francis Medical Center in Lynwood. Hart told me he'd thought I was dead with all the blood and being knocked out, but the paramedic had been correct. It was a graze. Francesca was getting ready to wheel me out of the hospital when Hart and LaBarbera arrived.

"Will you two please tell him not to play cops and robbers anymore," Francesca said. "He's just not good at it."

Hart laughed. "I would if I thought it would do any good, but, on the positive side at least he's getting better at it. First time, he got shot two times, this time he only got grazed."

"Whaddya mean 'grazed'? Man, I got shot in the head. I'm counting that as getting shot."

Francesca tenderly rubbed her hand over the bandage on the side of my head where I had chalked up another thirty-two stitches. "Sometimes, darling, I think you like getting shot."

Back at Francesca's home, I stayed in lockdown mode all weekend and wrote. No e-mail, no cell, no landline, no Internet, unless I needed to Google something for the six thousand-word cover story for the *Weekly*. The *Weekly*'s covers were never written this quickly, but this was a huge story, and I promised I would have it to them on Tuesday morning.

Francesca came home with a wild mushroom pizza on Saturday and lasagna on Sunday. She also brought a six-pack of the pizzeria's new house root beer, Capt'n Eli, my drink of choice when I wasn't drinking.

While I was taking a break and eating, I resisted the urge to check my e-mails, for fear I would be drawn into that quagmire. But, on late Sunday afternoon, while heating up the lasagna in the oven, I did finally check my phone messages. I had twenty. Most of them were from friends, six from media outlets wanting interviews. One was from Betty Desmond.

"Hello, this is Mrs. Desmond. Betty Desmond. Cleamon and Bobby's mother. That's Big Evil and Terminal to you," she said with the slightest of chuckle. "Sal gave me your phone number. I hope you don't mind. Well, I know we don't get along like best of friends, but I did want to call and thank you from the top to the bottom of my heart for what you did out there on my front yard. I know you know I was quite upset with that story you did on my son, Mr. Lyons. I remember talking on the phone to Cleamon about it. He told me 'Ma, don't worry about it. That reporter's crazy.'" She chuckled again, this time not so faint. "I guess he was right, thank God. They tell me you are already out of the hospital. That's good. Thank you and God bless you."

She didn't leave a number, but it showed up on my phone. I didn't call her back right then, but I would, both for the story and for what we had been through together. I'd finish the saga of Eddie Sims first, then call her Monday for some quotes. By then, I laughed, she'd probably be back to being pissed at me.

I was asleep by the time Francesca got home sometime after midnight. She was asleep, on her side, when I awoke at seven a.m. Monday and began kissing her neck.

Afterward, we showered and dressed and walked seven blocks to G&B Coffee on Larchmont. A double cap with whole milk for her, for me a large black coffee. From there, she went on her morning walk, but she had changed her course. The week before, a sixteen-year-old boy riding his bike at Clinton Street and Norton Avenue, part of her regular walk route, had been shot to death with the sun shining bright. It wasn't just the Southside. Even three blocks from Francesca's two-million-dollar home, kids were killing kids.

I went home and wrote all day. It was, along with getting a good interview, my favorite part of journalism. I had all the ingredients assembled, now I needed to put them in the right order, make it flow. Then I went over and over the story, cutting here, adding there, taking out a sentence, a word, an "and," a "the." Then, if it worked, if it was true, in went some poetry. Not too much. Sometimes I had a tendency to over season a story, but I had learned, from an unlikely source—Francesca—that it is usually best to let a great story alone, let it write itself, just get out of its way. She told me when she had the best ingredients—a tomato from a Fresno backyard, a prawn from old Dublin Bay—she didn't need any brilliant yellow saffron, just some good salt.

By ten, I was done for the night, satisfied and drained. I showered, changed my head bandage, then drove over to Zola where I had a glass of Barolo with Francesca and some staff.

Monday, I called Betty Desmond. It was a cordial conversation, her thanking me again. I asked her a few questions. How had she felt when she first saw Sims at her porch? Did she think she was going to die? Did she try to get through to sad, twisted Eddie Sims? She said she was terrified at first, but then, when she realized what was going to happen, she grew calm, was at peace. She didn't *think* she was going to die, she *knew* it.

She said Detectives LaBarbera and Hart had shown her where Edward Sims lived, just the other side of Central, about eight, nine houses down.

"When Sal and Johnny took me over there, I remembered that house, because it had these beautiful rosebushes. It was sad, though, because one of them was crushed, lying on its side like it was dead. Sad. I remembered that house from years ago. Way back when, before all this Bloods and Crips garbage got so terrible, Cleveland and I used to take walks and there was this man at that house. Used to be out there almost every evening, watering his yard, working on a car, throwing a football with this young boy I guess was his son. Very nice man. Used to always say, 'Good evening.' That's all he ever said,

'Good evening.' I bet that was Eddie and Payton. I know it was."

• • •

I turned the story in Tuesday and the editors at the Weekly loved it. They had some very minor edits and a few questions, but that was nothing, especially for a story that long. I felt grand.

That night, Francesca and I went to dinner at Jar on Beverly Boulevard. Usually when we go out, some foodie would recognize Francesca and say hello and tell her some dull story, all the while ignoring me. I was used to it. That night at Jar, a tipsy, face-lifted, bejeweled seventy-something woman approached the table. "Here comes one of your fans," I told Francesca. Instead, she directed her gaze at me.

"Aren't you the young man who got shot on television the other day?" she said with a slur.

"No, I didn't get shot. Just grazed."

When the story came out in the Weekly, it received lavish praise and attention. The only other time I'd received anywhere near as much notice for an article was years ago for a story about a gang leader known as Big Evil. The Weekly was so lauded, that they offered me a full-time staff gig. Much to Francesca's chagrin, I passed, saying I needed to think some things over.

"Like what?" Francesca asked.

"Just some things."

"Like what things?"

"I don't know yet, but there must be some things that need to be thought over."

"Just get a job."

Later, I got lousy news from my cousin Greg. He and Carly Engstrom and thirty others had been let go, given their walking papers by the Times. The Times was downsizing big time. Cutting staff. It was hard times for newspapers. I called Laurie Escobar at home and told her I would take the job offered. She was glad to hear that, and so was Francesca.

A week later, Francesca and I were heading up the highway. She had surprised me by taking off five days and reserving a room for three nights at the Post Ranch Inn on the mesmerizing Big Sur coast.

We left Los Angeles shortly before ten, timing it so we could be in Santa Barbara as the doors opened at La Super Rica, said to have been Julia Child's favorite Mexican restaurant. We were there in seventy minutes and had a feast for twelve dollars.

That first night we stayed 160 miles farther up the coast in Cambria near the Hearst Castle. Stayed at the Castle Inn on Moonstone Beach Drive. Made out across the street on the rocky beach, made love on the silken bed.

The next morning we set out on the magnificent odyssey up Highway 1 to Big Sur. I was going to relish the windy drive in the Porsche Turbo S. I wished I could crank it up and emulate my favorite race car drivers—Fangio, Moss, Clark, Stewart, Senna, Schumacher—but I knew it would scare Francesca, and a one-sided fight would ensue. So I planned to drive merely rapidly with just an occasional blazing burst.

The day Highway 1 beckoned was a glorious one. Cobalt sky, crashing waves. I thought of the other line I knew from the Iliad. *As when along the thundering beach the surf of the sea strikes beat upon beat as the west wind drives it onward.*

I said it aloud. She shook her head. "We have a long drive. Go easy on the saffron."

The road work on that part of Highway 1 had been constructed by inmates from San Quentin starting in 1919. Those killers, those early day Big Evils, built Highway 1. It was, in all the world, my favorite road. I stomped on it. The twin turbos whooshed and the famous chef and the crime reporter were gone.